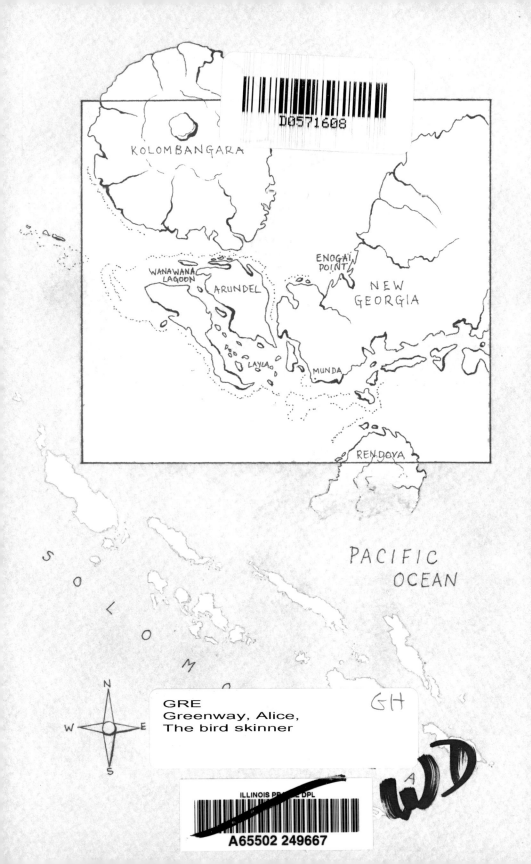

KOLOMBANGARA

ENOGAI
POINT

WANAWANA
LAGOON

ARUNDEL

NEW
GEORGIA

LAYLA

MUNDA

RENDOVA

PACIFIC
OCEAN

S O L O M O N

N
W   E
S

GH

The Bird Skinner

Also by Alice Greenway

White Ghost Girls

The Bird Skinner

ALICE GREENWAY

Atlantic Monthly Press
New York

Printed in the United States of America
Published simultaneously in Canada

ISBN: 978-0-8021-2104-2
eBook ISBN: 978-0-8021-9363-6

Atlantic Monthly Press
an imprint of Grove/Atlantic, Inc.
154 West 14th Street
New York, NY 10011

Distributed by Publishers Group West

www.groveatlantic.com

13 14 15 16   10 9 8 7 6 5 4 3 2 1

For my mother and father
and in memory of my grandfather

Set out, you people of Gele, you people of Lavalava, you people of Vonjavonja, you people of Elosana. Go up to Aku, launch four canoes; go down to Yombavuru, launch four canoes; go down to None, launch four eel boards, launch four embracing nights; cast out four hawsers. Shout people of Gele, shout people of Lavalava, shout people of Vonjavonja, shout people of Elosagana; let him come down sounding the conch, come down casting, come down casting. Go off to Mala Kinda, scoop the water four times; go off to Mbulolo, scoop the water four times; go off to Patu Lavata, cast four hawswers. Go off to the deep sea, backstroke; go off to Lolo te Pome, backstroke. Go off to the Stone that sits, and wait, that they may take you to go to Santo.

—Solomon Island Prayer for the Dead.
Adapted from A. M. Hocart, "The Cult of the
Dead in Eddystone of the Solomons," 1922.

CONTENTS

The Bird Skinner

PROLOGUE

They talked about it afterward, at the end of summer, after the summer folks had left and there was room to breathe again on the island. They talked slowly, hesitantly, in that drawn-out way you hear less and less down east, with long pauses between short utterances, as if, in the end, most things were best left unsaid.

Down at the boatyard where young Floyd was attending to some hitch in the electrics, resuscitating a bilge pump, adjusting a prop shaft that was shaking the engine something awful; down at the town dock where they tied up at the end of a long day, after hosing down their boats, shedding foul-weather jackets, high boots, oilskin overalls, rubber gloves, like lobsters shedding their skins; down at Elliot's Paralyzo too—the only watering hole on the island—they sipped the froth off their beers and talked of Jim.

The old man like an ancient buck, or an old, injured dog, seeking out a familiar hollow in the woods. Like Curtis's dog, who only the week before hauled himself the whole way down to the waterfront to slither in among a heap of traps, sniffing out the smells he loved best: salty rope, rotted herring, sun-soaked wood, the primeval scent of mud hauled up from the bottom of the sea. The way that dog lay, looked like he'd been hankering to be taken out one last time. Though Curtis, himself bent over, lame, rheumatic, hadn't lobstered in years.

"The old man must'ah felt it coming," Elliot observed, wiping down the long wooden bar.

1973. It was unusual then for summer folks to arrive much before the first of July or to stay beyond Labor Day. One or two kids, drawn to island life, might linger, then refuse to go home. But for the most part the summer folks followed a seasonal pattern. Like migratory birds, they flocked in, one generation following the other. Bostonians, New Yorkers, Philadelphians mostly. For two months, they'd stake out most every rock in the Penobscot and there you could see them: flitting and clambering round the islands; spreading towels and blankets, even in thick fog; unpacking handsome picnics of cheese, biscuits, thermoses of clam chowder, lobster salad, blueberry cake. They'd waft up and down the Thoroughfare, the tidal channel between Fox Island and Carver's, in their gaff-rigged sailing dinghies, their wooden Herreshoffs. Zip round in their flat-bottomed whalers, fouling their propellers on the ropes of lobster pots.

On land, they could prove even more troublesome. Getting het up about houses that hadn't been painted, fields that hadn't been mowed, pipes that hadn't been mended. Strutting up and down in their summer plumage, enacting age-old and highly evolved territorial displays—then flitting off again.

So it was unusual when Jim slipped ashore toward the end of winter. Stealthily, surreptitiously—so the islanders couldn't rightly say just how he'd come. Like a bird blown off course, he just appeared, then stayed, when the sailing boats were still hauled up onshore. March brought a late storm with four to six feet of snow. Snow heaped up in the backs of pickup trucks, plowed over to both sides of the road like a parting of white hair.

"Couldn'tah been Sarah brought him ov'ah," Floyd remarks. Elliot pours a last round for the men about to leave for the night. "No way she could'ah fit that chai-yah in her ca'h."

Sarah's the first to have a compact Mitsubishi hatchback, while the rest of them swear by Ford and Chevy pickups. "I suppose you put rice in the carburetor," Floyd likes to tease her.

If it wasn't Sarah, then it must have been her old man Stillman, lobsterman, dockmaster, and caretaker of Jim's family summer place. Even more taciturn and inscrutable than the rest of them.

They did remember the girl's arrival. Though she'd come later, mid-July with the rest of the summer folks, so that the only reason they'd taken note was the color of her skin. Which isn't to say anything particular, only there weren't many blacks living along, or even visiting, the Maine coast then. One fellow who lobstered out of Stonington. A few deckhands who worked the tall ships, sailing tourists up and down the New England coast out of Boston, Bar Harbor, or Damariscotta.

This girl was different though. Not just black but jet black, black as boat oil. Like she'd come right out of Africa. With that big halo of hair and a bright-colored dress with printed flowers, hibiscus flowers someone said, and an old-fashioned leather suitcase with buckles looking like one they might find stowed at the back of their mothers' attics. Even more peculiar, she'd come to stay with Jim.

Stillman drove Jim down to the ferry dock. It was the first time many of them had seen for themselves the old man had lost a leg. Sure enough, it was amputated just above the knee. He managed alone with a crutch, leaning back against Stillman's truck and smoking a stream of cigarettes.

"Guadalcanal," Curtis interjects from the far end of the bar. Slouched over, bleary-eyed, looking more ancient than his late hound. Curtis was a decorated war veteran, though most of them had forgotten for what.

"What's that you said?" Elliot asks, retrieving the glass Curtis shoves down the bar.

"She was from Guadalcanal," he repeats, his words slurred but emphatic.

Guadalcanal then—not Africa.

I
Summerhouse at the End of Winter

Yet some of the men who had sailed with him before expressed their pity to see him so reduced.

—Treasure Island

Fox Island, Penobscot Bay, Maine, July 1973

Jim wedges the chair into the kitchen doorway, forcing the screen door open, lights his third or fourth cigarette. The doctors told him not to. Cut down on the drink, right down, and cut out the smoking altogether. To hell with that. He lost the leg anyhow.

The nicotine leaves him edgy and overly alert. An irascibility that's hard to burn off, stuck as he is in a wheelchair. He could use a drink is the truth of it but he'll hold off for now. It's the least he can do—not meet the girl half drunk.

Go easy. Go easy, he mutters aloud. Shutting his eyes, he wills himself to concentrate on birdcalls. A habit honed since he was a boy. A surefire way of keeping emotions at bay, or safely battened down, which is how he likes them. Gulls—the leitmotif of the island, laughing or crying, however you want to take it. The scolding of a blue jay. The sharp chirrup of a robin. Crows—down by Stillman's place patrolling the fields, their voices grate, hoarse as smokers', and crack like adolescent boys'. There's no cacophony—it being midsummer and high noon—but he can hear the thin, come-hither whistle of a phoebe from the woods in front, the fish hawk mewling as it circles high above the point.

There are other sounds. The low diesel chugging of Adam Mac-Donald's lobster boat setting out late. Moments later, the dock creaks in the wash from its wake, rubbing against the wood stakes.

Clenching the cigarette between his teeth, Jim wheels out the door, over the uneven grass, and past the corner of the house. From here, he can look down the sloping lawn to the shore, where weed- and barnacle-covered rocks are exposed at low tide, across the brown-green water of Indian Cove, down the end of the Thoroughfare to the open blue of the Penobscot Bay. In the deepest water of the cove, a clutch of Stillman's orange and yellow lobster pots bob on slack lines.

"You can't live up there," his son Fergus protested when Jim announced his intention to move here to the old summer place in Maine. "You'll be too cut off."

"Damn right, I'm cut off," Jim snapped. He looked down at his stump. Transfemoral is the word they use when the leg is severed above the knee. Which makes it more difficult to fit a peg leg, or a prosthesis as the doctors insisted on calling it, though Jim had refused one anyhow.

"What if you fall down? What if you get stuck?" Fergus grew un-characteristically fraught. He felt guilty perhaps, being the one respon-sible for hauling Jim off to the doctor: the advocate for his father's operation. He implored Jim to be sensible, to hire a nurse or house-keeper. Pleaded with him to stay put, at least until summer.

"What if I get stuck here?" Jim spat back, banging his crutch on the floor. It was the one satisfying thing about being a cripple, having the stick to bang about.

The truth is, he was already stuck. He'd been stuck since the war.

He'd gone back to work, the museum in New York kindly offer-ing a position. There, he'd busied himself writing reports about other people's finds—buried himself more like it—for the past thirty years. His latest undertaking had been to catalog the department type specimens, the skins first used to identify new species and subspecies. The standard against which all new discoveries are compared. The museum had 6,300 of them, representing somewhere near a third of the world's known birds.

It was meticulous, painstaking work that involved delving into dusty archives, deciphering unintelligible labels, sometimes scrawled in French or German. It required encyclopedic command. Still, it was derivative, clerical.

He'd not initiated any original inquiry of his own. He'd not traveled, unless you count the daily commute from Greenwich into the city and back. He'd become a mothballed, dried-up skin himself. A shriveled specimen preserved by alcohol—gin in his case. His one book, his one valuable contribution to science, *Extinct and Vanishing Birds of Oceania*, published in 1960, was itself a compendium of loss, a rejection of life and living things.

Suddenly an amputee, he could no longer navigate the city. He couldn't get himself to the museum. He hadn't gone back, not even to say good-bye or to collect his things. He couldn't stand the idea of anyone opening doors for him, staring at the empty space where his leg had been.

"And no goddamned nurse!" he swore at Fergus. He'd had enough of that in the hospital. Enough poking and interfering, enough rules and regimens, enough mollycoddling. Not even allowing him a goddamned drink. He twirls the cigarette he has now defiantly between his fingers, associating it in his mind with a sort of freedom.

Early spring, Jim began to wonder if Fergus had been right about moving to Maine. He looked at himself in the mirror, eyes red-rimmed, thick stubble on his colorless cheeks, the deep creases in his forehead, the fishhook scar down one side of his face. His hair was thick, tousled, and uncut. His lips distinctly blue. He wondered if he was drinking himself to death. If so, there must be an easier way.

He flicks the spent cigarette, presses it into the grass with his single faded blue canvas sneaker. It's the first time he's worn a shoe in weeks.

Wintertime, Jesus Christ, he lived like a bear. Wrapping himself in a big fur coat he found in one of the closets. Piling goose-down covers and scratchy wool blankets on the bed, which was unmade and all scuffed up like a rat's nest. Sleeping. Drinking. Keeping the fires lit. Bottles and corks under the bed. Empty corned-beef tins that sprouted mold once the weather changed. Books left open with the spines straining. Half-smoked cigarettes stubbed out on the kitchen table. It's lucky he didn't set the goddamn house on fire.

Everything was new to him as he'd only come in summer. The island lay muffled in the snow of a freak storm. The weighted branches of spruce and fir bowed low over the white-clad rocks. Slips of birch trees shivered like cold bones. In the cove, disgruntled gulls hunkered on broken slabs of ice. An early snow goose with its black wing tips appeared one day on its way to summering in the arctic. *Chen caerulescens*—he noted it in a book he'd started, a record of birds on Indian Cove.

At night a pair of great horned owls hunted the point, filling the house with their bassoon-like calls. Scoters and rafts of eiders floated on the gray sea. When the temperature dropped below freezing, a sea mist rose from the water and wrapped the island in a mirage-like veil. He looked at the thin drift of snow lining the balustrade outside his bedroom and remembered that Helen had always wanted to come here for Christmas. They never had.

The house was cold. No matter how many fires you lit, how long you kept them going, you couldn't make it warm. Large, airy, built for summer, it had little insulation, no central heating. Instead it had a warren of rooms for guests, extended family, and servants. The original owner was one of a Boston elite, who called themselves the Rusticators. Businessmen, bankers, lawyers, architects, who flocked down along this coast at the turn of the century, seeking, like Emerson and Thoreau before them—like Jim now—a simpler life. Only for them, Nature was buffered by maids, cooks, and in-laws.

Cold leaked through places you wouldn't expect, right through the shingles and slated boards, right through the glass panes of the windows facing out to sea, right under the floorboards as the large front porch, jutting over the lawn, let the wind in underneath.

When Jim arrived, Stillman carried some ancient wood up from the basement, and they struggled to light the big cast-iron stove in the kitchen. The flue was clogged with a nest from the year before, which eventually fell down into the stove and burst into flame. Jim felt ashamed not to be able to look after himself as he watched his old boyhood companion light the fire in the dark wood sitting room, then in his upstairs bedroom.

Laboring up the stairs on his crutch, he pitched one-legged down the long hallway, shutting all the other bedroom doors while Stillman rolled mats against the thresholds to stop the drafts. Once the wood was stacked, Jim could stoke the fires himself. The stove was hot but if you walked any distance from it, you could see your own breath.

He remembers Stillman uncovering a family of field mice who'd claimed one of the big sofas in the sitting room. "Let them be," Jim said. No doubt they'd huddled here for generations. Its winter lodgers. There'd be mice all up and down the Thoroughfare doing the same.

Then spring with its own cruelty—mud.

"A-yup, mud season," Sarah said brightly, matter-of-factly, seeing Jim's tracks just outside the kitchen door. Deep muddy ruts. "Mud, lupine, lilacs, and it'll last till June." Just when it was balmy enough to go outside, the wheels of the chair stuck fast. Crutching back to the house, he managed to find a rope to haul it in, before Sarah found him—a god-awful mess.

Sarah, Stillman's unmarried daughter, strong-boned, strong-willed, freckled, thirty. She brings Jim his groceries each week: eggs, bacon, milk, cigarettes, corned beef. A bottle of Scotch or gin when he asks for it. He refuses anything more healthy or varied she might offer. She's Fergus's spy too, no doubt, checking up to make sure he's still alive. She delivers his papers: The *Rockland Courier Gazette* and the *New York Times*, a day late, carrying news of Watergate and Vietnam; Erskine Childers's son elected president of Ireland; Papua New Guinea's first elected chief minister; France testing its atomic bombs on Mururoa Atoll. Jesus Christ, hadn't they had enough of that?

Never you mind the mud. You could open all the doors and windows. You could sit in the sun. You could smell the whole island warming, thawing. Rotten seaweed, fermented leaves, wet grass. Listen to the sound of melt dripping off the eaves of the house and trickling down to the sea. He cleaned up. Leaning forward in the chair, he swept all the cans and papers into big black bags for Sarah to take to the dump in the middle of the island.

He watched migrants and then the summer birds flock in. Male red-winged blackbirds arriving first like military heralds with their red and yellow epaulets, then yellow goldfinches, and sparrows: the seed-eaters. Followed by the insect-eating bluebirds, phoebes, swallows, and warblers. The female blackbirds, the thrushes, and orange orioles. A smell of lilacs drifted in the kitchen door.

By May, Jim could walk outside, far enough to spread seeds and dried bread on the bird table. He needed both crutches at first, and placed them carefully so as not to slip and make a further ass of himself, though there was only Sarah to see. Then set himself to mastering one. The ground grew firm enough for him to wheel the chair around the house, and later Stillman came and laid a small path of crushed shell so he could wheel right down to the shore. He started to work, tapping out a long-postponed article he'd planned for the museum's *Natural History Magazine.*

Jesus Christ, he likes this place. He'd let himself be comforted by it, by all the sounds and the familiar smells from childhood—if it weren't for this goddamn girl about to arrive.

"Who's coming ov'ah?" Stillman asks, walking around the back of his pickup truck. It's the first time Jim's asked to go to town but, by nature undemonstrative, Stillman doesn't register any outward surprise.

"Hell if I know," Jim replies. He hoists himself into the cab, pulling up on the open door. Stillman knows better than to offer help. "You can leave the chair. I'll not get out of the truck," Jim says.

It was Stillman who brought the letter two weeks before. So that, damn it, Jim barely had a chance to reply. He remembers the envelope. It was festooned with big colorful stamps, like a missive in a bottle encrusted with barnacles and limpets.

"By God with that shoal of stamps, you can't tell where it's from," Stillman observed.

Jim nodded, though he could tell right away. He could identify each of the birds on the stamps: the Solomon Islands white cockatoo, the ultramarine kingfisher, Sanford's sea eagle. Jesus Christ, Finsch's pygmy parrot—a bird he'd collected. Official seals marked the letter's route from Honiara, via Port Moresby and Brisbane, to Washington, D.C. Forwarded to Jim from Greenwich by his brother Cecil.

Inside—a letter written on State Department paper with an embossed eagle and signed by a consular agent, whatever that is, with the singular name Sethie Bloom. *We know you will be pleased to host Ms. Baketi* (like hell he will!) *who will be arriving* (today!) *for a month before her medical training begins* . . . (a goddamn month!) *allowing her time to get accustomed to life in the United States.*

Jim doesn't see how anyone would get accustomed to anything staying here with him.

What the hell's he to do with a medical student from the Solomon Islands? He's too old, too drunk to *host* anyone. Besides he's a cripple. Jesus Christ, he should have wired straight back, just as soon as the letter arrived. *No. Stop. Won't have her. Stop.* He still doesn't think he ever said yes.

There was something else in the envelope. He'd held it up and two folded sheets of newsprint fell out, one showing a photo of a girl with a big circle of hair, a full head taller than the white, bespectacled teacher standing next to her.

New Georgian Girl Headed to New York.

Top Student at King George VI, Student of Fiji School of Medicine, Wins First-Ever Medical Scholarship to the United States.

It made front-page news in the official *British Solomon Islands Protectorate Newsletter* and merited a two-page write-up in what looked like a more popular, local rag called *Tok Tok.* Competing there with stories on plans to celebrate Fijian Independence Day, a feature on *kastom* magic, a photo of a local crocodile hunter.

"Jesus Christ," Jim swears aloud. He spits out a loose piece of tobacco.

Stillman watches Jim lift his foot over a hammer, a coil of rope, a wood clamp, all of which lie strewn across the floor of the cab, and wishes he'd thought to clean them out. Turning down the wooded road to town, he glances over at Jim, who stares grimly forward, chewing on the end of an unlit cigarette.

Jim looks fragile—even more so away from the cove. His shirt is clean and pressed, thanks to Sarah, who sends his clothes over to the mainland to be laundered each week. But still he manages to look disheveled, stick-thin, his eyes bloodshot. The scar down his cheek, where some other boy, Stillman remembers, had caught him with a fishhook. His leg missing. Old man.

In fact, they're practically the same age. They'd played together when they were youngsters. Jim had the grand family, the big summerhouse. He had the cigar-smoking grandfather, captain of a schooner with teak decks and shiny brass fittings that seemed to take up half the Thoroughfare. But Stillman lived close to the reed beds, which were their favored hunting grounds. He got to help his pa haul lobsters. Best of all, he got to stay on the island when Jim left—something he knew all the summer boys envied. During the war, he'd considered himself luckier too when he was sent to France while Jim, he heard, went to the Pacific.

Circumstance has separated them. Even so, Stillman feels the unspoken camaraderie of boyhood—of squelching through the bulrushes, hot mud oozing between their toes, the wide-brimmed summer hat his mother tied tight under his chin. They'd searched for frogs and birds' nests, crabs and June bugs, garden snakes, and the small globular jellyfish that floated in the millpond. Jim had always a purposeful intensity about him, insisting they memorize scientific names, then teaching himself to skin. While Stillman was content enough to catch critters, then let them go.

The sight of Jim sitting rigid and uncomfortable in his truck makes Stillman feel protective and wary of the fresh-faced groups of summer folks assembling in the small lot before the ferry dock. As he pulls in, he finds himself suffering from what he considers a long-outgrown adolescent resentment of these men with their 200-horsepower engines, their money and spare time; these women with their pretty legs. Then feels put out by Jim's family for letting the old man stay on his own, shunting their responsibilities onto Sarah and himself.

These thoughts surprise Stillman. He lives on his own too, and likes it that way. Besides, aren't these folks Jim's own?

To hell with it. They've all had their trials, their suffering, their luck. Islander or summer person, lobsterman or investment banker: he'd done with such distinctions long ago. His wife Esther died twenty years ago, after her long battle with cancer. He'd had a son too, who drowned. There's no reason he should feel sorry for Jim. Though Stillman does have Sarah down the road, which is a comfort, no matter how much he grumbles at her.

He parks, mindful to give Jim a clear view, so he'll be able to see the ferry come in without getting out of the truck.

"Boat's not in for ten minutes," he says, thinking he'll check in with Floyd at the boatyard, see if he's managed to repair an engine part Stillman left some days ago. "I'll be back once she's in."

Jim grins—a specter-like smile, twirling the unlit cigarette between his fingers. And Stillman feels a twinge of guilt and self-reproach, the kind he used to feel years ago dropping Sarah off at the island school.

It's a pity Jim's wife Helen isn't still around. She was playful and gay with no airs, so that she'd remember your name no matter who you were, even if she'd only met you once. Tall and regal with that lion-like mane of hair. The opposite of Jim, who's really an islander at heart—ornery like the rest of them.

Jim keeps a photo of Helen on his bedside table. Stillman saw it when be brought up wood for the fire, and noticed that the frame was turned to the wall. Well, it was no wonder if the old man couldn't bear to look at her; she was a beauty. He remembers Helen throwing her arms around Jim. Theirs was an outward, visible love, a thing Stillman's found to be surprisingly rare. His own and Esther's love had been more fraught, private, strained by her long illness.

People wave. Excited children wheel round the parking lot on bicycles, climb onto the bollards at the end of the pier, and hang out over the water.

Jim kicks the cab door open, letting the sun flood in, then fumbles in his breast pocket for a lighter. The small flame dances uncontrollably in front of his face. He can't say whether these shakes in his hands are due to nerves, old age, last night's drinking, or all three. Drawing in the smoke, he searches for some focus. Feels his fingers tremble against his lips.

The ferry blasts a horn as it enters the Thoroughfare, then rounds the red nun to avoid Post Man's Ledge. Tall and white, it dwarfs the yachts, the fleet of Herreshoffs and sailing dinghies moored closer in, then sets the lobster boats tossing at their moorings. Near the bow, a clutch of passengers gather at the rail. He sees the tall black girl among them, and looks away. Not ready, but will he ever be?

As he eases himself down from the cab with the crutch, a small girl in a sundress stops to stare openmouthed at his missing leg. He glares back until the girl's mother pulls her away. Jesus Christ, he looks as out of place here as she will. The sea churns a frothy white as the ferry's engines are thrown into reverse. The pier groans. Two eiders paddle furiously out of the way. A tern slips past.

Vehicles off before foot passengers. Jim's grateful for the extra minutes as each car drives off, making a distracting *kachunk kachunk* over the metal ramp. Volvo station wagons, a few Subarus, Fords, their roofs piled high with suitcases, cool boxes, duffel bags, bicycles racked on the back, reminding Jim of a stream of refugees fleeing some catastrophe—the Okies of the Depression. Hot, steamy children hang their heads and arms out of windows. In the midst of them, a long flat-bed truck carries timber. The ferry rises in the water as it disembarks. He breathes in hot tarmac, sea salt, fish, gasoline, carbon monoxide exhaust. Listens to the gulls.

She's tall, broad-shouldered, athletic-looking—like Tosca—even in her brightly colored dress with big flowers. Her hair tightly curled in a big wreath around her head like the Afro style popular in New York some years back. She's pitch black. This has given the other passengers something to ponder no doubt. It shouldn't surprise Jim, except that it does. Jesus, he can't be blamed, he's seen hardly anyone these past months, let alone a Negro. He corrects himself, not a Negro—a Melanesian from the South Pacific.

And someone must have told her to look out for a cripple because she walks straight to him. She has the same penetrating hooded eyes, the same slightly hooked nose as her father. Here she is, introducing herself in perfect English, which makes Jim wonder if she's been practicing.

"Are you Mr. Jim? I am Cadillac."

Christ, so that really is her name, not some sort of typo or misprint in the consular agent's letter. Tosca, his own name bestowed by an opera-loving copra trader, begets Cadillac. Named for what—the car, a pop song, a yearning for American largesse? A chance?

She puts out a hand to him and Jim recoils, a movement he instantly regrets but can't help. He doesn't like to be touched. To cover his rudeness, he drops his cigarette. Then forces himself to shake her hand.

She carries little. A small leather suitcase with buckles that looks as though it might have been lent to her by a missionary. A rolled-up mat, woven with pandanus leaf, the kind Solomon Islanders use for just about everything: shelter, sleeping mats, raincoats, wedding gifts. Good—the less she has, the easier it will be to send her back.

"Welcome," Jim says, nodding curtly. He'd help her with the bag, but she can see what shape he's in.

"Mr. Jim, he stop close up 'long sea, no 'long bush," Tosca had said, trying to explain where Jim lives, to reassure his daughter, and not just about the geography. The saltwater people of the Solomon Islands traditionally considered themselves superior to their brothers in the bush, smarter, cleaner and fiercer too—heirs of the headhunters. Though this sort of prejudice was discouraged by her teachers. It could cause fighting, even in her school.

Standing on the wide porch of Jim's house, Cadillac looks down across the cove and sees her father was right. The sea just there, almost the same distance as from the thatched platform of her mother's place at Enogai down to the water of the Kula Gulf.

She breathes in a great lungful of sea air—happy to be outdoors again, to have arrived after days cooped up in airplanes. New York had been crowded, with its too-tall buildings, reminding her of stacked cages of chickens! All vertical, with no horizon of sea or sky to orient herself, it made her dizzy looking up. There were so many people, she felt she couldn't move properly.

Here, standing on Jim's porch, she feels a childish urge to strip off her clothes, to run down to the water and jump in. She'd do it too, if Ms. Sethie, the consular agent, hadn't warned her emphatically about the water temperature.

Fox Island, Eagle, Burnt Island, Penobscot Bay: Tosca had remembered the names of Jim's sea after all these years. He'd traced a chart in the dirt with his toe. A few of the islands were large and mountainous like New Georgia, he'd said. Others were small wisps of places like the islands of the Wanawana. The Thoroughfare, he'd explained, was like a passage through the reefs. As if everything here would be similar or at least familiar, which she can see it's not. The blue of Jim's sea is a dark indigo and the shallows brown-green, rather than the brighter blues of New Georgia. The trees are pointy, needled, and sweet-smelling. The rocks along the coast, smooth, broad, and pink. And grass!

She remembers peering at grass through the wire fence at the Honiara Golf Club. Its lawns planted along the flat ground the Americans had used as a second airstrip. It was from here their fighter planes took off to shoot down the great Japanese Admiral Yamamoto, the same man who planned the bombing of Pearl Harbor, Tosca had explained, and soon after, the invasion of Guadalcanal.

She remembers the large red-faced Brits and Australian golfers in their hats and shirts, white socks pulled up to chubby pink knees. It's how she'd imagined Jim maybe. Not him. Thin, gaunt, he looks more like the bare-chested old Guadalcanal men who carry the heavy bags of clubs, the sinewy salvage collectors who pick up scrap metal from the war.

She turns to say something, then thinks better of it. "Mr. Jim, him nambawan man," her father had said, "alsem brother bilong me." She's happy to believe it, to look to Jim as a kindly and respected uncle. She'd grown up with war stories, tales of *Merika soldia*, in which Jim featured largely.

Behind her, he holds open the screen door as if he's not sure whether to come out or go back in. A crutch pinned under one arm, he squints into the sun.

Well, what had she expected—a handsome young marine in uniform still carrying his gun or radio? A mud-streaked GI from the war movies shown at Point Cruz? The cinema itself an old Quonset hut left over from the war, where sudden downpours of rain would erupt on the roof loud as machine-gun fire.

She can't remember her father ever describing Jim as young. Tosca had always spoken of him as an older man and teacher.

Looking at his sharp eyes, his tousled hair, one shoulder hunched over the crutch, the scar down his cheek, she can't help thinking of a mean dog, one of the lame strays you come across in the market at Honiara. One you need to step carefully around. She notices that he's taken off his shoe, how he ties the leg of his khaki trousers in a knot under his thigh.

Kicking off her own sandals, she walks down the porch steps, feeling the dry grain of wood against her feet. Then the grass all short, cool, and tickly between her toes.

She looks up to the sea, laughs, and swings her arms. A girlish joy that reminds Jim suddenly of Helen. Grunting, he swivels round on the crutch and turns back inside. Surely, by now, he's allowed a drink.

The *Laysan rail*, Porzanula palmeri

The small, sandy-colored, flightless bird, with green spindly legs and feet and sharp red eyes—not more than six inches from wing tip to wing tip—was nearly fearless. If you stood still, it would saunter right up to your boot and give the lace a determined tug, in case it might be something good to eat: a worm perhaps or some sort of grub.

Jim had seen the rails at Midway, the tiny atoll smack in the middle of the Pacific, defended from the Japanese in what was later seen as the most important naval battle of the Pacific war. The turning point at sea, just as Guadalcanal was the place the Americans pushed back the Japanese on land. At sunset, the birds would break out in a reedy chorus, the sound of which one naturalist had compared to a handful of marbles being tossed on a roof.

He remembers how if you put out a pail of water, the bird would jump in to bathe—reliant as it was on puddles and pools of rainwater. H. C. Palmer, a collector for Rothschild, who first discovered the bird in 1891, wrote of placing a dip net on the ground for the rail to walk right into. It was that inquisitive. *Porzanula palmeri*: the species was named for him. Bird collectors, as well as the occasional frigate bird, were the rails' only predators, which went a way to explaining why they were so fearless.

P. palmeri had certain human characteristics. Brave to the point of foolishness, suddenly terrified beyond reason. If you made a noise or quick movement, it would tear off at full speed, raising its wings to leap over small rocks and pebbles, like a girl lifting her skirts. You couldn't help smiling at this, whether you'd been there at Midway, or seen ships sunk in the Coral Sea, or if you were fresh like Jim, still anxious to find out just how you'd hold up. It's what they all worried about—how they'd hold up.

What made you laugh even more was to see the rail pull up short and swerve to one side if it happened to spy a fly or moth. Never passing up an opportunity to eat—another thing the men could sympathize with. Afterward, cocky with its full belly, the bird forgot any former cause for alarm and would saunter off, or right back toward you. Maybe the men felt reassured by this, the tiny creature's quick vanquishing of fear, its sassy reestablishment of poise. The possibility of forgetting.

To tell the story of the rail, you had to start with the guano traders of the North Pacific Fertilizer and Phosphate Company who rented the small island of Laysan from Queen Liliuokalani, the last monarch of Hawaii, before those islands were annexed by the United States. After fourteen years of excavating bird shit, one misguided ship captain devised an alternative scheme to raise rabbits on the island: English white rabbits and Belgian hares. The result was ecological disaster. The rabbits quickly set to work commandeering the ground nests of petrels and shearwaters, driving them off, then eating everything in sight. Things were worse for the rail, which couldn't fly away. Soon there was nothing left except a handful of half-starved rabbits. Shot by visiting naturalists.

As luck would have it, a pair of rails had been introduced to Midway, where they'd flourished. Managing to live in happy coexistence first with the workers of the Commercial Pacific Cable Company, who having little else to do, set about planting trees and turning the grassy atoll into a mini tropical paradise. Then with wealthy American tourists, who flew out on Pan American's *China Clipper* and stayed overnight at the Gooneybird Lodge, named for yet another endangered bird, the albatross.

And here's a piece of history—twenty-one marines sent to Midway by President Theodore Roosevelt, not only to guard the cable station but to protect the birds. Especially the albatross, as unscrupulous feather hunters would walk right up to their nests and bludgeon them to death.

The albatross survived, barely. The rails did not. By 1943 or 1944, some sailors who'd delighted at the tiny birds' antics might have noticed there wasn't a pair left. For the Battle of Midway, while marking the beginning of the U.S. Navy's victory at sea, also signaled the beginning of the end for the rail.

Rats, so often to blame, were the main culprits, brought in on navy landing craft that pulled right up to naval pontoons. Habitat destruction was a secondary cause, as the Seabees cut down the Norfolk pines and she-oaks planted by the cable workers, and leveled the ground to build their runways and docks. Even worse for the rail, the navy cut back the grass for mosquito control. Grass provided shelter for the small birds, and without it, they cooked to death as ground temperatures reached 150 degrees Fahrenheit.

The Laysan rail was just one small, generally unnoticed, casualty of the war, caught between the hatreds of the Americans and the Japanese, Jim had written in his book *Extinct and Vanishing Birds of Oceania.* Its case was particularly tragic as the bird had been extirpated twice. First from Laysan, then from Midway.

Some of their deaths were horrible, and some plain lonely.

Jim's not sure what makes him think of the rail now. Must be the girl reminding him of the place, or reminding him of the bird itself, with her forward, easy manner that might make you worry. More likely, it's a way of not thinking. He pours himself a gin and tonic.

A Cabinet of Auks,
American Museum of Natural History,
New York, July 1973

"**B**ad news about Jim's leg," Mann, the chairman of the Ornithology Department says, coming up behind Michael and laying a thick hand on his shoulder.

It's hot and stuffy in the sixth-floor lecture room, where the department's monthly meeting has just drawn to a close. Michael had *spaced out* as Americans like to say. Sometime after a presentation on Sichuan hill partridges, and before the inevitable budgetary bickering. It's incredible really how these men, who climb far-off mountains and trek deep into thick forests to locate rare birds, have difficulty securing lightbulbs and paper clips.

"Yes, very," Michael agrees, dissembling. Baffled as to why Mann mentions Jim now—half a year after his abrupt departure. Unsticking himself from the leather chair, smoothing out his linen trousers, he remembers clearly how his heart leapt when he heard the news Jim might not be coming back. Not that he'd wish an amputation on any-one, of course not. Nor any other infirmity. But at Jim's age, and with the old man's drinking problem, wasn't it was high time for him to go? The leg was just the final blow. Hadn't they practically assigned him a minder with Farrell, their Central American expert?

"I stop him biting," Farrell had said, grinning.

"Now that Jim's retiring, I'm wondering if you might write up one of your esteemed profiles," Mann continues. "Well, not officially retiring of course, but in practice."

Mann, an elder statesmen of evolutionary biology, is white-haired but jowly with the thick set of a boxer, a good six foot four. And Michael feels at a disadvantage standing so close. At least, he's well dressed, in his pressed linen suit and polished shoes. It's a thing he takes prides in: adding a touch of English class to this nest of khaki-trousered, tweedy birdmen. The other exception being Laina, the department's first and only female curator, an Australian who wears jeans and ties up her hair in a jaunty scarf.

He clears his throat, not sure whether to point out that the *profiles* he'd written for the ornithological journal the *Auk* were in fact a series of obituaries.

"Maybe you could get Laina to help you with the legwork," Mann suggests. "She's close to Jim."

Michael weighs the tastefulness of a wry retort, then decides against it. Mann must be Jim's age or a little older. Instead, he finds himself nodding banally. His nostrils flare at the trace of human sweat which hangs in the room, overlaying the academic smells he loves: the aroma of old leather, musty books, the sharp mothball scent of dichlorobenzene used to keep insects out of the skins—smells that tie him to his career. Two black os-cillating wall fans strain to stir the stultifying heat. He listens to the desul-tory twittering of caged meadowlarks from the sound lab next door and wonders if it's possible to accurately study the songs of captive birds.

It's another thing that bothered him about Jim—the way the older man had begun to monopolize Laina's time. He blushes to think now how he'd lectured her on women's equality and her responsibility as a role model. Warning that she risked sidelining her own important work on New Caledonian birds; that she shouldn't allow herself to become an older man's uncredited dogsbody, which had been the fate of some brilliant female ornithologists before her. Just why she'd agreed to help Jim with the onerous task of cataloging the department's type specimens, he couldn't understand.

He blinks, smooths his mustache down with a thumb and index finger.

Retreating to his office, Michael sees Laina's door invitingly open. Unsure whether to approach, he pauses a moment, running his hands along the top of a cool glass cabinet. It's a display case he passes many time a day, hardly taking note. But now, flustered and put out by Mann's assignment, he finds himself peering down at some yellowed news clippings and a large stuffed auk.

Rothschild's Birds to Be Brought Here, a headline from the *New York Times* gloats. *Famous British Collection Acquired by the Museum of Natural History.*

March 13, 1932, he reads on. *Over a quarter of a million skins to be sent in some 200 crates from England. Including the extinct great auk, the Labrador duck, the Solomon Islands blue-crested pigeon—a specimen so rare that none is known to exist in any other museum.*

It was a coup for the department, securing its reputation as one of the best, but a huge loss for Britain, Michael thinks with a rare twinge of patriotism. And a tragedy for the tall, shy Lord Walter Rothschild, who'd spent his life collecting. Rothschild had more than fifty birds named for him, hundreds of butterflies, as well as a giraffe. There were photos of Rothschild driving a carriage to Buckingham Palace behind a pair of zebras, to prove the animals could be trained. Of the top-hatted lord sitting astride a giant tortoise.

The 1930s—when Jim came of age. Surely those were the department's golden years. Its collectors, dispatched across the globe, led the way in a frenzied transatlantic race to acquire as complete an inventory as possible of all the world's birds. It was imperial in scope.

Jim had been part of that, if at the tail end—entering the profession at a time when science, exploration, and hunting went hand in hand; when ornithologists sought birds through the sights of their guns rather than by looking at cells through microscopes. He was one of the old guard. One of the last of a dying breed of gentlemen collectors: Rothschild; the French textile heir Jean Delacour; even Theodore Roosevelt might be counted among them if he hadn't become president. Men who didn't have to work for a living, Michael thinks with envy. Instead, they lavished their family money and sometimes their friends' fortunes on birding. The way museum trustee Leonard Sanford persuaded his philanthropist pal Harry Whitney to build a new wing at the museum, then to fund the ambitious Whitney South Sea Expedition.

As the department's self-appointed historian, Michael usually enjoys writing about these men. He'd have had some fun with Mann's assignment—if the focus wasn't on Jim. It worries him that Mann doesn't think he has better things to do.

Jim's largesse was on a lesser scale. Still, hadn't he financed the museum's bird-banding project on Great Gull Island? Hadn't he paid for all the back copies of the *Auk* to be bound in rich Morocco? It had become departmental lore, the night Jim lifted all the cracked leather chairs from the library and had them reupholstered after the union refused funds. He'd paid for Farrell to study parrots in Guatemala and for Laina's salary before she was appointed curator, which is perhaps why she remained so loyal.

It was part of the problem too. Jim was a benefactor, not an employee. No one had the right to tell him to go. It's why he was allowed to linger so long, stalking the hallways, slapping schoolchildren's fingers when they pushed the buttons in the elevator and slapping just a bit too hard, insulting people. Insulting Michael. It had taken a medical surgery to get rid of him.

Glancing once more toward Laina's door, Michael taps the top of the glass case decisively, then withdraws to his own office. He feels resentful, discouraged. A monkey's ass, Jim had called him. The memory still smarts.

The truth is, there's no one he'd less like to write about than Jim.

Fox Island, Penobscot Bay, Maine, July 1973

Damned considerate of her to keep out of the way, Jim thinks, happy not to be watched stumping down the stairs. Some mornings he can manage, negotiating each step with the crutch. Other times, he's reduced to going down on his ass. Bump. Bump. Bump. Like goddamn Winnie-the-Pooh.

Good, she's not here in the kitchen either.

Swinging across the wide, painted floorboards, he kicks the door open with his foot and stands for a moment in a pool of sunlight, letting it warm the bare skin of his hands and face. This is the time of day he likes most to be alone. Even as a boy, he'd felt cheated if his brother or sister Ann woke before him. He remembers jealously hoarding the early hours: the long day stretching itself languorously out before him, offering the promise of sailing and exploration, and jumping into the cold sea.

Summer, best time of year—bringing with it the tattered vestiges of childhood pleasure.

Hobbling across to the kitchen sink, he leans in against the counter to fill a blackened kettle. Listens to the buzz of a cicada warming up, a lone trill that will become a deafening chorus later in the day. The fish hawk's high-pitched whistle as it patrols the flat sea.

He lights the gas stove, then takes a battered tin mug and measures out two spoonfuls of instant coffee. There are other cups in the cupboards, proper teacups with saucers, shelves full of them, but he prefers this mug with its chipped blue enamel, part of a set he used to take sailing and camping. Perhaps it's a statement that he's been camping out, all these years without his wife. Damn that.

The water steams and he pours, watching the coffee granules spin and dissolve. He has to wait for the tin to cool so he won't burn his lips. He's not particularly hungry but he'll make breakfast anyhow and leave the girl's on the counter. It's too bad if it gets cold.

He's eager to get back to his work on the museum piece he's been writing; his routine thrown off during the past week by the anticipation of her arrival. He'll start anew, try to steer clear of diversions and confusions that have beset his past attempts. The effects of hangover. He has until noon or one at the most, he reckons, before the gloom and bad temper set in. The *black dog*, Churchill called it. For Jim, there are physical symptoms, bouts of shaking in his hands, cramps and spasms in the stump. Best way to deal with those—a stiff drink, or two.

Isla de Providencia. Province of Pirates, Jim types at the top of a fresh sheet of paper, then rips it out and begins afresh. He sits at a heavy wood card table he's shoved up against one of the big bay windows in the sitting room, with a good view over the cove and out to the end of the point. His chair positioned where he can watch the ferry gliding past, half past the hour at seven, twelve, and three, and set his watch by it. So that he can keep an eye on the fish hawks in their large, ungainly nest lodged at the top of a dead pine. The pair successfully hatching chicks this summer after years when their eggs had been too thinned by DDT.

Old Providence. The True Treasure Island—clearer and more to the point. He scrolls down. *Old Providence, an island in the western Caribbean Sea, is the true Treasure Island. And you may "lay to that,"* he types—employing the turn of phrase Stevenson's pirates use when they swear to tell the truth. He sips the bitter coffee, tugs thoughtfully at his left earlobe.

The idea for the article had come to him many years ago when he sailed to the Caribbean on the research yacht *Utowana*. Maybe someone had even suggested the likeness of the islands to him then; he can't remember.

He does remember his first sight of Old Providence with its volcanic-shaped hills rising from the sea: *fore, main, and mizzen,* Stevenson playfully named them. *All three seemed sharp and conical in figure.* The distinctive split hill with the two peaks: the place the marooned pirate Ben Gunn stowed his treasure in a cave. The snug, perfectly round harbor—*this pond,* Stevenson wrote—protected from the ocean by an off-lying islet.

Jim had rowed a small skiff across from the main island to Catalina. The distance fit Stevenson's estimate: *about a third of a mile from either shore, the mainland on one side, and Skeleton Island on the other.* Skeleton being Stevenson's name for Catalina.

Birds rose from the green trees, just as they did when the *Hispaniola* dropped anchor, *wheeling and crying over the woods.* In the small trees and thickets along a path, he'd found a golden warbler he later named for Helen, *Dendroica petechia helenai.* Its yellow crown and the small chestnut patch on its breast, distinguishing it, just as he suspected, from the brown-capped warbler on nearby Saint Andrew's.

Any recent visitor will see how much the anchorage resembles Treasure Island's, he types.

Cadillac walks across the wet grass of the early morning, ambles along the rocky coast until she comes upon a small beach. The sand had been submerged at high tide the day before so that she hadn't noticed it. But at low tide, there's a tiny fan-shaped cove. She clambers down eagerly. The fine pale sand is strewn with mussel shells. She picks up the sun-bleached exoskeleton of a sea urchin, an orange crab shell.

Looking back, she sees how the small drop hides her from the house, making this a private place she can lay claim to. The way Solomon Islands women stake out a certain beach for bathing—a place that's taboo for men. This shouldn't be a problem, as she doubts Mr. Jim could make it down the rocks on his one leg or in his wheelchair.

It had surprised her to find Jim was an amputee. Tosca hadn't mentioned it, but perhaps he lost his leg after the fighting in New Georgia, when the war moved on to Bougainville and to the Philippines. That would explain why Tosca hadn't known. This in itself is a new concept, as up to now it seemed her father knew just about everything.

Here's something else: the size of Jim's house—big as Mendana's or Bloom's Hometel, bigger than the Point Cruz Yacht Club. The way the old man lives in it all alone. In the Solomons, if you had a house even a small fraction of this size, it'd be filled with *wantoks*, relatives or people who come from the same island or who speak the same language. And children would be everywhere—running up and down the stairs, spilling out along the upstairs balcony, dangling their legs over the porch steps, trying out their balance on its flat balustrade.

She walks down to the sea, steps into it. *Owee.* The water's like ice, so cold it burns. She manages to put both feet in, then forces herself to wade up to her calves, the chill shuddering up her legs. What would her brothers say and the other boys, always teasing the girls who didn't dive right in? Suggesting they were bush people. They'd never felt *this* water. The shock spreads to a numbness so she has to rub her shins vigorously to get some feeling back.

Stevenson, it must be acknowledged, never traveled to the Caribbean. He had yet to sail to the South Seas when he wrote *Treasure Island.* He'd once described the flora of his island as *part California, part chic.*

It's Jim's contention though that the author used Old Providence as a template. He believes Stevenson read of the island, first in a highly popular, if slightly suspect, account of an eighteenth-century shipwreck, penned by Sir Edward Seaward and discovered posthumously by one Miss Jane Porter. Also that Stevenson would have read the far more discerning survey conducted by Mr. C. F. Collett of the Royal Navy and presented to the Royal Geographical Society in 1837. The survey attracted public notice as it persuasively identified Seaward's island as Old Providence.

Robert Louis (or Lewis as he was christened) Stevenson most likely read the Seaward Diary when he was a sickly lad growing up in Edinburgh, Jim types. *He no doubt read Mr. Collett's account; he was an avid reader and drawn to sea tales. Both his father and his grandfather built lighthouses.*

Indeed, Stevenson tipped his hat to Collett when he named the captain of the Hispaniola *Smollett. Or was that mere coincidence?*

Jim looks out the open window at his own smattering of islands, his own lighthouse across the Thoroughfare at Goose Head. It's a still, bright morning with hardly a breath of wind. Soon the small sailing school dinghies will be floundering about, caught in irons at the entrance to the cove. These morning lessons must put children off, the prevailing sou'wester often not picking up till noon. The day is set to be a scorcher as a heat wave wends its way east. Good news for the girl, accustomed as she is to the equator.

The similarity between Treasure Island and Old Providence had greatly excited Jim, when he visited the island some forty years ago. He'd set down all the main points in his field notes, planning to take it further when he returned home. But somehow he'd let it go, with crates of birds to identify, new species to describe. With Helen to propose to.

It was his son Fergus who unwittingly rekindled the idea, when Jim was still in the hospital, when he felt his lowest. He was bedridden and in pain, what was left of his leg strapped down to a lathe of some sort to keep the muscles from retracting, when Fergus had thoughtfully brought in some of Jim's books to cheer him up: Conrad, Hemingway, Stevenson. That morning, after rereading the tale and drinking copious amounts of coffee—it was the one palatable thing they offered in that place though it was cold and served in a Styrofoam cup—the likeness and the particularities of each island resurfaced. And he became so bitten by the notion that his doctor proclaimed he'd turned a corner. Well, perhaps he had.

He grasped the idea like a lifeline.

She looks up across the cove and takes note of the birds, so she can describe them for Tosca. Cormorants perching on some rocks, wings outstretched. A tern skimming the flat surface of the water. Doves— she can hear their mellow cooing from someplace inland.

But here's something new—gulls. She hasn't seen gulls in the Solomons and Tosca would be impressed by their loud squalling and wheedling, their gleaming white feathers, their bright yellow eyes and legs. They're cocky too. One careens in to land on a rock nearby, fixes her with its eye, and she has to chase it away before it makes off with her comb or toothpaste.

Gathering her belongings, she squats at the edge of the water to brush her teeth. She spits. The white foam washes in and out on the flat sea.

In the Thoroughfare, a lobster boat heads out to haul traps. The diesel chug and the gentle wash of the sea make her daydream of the rickety old Chinese trading boats that putter about the South Pacific and she finds herself wondering if she might travel back to Honiara on one of those boats but shakes her head. Of course it would be impossible. A boat like that would never make it. It's a wonder they stay afloat between the islands.

When she spits, a good-size fish lurking just below the surface darts up to suck down a bubble of the toothpaste, mistaking it for the larva of a small bug, or spawn of some sort.

She stands, searching the edge of the beach for a sharp stick suitable for spearing.

Jim runs his hands over the smooth grain of the table, rests them on the chunky keys of the typewriter.

"Just like Hemingway's," Fergus had said, presenting him with the machine, a portable Corona 3. And Jim, who's not good at accepting presents, has to admit it's a godsend. His handwriting shot to hell.

To prove his theory about Treasure Island, he's squandered a good deal of time trawling through the three-volume Seaward diaries and the more succinct naval survey, jotting down nautical and geographic clues. Flipping through these now, he sees his notes and page references are as shaky and illegible as Billy Bones's book of sums and crosses—the illiterate pirate's attempt to keep track of the ships he'd plundered, the share that was his due.

Fergus, no doubt, intended the typewriter for more practical uses. Bills and correspondence for instance, rather than more ranting on obscure topics of natural history and minute physical distinctions, which might be how the boy would see this too. A taxonomy of islands, not unlike comparing different bird skins, which is maybe what Jim likes about it, why he might be good at it.

He reaches out to retrieve the twisted butt of a half-smoked cigarette. No use letting it go to waste when Sarah has to bring them over from the mainland. The keys of the typewriter make a purposeful telegraphic sound in the empty house, like a wartime code transmitter.

He hears her before he sees hers. She's singing a catchy tune in pidgin. *Time you go 'long way 'long sea, supposim you no lovim' me*—the words as far as he can make them out through the open window.

He remembers how the Pacific Islanders could sing. How they sang all the hymns and church music the missionaries taught them. Though their talent was a far older one. A gift passed down by mothers singing to their babies. Headhunters ululating as they paddled their grisly trophies home.

Me writim letter 'long you. Supposim you no lovim me turu.

Her voice is rich and high. If she were back home, no doubt, the others would join in, taking up different points of harmony. He remembers coming into a small Catholic mission at Marau Sound after they'd pushed the Japanese from Guadalcanal. The villagers had returned to repair an abandoned church and were weaving an altar from sago palm fronds and bamboo. He'd stopped, pleased to accept a man's offering of a coconut and sliced papaya, when some women started singing. It was Schubert's *Ave Maria* and their voices spread out, washing across the water like sunlight as they escorted a carved statue of the Virgin Mary off into the sound in a small fleet of canoes.

It was the most beautiful singing he'd ever heard.

He looks up from his table and sees Cadillac walking up from the shore, her skin so black she looks purple against the green of the grass. Barefoot, with that unexpected blond streak in her mass of hair, a natural lightness the islanders sometimes accentuate with lime.

Time you go, you must think back 'long me

She's carrying something in her hand.

When she comes in the door, he sees she's caught a fair-size flounder, and that she's stuck her comb and toothbrush through her hair.

"Summer flounder," Jim says, thinking she might want to know.

Standing up and crutching into the kitchen, he opens the drawer for a knife, hesitates, then hands it to her.

"Also called a fluke." *Paralichthys dentatus*.

He leans against the counter and watches as she lightly scales the fish fresh from the sea: first one side, then the other. Running the blade of the knife from the tail up to the head, she scrapes under the gills, then rinses the fish under the tap. No longer singing but gently humming to herself.

She wears a sarong, a colorful cloth the islanders call a *laplap*. He watches her run the knife in a red streak up the middle to extract the fish guts, severing them neatly. She'll make a good surgeon, no doubt— tall, authoritative, confident, steady. He imagines her in his own doctor father's white coat with his stethoscope around her neck.

He admires the sureness of her hand.

I used to do this. I could scale and gut as neatly as you. I could skin a bird in minutes. As fast as any of Delacour's native Annamite skinners, whom the others could never match.

Fish scales stick to the sink and counter. The bright sun catches them as it streams in the window, scattering specks of broken light onto her face and arms. Into his eyes. Dazzling him.

He looks away. Shuffling sideways to the stove, he takes down the skillet, spoons in a bit of the bacon fat. Here he is fixing a second breakfast, just what he swore he wouldn't do. But then, he didn't expect a fish. He takes the gutted flounder from her hands. Laying it sizzling in the fat, he sees the ragged tear, a bloodied hole just behind the gill. Jesus Christ, she speared it!

Tosca standing barefoot, poised on an outcrop of coral, spear in hand. Swarms of reef fish swim about his feet, red, pink, blue. He is fifteen years old. The boy's delight when Jim obtains a navy diving mask and they can watch the fish underwater. Bright green and blue parrot fish tearing off whole chunks of coral with their beaks.

Tosca sauntering up the beach with an impressive barracuda, all silvery blue. He lays it on a wild banana leaf and Jim insists on measuring it. He uses the dividers from his skinning set, swivelling them back and forth. A small instrument designed to measure the wings of songbirds.

"Mr. Jim, did you lose your leg in the war?" Cadillac asks, moving to his side to watch him cook. So that he's glad the empty space where his leg should be faces away from her.

Well, that's a change, as his family, Stillman, even Sarah, politely ignore the stump, trying their best to act as if he's not stumping around on a crutch or sitting in a goddamn wheelchair. Strangers too, he's noticed, generally turn away abashed, or stare. Or worse, speak too loudly, as if he were deaf or imbecilic rather than a cripple. The war—another taboo. Jesus, people just don't ask him. She tramples right in.

"No, nothing so glamorous," he mutters, flipping the fish.

Jesus, did he really use that word? No wonder he prefers not to talk about the war, if his words are so wrong. There was nothing glamorous about what he saw.

She's too young, too foreign, to read the signs he so painstakingly erects around himself. Invisible markers signaling reefs. Like the warnings that ward you off when you sail into Stonington or some of the other more insular harbors of Maine: *No Docking. No Trespassing. Private Mooring. Go Away.* It's one of the reasons he likes the place.

He looks down at their bare feet and remembers another foot, a strange prefiguring of his own missing leg. A man running toward him, an explosion, the man jerked into the air like a marionette.

A piece of the man's body lands next to him. A foot. He picks it up and carries it over to the medic, who is already leaning over the hit Seabee, extracting a vial of morphine from his kit.

"It's not yours, not yours," the medic mouths, waving Jim away as if he's an interfering schoolboy, a goddamn nuisance. The Seabee stares up in horror as Jim holds the foot out. Christ, he doesn't need to take another look to see the man won't be needing it. The medic sucks the drug into the syringe, plunges it into the man's side.

And now, a belated wail of an air-raid siren and the whole world erupts. Bulldozers, trucks, jeeps, trees, tents flip and blow apart. Great holes are torn from the earth as a swarm of planes darken the sky. Some thirty or forty Jap Betty Bombers, red suns painted on the undersides of their wings.

The foot is naked, smooth; sock and boot have blasted off. Jim feels the rounded heel, the curved arch. Ligaments, bone, veins severed right through. He's in shock, deafened from the noise of the explosions, splattered with mud and God knows what else. October 1942, two days after his arrival on Guadalcanal.

The medic yells at him—For Fuck's Sake Get Down! Jim can't hear a thing but it's impossible not to read the medic's lips, his hand gestures. Get Down In The Fucking Foxhole! There's a dead man there. Later, he'll get used to that, callously using bodies to shield himself. He'll grow more used to the bombing raids on Henderson Field.

The medic waves angrily. It's his job to stay out in the open if needed, not Jim's. He doesn't relish the prospect of another casualty, especially a stupid bastard greenhorn. For Fuck's Sake, Put The Fucking Foot Down! Jim puts it down.

He steps away, glaring at Cadillac for making him think of that. It's what can happen if he isn't careful. But the girl just smiles, straightforward, good-looking, waiting for his answer. As if she doesn't consider his leg or even the goddamn war to be so all-important.

Sitting down with her at the kitchen table, he reels off the angry litany to himself, all the reasons the doctors gave for taking his leg. Restricted circulation in the artery (clogged up like old plumbing). Likelihood of a blood clot. Ulcerated infection of the shin. The onset of gangrene. He stares at Cadillac as if it's her fault. As if, an aspiring doctor, she's already part of the medical cabal ganging up to play this ugly trick on him. His own particular situation aggravated by drink and smoking, his careless neglect of a skin infection.

"Old age," he says quietly.

The fish is cooked to perfection, its skin charred, its flesh fresh and delicate. A back fillet for each. Cadillac mixes hers with the congealed corn beef and bacon he left earlier; this makes him feel bad. She drinks down the cold coffee, wasting nothing.

Jesus Christ, he can't blame her. *Bikfala Faet*, the bigman's fight, was the islanders' slang for the war. How else would you describe the inexplicable violence that descended on them from nowhere, like a plague? A war fought among their own islands by two peoples they hardly knew. The Japanese, who'd sometimes fished their waters. The Americans, whom the British told them were friends.

He picks a bone from his teeth, and stands. Jamming the crutch under his arm, he turns his back to her to scrape the plates and clean the fish guts from the sink.

Not sure what to do with her, Jim's relieved to find the girl takes herself off. He sees her walking down by the shore. When he wheels out to the porch in the afternoon, she's draped like a cat over the low branch of a beech tree.

The next days, she takes longer walks, each time bringing back some find or other. To his surprise, he can tell where she's been. The floppy leaf of skunk cabbage and branch of sumac from the brackish, swampy end of the cove. A bulrush from the reed beds near Stillman's place. A clump of moss and toadstools from the wood behind the house. A rounded beach stone, which means she's been to the north side of the island—a good two-hour walk, where the stronger surf rubs the stones smooth.

Feathers too. He stuffs them in a jar near the kitchen sink. The glorious red of a cardinal, the black and blue banded feathers of a blue jay, the tawny feathers of a barred owl. She shows a particular interest in birds. Later, he'll identify them for her, which feathers come from which bird.

Sometimes she comes in so quietly he doesn't hear her—like Tosca all over again, who would appear from nowhere. He'll look up from his work to see she's left a piece of sea glass on his table. A rare red, which most likely came from the pane of a lighthouse. A piece of flint that might be an arrowhead. A clamshell covered with barnacles. A black stone. Objects that fill him with an unidentifiable longing.

Other times he hears her singing. *Auki Love Song* and *Walkabout 'Long Chinatown*—she tells him the names of her songs. Another tune with a surprising refrain, *Ha ha, Japani, ha ha!* She sings it slowly, so he can make out the words.

Me lukuluku longo landi 'long sea. I look over the land and sea. *Ha ha, Japani, ha ha! Mifela comu downi longo mi parasuti.* I come down with my parachute. *Ha ha, Japani,* ha ha!

A Coastwatchers' song. A *kastom* song, she calls it, often played on Honiara radio.

"*Juniperus virginiana.*" Jim's sitting at his worktable in front of the open window. He takes the sprig of juniper she holds out. Picking off one of the unlikely blue fruits, he flicks open the jackknife he keeps in his pocket, peels back the tight scales to show her the tiny seeds inside.

"Cones, often mistaken for berries," he explains. "From the cypress family Cupressaceae."

He crushes the needles between his fingers, releasing the thick, sticky sap and a sharp scent of pine. A smell that conjures the image of his mother and Frau Leiber, their German housekeeper, packing away summer sweaters and blankets, laying them in big wooden cedar chests in the linen closet upstairs. A smell of summer's end.

"The juniper wood's used to repel bugs," he tells the girl. "Its cones are used to flavor gin." He smiles mischievously.

Swiveling the chair around to the bookshelves, he selects some books for her: Frank Chapman's *What Bird Is That?* from his youth; a newer, glossy *Field Guide to New England Plants*. She leans over his shoulder to look at a picture of sumac and witch hazel. So close that he can smell her skin, soap, and some coconut oil she must use. Too close. He snaps the book shut and thrusts it at her, wheeling back.

Then is alarmed by the look on her face, her reluctance to take it. Christ, he shouldn't be so rough.

Jim's books. Books stacked on his table; sprawled along the cushioned window seat; left, spines straining, on the kitchen table, on the floor. The shelves in the big room that run right up to the ceiling, like no library she's ever seen.

When he thrusts the book at her, she jumps back, half-expecting the sharp hand of her primary school teacher to come slapping down on top of hers.

"Don't touch. Don't touch," her teacher admonishes shrilly. It's at the small Methodist school in Munda. Cadillac and her schoolmates clamber round, pulling their low wood stools forward or kneeling on the thatch floor to see the book she holds out, forcing their grubby hands down into their laps.

Knights and Their Armour. She remembers the title. It arrives in a charity package from England. They listen attentively and admire the pictures. But afterwards, out on the school grounds, there's a hot debate about whether the English were seriously deluded. A boy Cadillac likes staggers about in front of the schoolhouse with an empty petrol can over his head. "Hey, look, I'm a knight! I'm a knight!" His voice echoes inside the can as he walks with stiffened arms and legs.

The knight's armor was impressively shiny, but how could you possibly fight in all that metal, they ask. You'd boil up. Even the petrol can on your head makes you hot and dizzy, the boy testifies. He sits next to Cadillac and grins; he's a little high on the fumes.

And what happened if a knight's canoe tipped over and he fell into the sea, someone points out. He'd go right down to the bottom.

Remembering this, she laughs aloud, then takes the books. Jim's relieved to find he's forgiven.

"It's hot inside, Mr. Jim," Cadillac says. "Would you like me to push your chair outside?"

"No," he snaps rudely. For God's sake, he doesn't want to be pushed. He likes it here, half in, half out the door, nursing his one-o'clock gin and tonic. He wheels backward to let her past. The heat wave has settled in, with temperatures in the nineties, more like what you'd expect in Boston or New York. He smells the heat radiating off the cedar shingles of the house, the cut grass, the dank smell of seaweed.

Even the birds have retreated, all except the fish hawk circling above the house, both parents working to feed their chicks. Sarah's hot-weather flowers droop in the flower beds: black-eyed Susans, purple echinacea, feathery cosmos, tall hollyhocks, sunflowers already shoulder height. He looks out at the grove of apple trees and the woods beyond.

"Do you want me to take you for a walk?" she persists. "I could push your chair down the road."

"No, goddamn it!" She won't know that he doesn't go anywhere, that he hasn't left this place since he arrived, except the once to pick her up. And how would he explain it? A self-imposed exile or self-incarceration. A useless protest that punishes no one but himself, unless he intends it to punish Fergus, who insisted on the operation.

To the girl, he'd seem like a petulant boy who refuses to do what's good for him. Holed up here, drinking, smoking, sulking—doing exactly what the doctors said not to. Unless it's a mild agoraphobia, something they failed to warn him about. Though, for Christ's sake, they regaled him with every other possibility.

Watching her walk round the side of the house, he pulls a crumpled cigarette pack from his top pocket and taps it lightly on his knee to loosen one. Christ, he can't be blamed. He didn't ask for this. He'd just as soon have died of a heart attack, or rotted, or whatever else they were worried about.

Lifting the stump to stretch the muscles, he feels a damp patch of sweat between his thigh and the nylon seat of the chair and wonders whether he should have at least tried a prosthesis. If only they'd offered him a timber leg with piratical appeal, instead of that newfangled fiberglass contraption. Still, he might have got around better.

The scars itch in this heat. He lowers his thigh back down, presses his bare foot against the wood threshold of the door, and feels the roughness of the dry weathered grain so distinctly in the missing foot, he glances down to make sure it's not there. The doctors warned him of this too. A phantom limb—like an overly vivid memory of things past. He'd like to push down the missing toes, stretch them with simian dexterity. He'd like to walk.

Wheeling himself back to the drinks table for a second gin, Jim notices distinct ruts drawn in the weave of the oriental rug like a well-worn path gouged by an animal. Signs at watering hole: three-quarters-empty clear bottle of Talisker's Scotch, half-empty green bottle of Tanqueray gin, green bottle of French vermouth in similar state, clear bottle of Mount Gay rum.

A package arrives for Cadillac. Sarah delivers it along with Jim's newspapers, a postcard from Fergus, and Jim wheels it in to her when she comes back from a walk.

Cadillac's hardly ever received mail, only short, infrequent letters from her mother when she was studying in Fiji. All correspondences from Yale had come through Ms. Sethie, the American consular agent. So her heart leaps when she sees her name. The words *Yale School of Medicine* printed in blue letters along the bottom. This means they know she exists! They're expecting her.

She unsticks the envelope carefully, so as not to rip it. A thrift Jim associates more with his own generation. Inside, her own book—*The Yale Medical School Course Prospectus*—and a letter welcoming her and explaining the undergraduate courses she's to complete during a premedical first year designed specifically for her.

She sits on a chair at the kitchen table and reads the letter to Jim. "Introduction to Anatomy, Genetics, Biochemistry, Mathematics."

As if it were goddamn poetry. He stumps back into the big room.

She knows the need for doctors. The advances made during her own childhood. First the cure for *soreleg,* or yaws, the open pus-filled sores that covered the legs of so many children in school and could infect and warp the shinbone. A British medical officer and his New Georgian assistant had traveled by boat delivering single injections of penicillin—a miraculous treatment Cadillac's mother called *the needle.*

When Cadillac was twelve, a malaria eradication team arrived. Her mother scolded the men from Honiara as they handled her clothes, baskets, and cooking utensils, removing everything from the huts. But Cadillac remembers admiring their official-looking badges, which showed an X stamped over a blue sickle shape. It was the Plasmodium falciparum parasite she would later become so familiar with, examining blood slides in Fiji.

The spray left the walls damp with a milky solution of DDT. It had a strange smell. Bugs, insects, and dead geckos fell from the leaf roof, and her mother had to sweep them up. Cats died. But the chemical had useful properties. At school, they found that if they rubbed their heads against the damp thatch, they could relieve themselves of head lice. Cases of malaria dropped eighty percent in one year. Lives were saved.

It turned out there were vaccinations to be given against tetanus, polio, and whooping cough. Cadillac remembers the time before the clinic was built at Enogai, when her own baby sister died.

She looks down at the Yale book, studying the cover photo of students peering through microscopes, books, and petri dishes spread in front of them on wide counters, and is relieved to see that there are one or two black students, and a number of Chinese and Indian too. That almost half are women.

America prides itself on being the melting pot of the world, Ms. Sethie had promised, at the same time warning Cadillac that she wasn't likely to find any fellow pupils from the Solomon Islands. We don't usually make it this far, she thinks.

At George VI, and at the Fiji School of Medicine, students shared a few coveted pieces of equipment. The shelves in the library were half empty.

A Drawer of Parrots,
American Museum of Natural History,
New York, July 1973

"I think I might have what you need," Laina says, peering round his office door.

Michael can't help but take this in a way it's not intended. He follows with an expectant lope in his gait.

Wearing calf-length jeans and a plaid shirt tied casually in a knot around her waist, and carrying a shallow drawer from the collection cabinets, Laina might be mistaken for a pizza delivery girl, except that a sharp smell of mothballs wafts down the passage after her. Her Australian inflection.

She puts the drawer down on a long table in her office. It's filled with parrots: skinned, stuffed, and laid belly up, side by side, like plump colorful cigars. At one end, a pygmy parrot, which can't be more than three inches from beak to tail. It's green with a blue crown, the yellowed field label tied to its leg half as long as it is.

"Finsch's pygmy parrot," Laina says, picking it up. He takes the bird in his hand, expecting her to address some irregularity on the label, a possible misattribution. Of all the curators, Laina's the most exacting, tirelessly checking and cross-checking field notes and journals to determine, for instance, whether a collector actually shot a bird himself or whether the specimen might have been brought in by a tribesman eager for a plug of tobacco. In which case, as she rightfully points out, the data may be questionable owing to gulfs in language and understanding.

Having assumed these are New Caledonian birds or some of the type specimens she's been cataloging, Michael is surprised to read Jim's name scrawled on the label.

Micropsitta finschii tristrami. ♂ *juv.*
Layla Island, New Georgia. Solomon Islands.
June 19, 1943.
Lt. Jim Kennoway

She smiles and hands him another parrot as if she's letting him in on an intimate secret. He wishes she were. This one's a red and green lorikeet with a bright yellow band across its chest.

Vini margarethae Tristram. ♀.
Lunga River, Guadalcanal. Solomon Islands.
December 26, 1942.
Lt. Jim Kennoway

A whole drawer of parrots collected by Jim and by a T. Baketi, who must have been with him.

Leaning over, Michael picks out the largest. *Larius roratus*, a bird he remembers from his graduate studies. The male's a beautiful green with blue wings and tail feathers, and a brilliant red patch under its wing. The female, an equally striking red and blue. Together, they represent a classic example of sexual variation in plumage. For many years, the two sexes had been mistaken for separate species.

Cape Esperance, Guadalcanal, February 11, 1943, he reads.

"Don't you see?" Laina pipes up cheerfully. "The skins establish where Jim served, and provide dates. It's all here in the collection rooms." February was the month the Japanese secretly evacuated their troops from Guadalcanal, she reminds him.

He's astonished, stunned by her resourcefulness. He remembers moaning to her, but not in any serious way, about not being able to pinpoint Jim's military record. Here's a way to track it, though he's not about to spend hours searching through the skins.

"Jim wasn't the only one who sent back specimens during the war," she says. "Oliver Austin and Tom Gilliard also collected." Laina's parents had lived and worked in New Guinea soon after the war, he remembers. Her father was an ethnographer, her mother an amateur Lepidopterist. Gilliard had once joined them on an expedition and taught the young girl to skin. Oliver Austin had stayed on in Japan to serve as chief wildlife officer in MacArthur's occupation government. What opportunity they'd had despite the adversity of war.

"Though so far I haven't been able to find any of Jim's specimens sent after the Solomon Island campaign." Her voice, high and girlish, belies the serious nature of her professional accomplishments. Her thick auburn hair is piled ingeniously on top of her head.

"Perhaps Jim just got busy fighting the war," Michael suggests, half-heartedly. It seems reasonable enough. After all, his own life, though far less grand, has interfered with his work. Resting his hand on a tall wood sculpture, he looks down to see a painted man standing rigid and upright, his head caught between the jaws of a shark. A carving from the Eastern Solomon Islands. Her office unnerves him with it Aboriginal bark painting, its baskets arranged on top of bookshelves, its Pacific Island masks, carved clubs, axes and shields decorated with feather, fiber and shell hanging from the walls: objects more suited to the anthropology wing. Its general disorder.

At first Laina had seemed put out when Michael mentioned his profile of Jim. Touchy enough to make him wonder whether she'd taken offense that Mann hadn't given the assignment to her. It would surprise him. As sole woman curator, Laina's always been enviably immune to interdepartmental rivalry.

Certainly, she has enough work, judging by the piles of books and papers on her desk, Michael thinks enviously. His own compilation of the vernacular names of South American birds has been put on hold. The fact is he needs to go back to Argentina to finish it, but that's just where Nita is. His wife having quite justifiably left him to return to her home.

"Of course, you could just call Jim and ask where he served. That would be easier," Laina admits. She looks at him over the drawer of parrots, suddenly prickly and self-conscious, embarrassed perhaps by her overabundant enthusiasm.

Michael can't imagine asking Jim about the war, especially without the basic facts to fall back on. He can't imagine Jim taking kindly to being asked about anything.

She has something else. Riffling through her desk drawer, as messy as the desktop, she pulls out a small six-by-four photo—another thing Michael has had trouble locating.

"Voilà," she says more brightly. "One photo of Jim." She holds it under her desk lamp, so they have to stand side by side to see. Can he read this as encouragement?

He reaches out to take the photo, but is surprised to find that Laina holds on tightly.

Jim acted like a hunted animal, Michael scribbles on a piece of paper. *He covered his tracks.*

An unpromising beginning for an obituary of a man not yet dead. He crumples this up and tosses it aside.

The man was obsessively secretive as well as unpleasant. That won't do either.

He starts again, this time simply noting the facts he's established so far.

Jim Kennoway. Born Greenwich, 1903. Graduates from Yale, 1925. Accompanies Jean Delacour to Madagascar and Indochina, 1929. Appointed Assistant Curator, Harvard Museum of Comparative Zoology, 1932. Collects in the Caribbean 1932–1938. Joins Delacour's last expedition to Indochina, 1939. Studies Drepanidinae in Hawaii, 1940.

Somewhere along the line, Jim had got married and had a son who, Michael has heard, is a successful investment analyst here in New York, quite different from his father.

"What happened to Jim's wife?" he'd asked Laina. Was it his imagination, or did she flinch? He doesn't need to write much about Jim's wife but he should at least mention if she died or they were divorced. Or had she just got fed up with him and walked out, like Nita?

Laina had handed him the photo, then turned away with a deflated shrug, so he almost wished he'd kept quiet.

Swiveling around in his chair, Michael examines the framed departmental photos on his wall. It's surprising that he'd never noticed before Jim's absence from every one. His refusal to pose for even a single official portrait.

A pity. It might have been intriguing to examine past images. Though Michael can't imagine that Jim changed very much. A few scruffy jackets, tweed or seersucker, and a battered cloth hat were Jim's only variations on museum dress code. He'd served as a naval officer in the war. He kept his hair short.

It'd be more interesting to find out what Jim thought of recent changes in the field. Sibley's controversial egg white protein studies and DNA hybridization threatening to overturn the taxonomic order Jim and his forebears had spent their lives perfecting. It's a sea change Michael himself finds hard to adjust to.

There'd been improvements too, of course. A new interest in field identification that coincided with the improvement of binoculars. A growing interest in bird behavior, life cycles, and ecology, which could make the earlier preoccupation with skins seem dull. The entry of more women into the field. Like Laina. Like this pretty Japanese woman in the staff photo from 1966, lithe and neatly dressed in a fitted silk jacket, while the rest of them wear loosened ties and sideburns in a nod to the times.

What was her name? He peers at the typed caption. Ms. Misako Yamatori. Yes, he remembers her now. She was a visiting student from Hawaii, writing her dissertation on, of all things, the tongue shapes of Hawaiian honeycreepers, Drepanidinae.

He recalls his crush on her at the time, one he'd had to stifle pronto—being engaged that year to Nita.

"You should talk to Delacour," Laina had suggested after Michael asked about Jim's wife. "He knew Jim best from those days."

Of course, she's right. He should have thought of it himself. Delacour, the esteemed French ornithologist who'd taken the young Jim under his wing, spiriting him away to Madagascar, then Indochina. Who'd kept a desk in Jim's office.

Kagu, Rhynochetos jubatus

She looks down at the itinerary for her expedition to New Caledonia, the small French-ruled archipelago lying to the southeast of the Solomons.

It's astonishing how she can remain levelheaded in the field, calmly dealing with the crises that will occur—porters deserting, students coming down with dysentary or skin rashes, village chiefs taking offense or just being difficult—but her concentration will fall to pieces if she thinks about Jim.

As soon as she handed Michael the photo, she regretted it. She must make it clear she'll want it back. Not that she needs it. All she has to do is shut her eyes and there is Jim standing in the door of her office. His eyes bloodshot, his eyebrow arched, they way he tilts his head slightly as if challenging her. Shoulders hunched. Edgy. Bristly.

She draws her hair out of her face, retying her scarf. She and her group of students will spend three weeks trekking in mountain forests along the Blue and White Rivers, then move up to the forests above La

Foa, surveying numbers of kagu. A quirky, spirited ash-gray ground bird, the kagu, she's argued, may represent an intermediate between a small heron and a crane, with its wispy crest and long red legs. It's the sole surviving species of the family, Rhynochetidae, named for the small corn-shaped flaps above its nostrils. A group of birds thought to date back to the time when New Caledonia, far older that the other volcanic and coral islands of Melanesia, was part of the Gondwana Continent. Now highly endangered due to the introduction and predation of dogs. Her own estimate is that barely 700 remain.

She's been studying kagu populations for years, advising both French officials and the local Kanak chiefs on conservation measures, and often acting as a go-between. Relations between the two had been prickly since the days of blackbirding, when islanders were lured onto trading schooners and forced to work on Queensland Plantations. In 1878, a native revolt ended when the French decapitated the Kanak leader and put his head on display in the Paris museum.

This year, she will have with her two students who are technical sound experts, eager to make high-quality recordings of the bird's extended predawn call and response. Most usually described as a crowing or barking *gwa-gwa* or *waa-waa* but sometimes including a territorial hiss or shriek. Calls the Kanaks once believed were messages from the spirit world, to be deciphered by chiefs.

After New Caledonia, she and her students will fly on to Papua New Guinea to meet up with her colleague Ian Opal, an expert on birds of paradise.

She should never have let it go so long. Somehow naively assuming she'd have a chance one day. Like that wonderful book she'd read later by Gabriel Garcia Márquez, in which Florentino Ariza waits fifty years to consummate his insuppressible love for Fermina Daza. What she'd failed to take into account was Jim's age. The fact that he was a generation older, seventy to her thirty-five. Which was part of the problem. She worried that she suffered from a schoolgirl infatuation, that he wasn't suitable.

She looks down at her papers. It's important to give her students some downtime, as most won't be used to the tropics. For this, she's planned some scuba diving in the beautiful Ile des Pins and, when they get to New Guinea, rafting on the Wagi River. Her more serious students will prefer the days spent in the field. Lying in their tents at night, trying to identify the calls they hear: the loud, explosive snorts of the cuckoo shrike, the screech of the Eastern barn owl.

She remembers her first expedition as a PhD student: waking one morning to the haunting calls of kagu from the hills all around. Her own delight the first time she spotted the bright, eccentric-looking ground bird tearing through the understory.

She remembers herself age twelve, crouching in the bush near a displaying tree of *Paradisaea rudolphi*, the blue bird of paradise. Not far from her father's camp at Ubaigubi. Her amazement as she watched the male bird swing upside down and spread his iridescent blue wings. The strangely stirring, otherworldly buzzing throb, unlike anything she'd ever heard. Underneath, his black head with its distinctive white cowrie eye-rings, like a painted mask, while his two long tail feathers quivered above, each with a blue dot at the end.

It strikes Laina all of a sudden that she'd failed to learn anything from the fantastical birds she's grown up with and studied. That she's never taken a single cue from their extrovert courtship displays. Unlike the native highlanders, who adorn themselves in feathers and mimic the birds in their dance and songs. Even from the quirky, flightless kagu, which she has seen lift and fan out its crest feathers, display its barred wings, and perform a mad dance. Throwing its wings above its head, as if using them as shields, and skipping back and forth.

She should have taken a chance with Jim. She should have reached out and pulled him toward her, closing the office door behind them. Never mind the differences between them. She should have at least taken his hand. Run her hand along the sinews of his neck, up through his thick hair.

II
A Girl Named After a Car

Fox Island, Penobscot Bay, Maine, July 1973

Jim wakes, groggy and hungover from the night before, the pounding in his head aggravated by a gull screeching from the railing just outside his bedroom. *Jamie, Jamie, Jamie.* In his half sleep, it seems to him they call his boyhood name.

He rolls over, tries to sit up and swing his legs over the side of the bed, forgetting he only has one. The stump like a dead weight holds him back.

It's the same each morning. He has to get used to it all over again. Grapple with his own self-pity and disgust. His fingers recoil as they reach around the smooth stretched skin, the hard ridges of scar.

He's seen worse, much worse. Bellies torn open, guts strewn. Arms, legs twisted like contortionists', sometimes heartbreakingly graceful. There are faces he still dreams of, black and swollen with rot. A man, face fully bandaged, sucking through a straw, like H. G. Wells's Invisible Man. Jesus Christ, what did he see when the bandages came off?

He should feel grateful. His own dismemberment put off till now. His operation undergone with the luxury of anesthesia. His blood cleaned away so he hardly saw any of it except a few stains before they changed the gown. The pain, Jesus Christ, you couldn't compare. But perhaps that's why he forgets it's gone. He hadn't suffered enough to make it real.

Nudging himself upright, he flings his hands in the air and swears loudly at the gull, still screeching from the balustrade. And looks around the room with its familiar Spartan furnishings: his dark wood bureau and desk, his bed with the tarnished brass rails and knobs, the sea-facing windows and French doors that lead to the veranda outside. The soapstone sink in the corner.

Lowering his foot, he stretches his toes against the rough, scratchy weave of the sun-bleached kilim rug. Catches an unwelcome glimpse of the stump in the bureau mirror. The ugly, blunt rounded shape of the thing. Its grotesque pink hue. Nestled against it, his unaroused penis curled in its nest of gray hair.

Welcome to old age, the final decline. He's still got his mind, as far as he's aware. He's not sure in what order he'd like to lose his other faculties: eyesight, hearing, bladder. The inevitable slide. His set of toes looks lost, unmatched, unsymmetrical. His one thin leg unfit for the task of hopping.

He reaches for the crutch and remembers the other thing he's forgotten—the girl.

Goddamn it! He grabs the stick from under the bed and bangs it on the floor. His head throbs painfully from the sudden rush of blood. And goddamn Tosca! It was utter foolishness of him to send the girl. What the hell was he thinking, letting her travel across the world to a man he hadn't heard from in thirty years?

Pulling himself up, he clumps over to the soapstone sink. Splashes cold water up onto his face and rubs a washcloth behind his ears as he has since he was a boy. Running his hands through his short, thick hair, down the knobby vertebrae of his neck, he examines the lines of his face, the veins of his bloodshot eyes in the chipped mirror. Counts off the reasons why she shouldn't be here. One, he's too old. Isn't this why Fergus threatens him with a live-in caretaker, or even worse, a nurse? Two, he's a drunk, and judging by his face this morning, not a pretty one. Third, and most important, he'd like to be left alone. He doesn't want anyone else in the house. To have to consider anyone else's needs, or worse, their opinions. He'd like to be allowed to retreat. Is that too much to ask?

He cups his hands under the tap and brings them to his mouth to drink, tastes the slight metallic tang in the water. Looks down at the blue-green stain of copper under the faucet. A taste and smell of his childhood.

Jesus Christ, it's his own goddamn fault. He lowers himself onto the wooden chair next to the sink where he sits to wash the stump each morning, and every night if he's not too drunk, and casts his mind back—trying to remember exactly how it was she came.

A year ago, July, it must have been exactly that, when a man from the bank had made a trip up to Greenwich from the city to discuss Jim's inheritance. Another matured investment from his maternal grandfather, a man Jim had loathed, consequently loathing the money too, which seemed designed to be parceled out throughout his life, so that he can never escape his boyhood fury, rising again each time.

He remembers how he'd stood, skulking in the doorway of his house, wary, drunk—two-legged. The banker in his expensive suit, which was too dark for summer. His too-tight brogues crunching on the gravel and bread crumbs Jim had tossed out the door for the birds. His silver BMW pulled up next to Jim's beat-up Chevy. Jesus Christ, was it only a year ago he could still walk, still drive?

"Your brother Cecil's considering investing in the Hawaii Sunshine Plantation," the banker spluttered. He was puzzled no doubt not to be invited in. Curious why Jim lived here in the groom's quarters, while Cecil lorded it over the family mansion, a Gatsby-era extravagance, an architectural mishmash of shingle, German baronial, and windowed Versailles.

By comparison, the grounds around the disused stables were ramshackle and unkempt. Sassafras and sycamore saplings pushed up the paving stones. It looked more like what you might expect to find on a clapped-out farm upstate, rather than on prime Greenwich waterfront. Good cover for the birds, Jim liked to say.

"There've been reports in the local press that a Japanese firm's about to take ownership. If that happens we can expect shares to skyrocket," the man informed him.

"Are you telling me, young man, that you want me to help the Japs take over Hawaii?" he'd shouted. He was drunk. He felt like a fighter plane careening off the deck. Though he realized, even as he spoke, that he was serving up another story for Cecil to dine out on. Stories of his misfit, drunken brother. He's well aware it's not acceptable to use the word *Jap* anymore, that it makes him seem mean and coarse.

Jesus Christ, it was Cecil's fault too. His brother knew better than to send anyone over unannounced, especially after one o'clock, by which time Jim would have treated himself to a cocktail or two. Unless Cecil had done it for a lark, which was entirely possible. But surely someone at the bank would have briefed the emissary, warned him that a Pacific war vet, a man who'd served at Guadalcanal, might not take kindly to Japanese investments—whether it was in pineapples or the goddamn U.S. car industry.

He lathers the stump with antibacterial soap, rinses it, and waits for the skin to dry before sprinkling on talcum powder. Taking the elastic bandage he'd washed the night before, he lattices the stretchy fabric the way the nurses showed him, to prevent swelling.

The banker had blinked, backpedaled fast, staring down at Jim's feet. No longer seeing an eccentric rich man before him but an unpredictable lunatic. Damn right. Jim wonders if he could intimidate so easily now, from the wheelchair.

"Wait here!" he'd barked, stomping upstairs, letting the screen door slam behind. Why he thought he'd have an address for Tosca, he has no idea. Nor has he any idea how long he took rootling around for one. He came back down empty-handed and even angrier.

"If I've got any more of that bastard's money coming to me, send it to Tosca Baketi in New Georgia."

The banker looked confused.

"A hundred and eighty miles northwest of Guadalcanal," Jim explained. From the blank look on the banker's face, it was clear he'd never heard of Guadalcanal either.

"Tosca Baketi," he shouted as the man retreated to his BMW. "B-A-K-E-T-I. Write it down!"

"I had to offer the poor man a stiff drink," Cecil teased Jim later. "He looked like he thought you might have pulled out a shotgun."

"I might have," Jim said.

He had to give the bankers their due. They'd found a contact for Tosca, sent Jim a copy of the wire transfer. He hadn't thought of the matter again. Until just a few weeks ago, when the letter came, festooned with stamps, interrupting his solitude, shattering his peace.

Sending his girl was how Tosca chose to spend Jim's money. Supplementing her scholarship. For Christ's sake, how could Jim have foreseen that? He'd thrown his inheritance at plenty of things before. Paying Laina's salary. Paying for Farrell to study his parrots. In not one of those cases had he ever been expected to play any further role. Jesus Christ, he can't be expected to babysit. How the hell had Tosca tracked him down? No doubt with the help of that damned consular person.

Stump bandaged, he hops over to the dresser and rummages in the top drawer, where he keeps a flask of Scotch. He takes a good long swig, hair of the dog. Then another, and another. Feels the alcohol seep into his veins and feed his anger. He struggles with the trousers, which only makes him more furious. Having to sit and stand and sit to get the one leg in, the belt buckled round his waist, then to tie up the empty leg. Jesus Christ, he'll not bother with a shirt.

He's still drunk from the night before. He shouldn't drink so much with the girl in the house. But isn't this precisely his point? He wants to be able to do as he pleases. Drink. Smoke. Walk around naked reciting poetry if he feels like it. Isn't that why he came in the first place?

He doesn't want her here.

To hell with it, he won't put up with it any longer. He'll tell her to go. He'll tell her to pack her bag and get out. That easy. And if she won't agree to going all the way home, she can go to New York, or to Yale. Surely, there'll be someone there eager to take her. Goddamn money of his goddamn grandfather cursing him again. He won't have her in the house one minute longer.

"Girl!" Jim shouts. Jamming the crutch under his arm, he swings down the hall like an ape. The rubber top chafing his skin as he negotiates each step. Clump, clump.

The chair waits for him at the bottom, but when he reaches out, it rolls back so that he almost stumbles and has to grab hold of the railing to stop himself from falling. He forgot to set the brake, damn it.

"Girl!" he shouts again. She's not down here. Now he's struggling back up the stairs, down along the hall. Leaning against the wall opposite her door, he summons racist slurs, the discredited terms of his youth, to fuel his determination. Darky. Pickaninny. Negro.

Who says you're not lucid when drunk? He feels a sharp clarity of purpose and determination.

No answer. In that case, he'll force her out. His heart racing, his stump throbbing with pain, he pushes open the door with his shoulder and steps in. Empty. The bed neatly made. Not only made but not slept in. The top sheet folded exactly as he himself folded it a few days before.

He looks around her room, suddenly confused and disoriented. His anger undercut by a riptide of grief. The bed's his own, the bed he made after the war and couldn't sleep in without Helen. Those nights when he rolled himself in a blanket and slept on the hard floor. He wonders if he's got it all mixed up somehow. Whether Tosca's girl even exists or if he's invented her: some immaterial figment of a drunken, febrile imagination. The onset of senility after all. The side effect of loneliness.

I made this bed for you Helen. I limped down the hall with sheets, pillows, blankets. One at a time. The linen smells of cedar and mothballs. I pulled up the chair and sat to tuck in the sheets and smooth the blankets. Why did you not come home?

The bed too soft, too easy, too lonely.

He looks around trying to find his bearings. The brass bed rails, the French doors open wide to the balcony, the fireplace, desk, chest of drawers, the soapstone sink, all like his own room. Then starts to focus. Small things, distinct, exaggerated, disconnected, present themselves to him like a series of close-up slides. At the end of the bed, the girl's small missionary suitcase. Along the windowsill, a row of sea glass and shells she's brought from the beach. On the desk, the books he'd lent her, the Yale prospectus. In the open closet, two colorful skirts and three shirts hang neatly. A pair of flip-flops.

The paltriness of her belongings fills him with humility. Testifying quietly to the lightness of her existence, the enormity of her ambition, her leap across the world. The girl owns so little, less than him. And he's chosen to live this way: a squatter spurning the family splendor.

Lurching to the French door, he almost trips over the girl's pandanus mat, rolled up with a pillow and blanket folded neatly on top. Jesus Christ, she's been sleeping here on the floor.

He feels the smooth weave of the pandanus leaf against his cheek, the smell of wet fiber. He turns his face toward it in the dark, breathes in cooking smoke, the salty tang of seawater, the freshness of rain.

"Mr. Jim. Mr. Jim." Tosca shakes him gently, whispering. It's not yet dawn and he's chilled from a downpour in the night that's left everything damp. He wakes, fully alert, aware of a noise that had already begun to penetrate his dreams. The quiet grumbling of a boat approaching the island.

Now Tosca is kicking down the small lean-to, scattering leaves and dirt to erase any trace of their camp. Jim shoves his feet into his hard boots. He's got used to going barefoot these past weeks and the boots are stiff. He grabs his rifle, passes Tosca his captured Japanese gun, and they hurry down a small track they've cut through the undergrowth to the shore. Slither on their bellies up to the edge of a jagged coral outcrop where they've constructed a small blind of palm fronds.

There—just a few hundred yards out—a Jap whaleboat. A searchlight like the eye of a cyclops sweeps the beach, then blinks off, leaving the night even blacker than before. Across the water, they hear the harsh guttural sound of Japanese. The splashing of boots.

Silhouettes of three men wade in across the reef.

Cadillac knows drunks. The boys that leer at her from the safety of the bars at Munda. Afternoons after school, she'll stroll through town to pick up supplies for her father at the old Chinese trading shop: more thin netting for trapping birds, arsenic for his skins, a spark plug for the outboard motor.

"Hey pretty brown girl," the boys call. "You-mi go walkabout 'long bush." Lines they've picked up from radio hits, as if they themselves weren't brown. The boys her brothers know turn away, pretending not to see her. At the airstrip, the old man in his shorts, so tattered that you don't want to look too closely, and his rubber gum boots, waiting for Megapode Airways' twin-engine Piper Aztec to fly in, or the larger DC3s from Fiji and New Guinea, spitting at her or anyone else who comes close.

The Australian divers too, large and garrulous. "Hey Agnes beauty, bring us s'more beer will ya?" they call out from the veranda at the Agnes Guest House. Carousing under a single bare lightbulb and a slow ceiling fan. Singing their drunken songs late into the night: *Waltzing Matilda*, *Tie Me Kangaroo Down*, or Slim Dusty's hit, *The Pub with No Beer*. Or if they're feeling maudlin, *The Skye Boat Song*. Drinking their way through crates of Four X and Victoria Bitter or, if forced to, the local Solbrew, brewed and bottled in Honiara.

Round the back, their heavy oxygen tanks stand propped up against the house, metal canisters of air that let them stay underwater for hours. Their black rubber suits hang from the line like sharkskins. The shiny glass masks that cover their eyes and nose—how she and the other kids would like to try those. And the flippers for their feet!

So Cadillac's not afraid when she finds Jim in her room, shirtless, looking disoriented and confused. Stuck, as if he can no longer manage the crutch.

"Mr. Jim, do you want to sit down?" she asks, coming into the room. She heard him shouting from down at the beach and rushed up, worried he might have fallen.

"No," he says, his words slightly slurred. "Just help me to my room." Not bothering to explain why he's here or why he called. She reaches out to take his arm, the one on the side of the missing leg, turns her palm up under his, lays her other hand on top for support.

His grip is strong. There's surprising strength in it. She can feel the bones of his forearm, the sinewy muscle and tendons. He was never a big man, not tall like her father. Physically he was more like her brothers, slight and lithe. His bare chest is thin, with white hair, but his skin is firm, not yet wrinkly or saggy. His shoulder blades jut from his bare back like wings.

"All right, that'll do," he says when they reach his door but she helps him across to his bed anyhow. He sits and she pulls up a pillow behind him, straightens the sheets, and picks up a shirt draped over a chair.

On Jim's dresser, she sees a framed photo of a woman twirling across a great, long beach. Her arms are spread out. The woman looks right out at the camera. You can tell she's twirling because of the way her dress and hair fly out.

She picks it up.

"Leave it alone," Jim snaps.

USS Copahee,
En Route to the Solomon Islands, October 1942

The pilots are young and eager and already tanned a dark brown from going shirtless. They try to keep fit, running laps up and down the flight deck, doing pull-ups from the wings of the planes. Twenty Grumman Wildcats parked wing to wing, bound for Guadalcanal.

He remembers how they look up to him. He's older, married. He's assistant curator at the Harvard zoology museum while many of them have yet to hold a first job. Jim is jungle veteran, hoary lieutenant. Long John Silver. Their Ancient Mariner.

Except no, he wasn't old then, or crippled. He was a boy himself, thirty-eight to their eighteen. A teacher, a young uncle, which is maybe how they relate to him.

Too old to be commissioned, he'd wangled his way in through Naval Intelligence, like so many other East Coast Ivy League men, all determined to sign up after the carnage at Pearl Harbor. He'd been assigned to the Pacific front, to the USS *Copahee*, a civilian boat hastily fitted out as escort carrier. She is top-heavy and unwieldy.

Strong, muscular, any one of those boys could have knocked him down. Jim was thin and slight but tough. He'll come to find that he can survive on almost nothing. He can outlast them. He's not homesick either, even though he has a wife and baby. He's hard that way. Professor they call him. Pappy. Later, on *the Canal*, they call him Jungle Jim, owing to the fact that he keeps volunteering to scout alone, to go off into the jungle. They call him Bird Man, after they've pushed the Japanese west toward Cape Esperance and established safe perimeters and he starts shooting birds and drying the skins in his tent.

In the port of New Caledonia, he fishes a coconut from the sea, splits it open with a rock to let the boys get used to sucking out the milk and eating the sweet flesh. In town, he goes to the market and buys breadfruit and mangoes. He finds cassava root with the stalks still on, so they will know how to recognize it. Shows them how to mash and cook it to remove the natural toxins. He won't let them starve just because they don't know what to look for.

What really impresses the pilots is how Jim can shoot a tern from the moving deck, take out a flying fish mid-leap. They admire his .410 shotgun. A Harrington and Richardson folding model. Single-barreled, which makes the target harder to shoot. Trickier than a 12-gauge but smaller and lighter to carry. He doesn't point out that birds are all he's shot until now. That the jungles where he collected with Delacour were never more than a week or two's journey away from the decadent luxuries of French Indochina: the Metropole Hotel in Hanoi; the splendid villa of Jabouille, Resident Superior of Hue, with his cages and aviaries, his tame leopard chained to the front steps. Where five-course meals were served on eighteenth-century Bleu de Hue porcelain. The luscious scent of frangipani mixing with the more earthy and human smells of the Perfume River and the smoke from wood fires.

That alongside his experiences of jungle campsites and arduous treks through thick undergrowth sit other memories that might surprise them. Playing tennis in the highlands of Tonkin with the French resident's wife. His delight at her Parisian airs. How she turned out in immaculate whites as if going to her club and playfully scolded her pet gibbon, chastising him like a wayward child as he scampered back and forth in the trees above, excitedly following the trajectory of the ball.

He doesn't point out that it can be bad luck to shoot a bird at sea. Remind them of their Coleridge:

> "God save thee, ancient Mariner,
> From the fiends, that plague thee thus!—
> Why look'st thou so?"—"With my cross-bow
> I shot the Albatross."

No, he will let them look up to him, milk some confidence. It may be all he can give. Gourmand of the jungle. Connoisseur of wind, reef, and tide. He briefs them on the southeast trades that blow steadily from May to November lashing the islands' so-called weather coasts, on the less predictable northwesterly monsoons that set in after. The likelihood of squalls when the wind backs from north to west.

Solomon Islanders forage for more than half their diet, Jim instructs the pilots. He reads the sentence aloud from some handbook printed hastily by Naval Intelligence, or perhaps he makes it up, surmising. Chestnuts, almonds, ngali nuts, wild roots, and edible fungi. Fish, turtle, wild pig, crocodile, the possum-like cuscus, snails, ants— all can be eaten. Fresh water collects in natural bowls at the hearts of tree ferns and epiphytes. You can survive solely on coconut milk and meat for days.

He has talismans too to pass around. Silk maps from the Hydrographic Office. The islands crisscrossed with minutes of longitude and latitude, stamped with compass rose and magnetic variations, arrows and isobars depicting average wind force and speed and directions of currents. As if all this could impose some order. As if wet and soggy, struggling with hatches of cockpits and parachute strings, escaping fire, fearful of sharks, the pilots would have time to consult and plot. He gives them fishing line, iodine tablets for purifying water, waterproof matches. Tiny compasses, small enough to hide in their assholes. Thin phrase books of Melanesian pidgin. Cards printed with British, American, and Dutch flags with instructions to natives:

Dispala masta i gifim pas long yu 1 peren bilong Gavman! The white man holding this paper is a friend of the government.

Gifim wara bilong dring olsem kulau. Bring him drinking water and also coconuts.

Gifem kaikai, olsem kokuruk nau kiau nau banana mau nau popo nau ol gutpala kaikai. Give him food such as fowls, eggs, bananas, pawpaws, and other suitable foods.

Sapos Japan ikam kilostu yupala. If the Japanese come. *Haitim.* Hide him.

The cards are no doubt useless. Few of the islanders can read. Most of them are on our side anyhow, instructed by their colonial rulers before the fighting broke out. Organized into scouting patrols by the British, Australian, and New Zealand Coastwatchers. Traders, planters and district officers who'd stayed behind, risking their lives to spy on the Japanese.

Still the pilots hold on to the cards. Carefully, they slip them into navy-issued waterproof wallets, secret them away in the inner pockets of their flying jackets—the same way, Jim remembers, Hemingway kept a lucky rabbit's foot or stone or horse chestnut.

Cadillac's back. She's brought some coffee in the tin mug. A cup of water, which she puts on the table by the bed. She wraps her fingers over his, making sure he has a good grip.

Damn nice of her. The coffee's strong and bitter, the way he likes it.

"Some of our boys were scared of your people," Jim says. He remembers pilots asking him about cannibalism and head-hunting. He'd had some fun, reassuring them that the missionaries had long put a stop to all that—the ones who weren't eaten, at least.

"We didn't know then how many pilots would be rescued," he says. He's unsure if he's making any sense.

Card or no card, map or no map, dozens if not hundreds of Americans were pulled from the sea, carried into the bush, fed, washed, cared for by natives. Secreted back to American bases or to the Coastwatchers. Some of the islanders paddled hundreds of miles to carry wounded men to safety, skirting close to the shore at night, putting into mangrove swamps during the day.

He sips the hot coffee and wonders what it must have been like to make that journey, to travel by night bundled in the shallow of a dugout canoe, faint, feverish, wounded. He imagines the splash of the paddles, the canvas of stars, the ominous shapes of huge warships slipping past in the dark.

He must remember to tell the boys how the islanders turned out to be friends. Not only because the British said we were allies but because of their own bravery and kindness. Besides, they liked the Americans, especially the black soldiers. They liked the way American *Joes* would sit and eat with them, sharing food and provisions, learning enough pidgin to swap songs and stories.

He must tell them how PT boat captain John F. Kennedy was rescued by two New Georgians. By Biuku Gasa and Eroni Kumana, sent by the Australian Coastwatcher Evans on Kolumbangara. How Kennedy and his men had survived on coconut and water for six days. The Americans had given them up for dead after their PT boat, cut in half by a Japanese destroyer, went up in flames.

It had become legend—the story of how Kennedy had swum for hours towing an injured crew member by gripping the life jacket strap between his teeth, then carved his S.O.S. on a coconut husk. *Native knows position. He can pilot. 11 alive. Need small boat.* Less well known that Gasa and Kumana paddled that message some thirty-five nautical miles to the Americans on Rendova. And later returned to take young Kennedy to Evan's hideout, from where he coordinated the rescue of his men.

In this way, Solomon Islanders helped set the future of American history. But of course, Jim wouldn't have known that then.

And what if you were one of the pilots who didn't come back? What if you were one of the men who caught fire and fell burning into the sea? What if you were too badly injured, or too sick? What if you got lost, or stumbled into a Japanese camp or patrol by mistake? Jesus Christ, he'd seen what could happen then.

The coffee's strong and hot. The sun, coming in the window, is hot on his face and bare arms and chest. It works its way like fingers through the khaki trousers, massaging the cramped muscles of the stump. Cadillac sits at the end of the bed. He likes her there.

He remembers the pilots, how they all took off their shirts. Lean, brown, muscular, clean. Not sick and dirty yet, like when they went ashore. Not shell-shocked or bandaged or mutilated or dismembered.

"I was in Hawaii," he tells her, hoping he might make some sense if he goes back to the beginning, to Pearl Harbor. "I was looking for honeycreepers, at their tongues." He'd been working with Bryan, a curator at the Bishop Museum in Honolulu, examining how the tongues of different species evolved to adapt to the different flowers of particular islands.

"At home, our sunbirds and honeyeaters have long tongues like straws, to help them suck nectar from orchids and hibiscus flowers. Some have little brushes on the ends of their tongues."

Did she really say that, or is he imagining it?

Glossy Swiftlet, Collocalia esculenta

When Jim shuts his eyes, he's on Guadalcanal, near the Matani-kau River. There's a cave he wouldn't have seen except for the tiny blue-black swiftlets darting in and out, the way their feathers glimmer with a bright metallic sheen as they catch the sun. Glossy swiftlets with their blue green feathers, white bellies, and long pointed primary feathers, performing lithe acrobatics. Not unlike the barn swallows that nest over at Stillman's place.

He enters entranced by the birds and shines his flashlight up along the nests that plaster the cave roof. Pale pouches made from spit with small openings through which the adults hunch in and out. He listens to the thin, high-pitched twitterings echoing in the dark wet.

As he lowers the beam along the cave, it falls on a low natural shelf and illuminates something there. A small stash of rations—Japanese. He fumbles, struggling to switch off the light. At the same time, dodging to one side in case someone has already taken aim. Crouching against the wet rock.

As his eyes struggle to adjust, he imagines another man leering at him, a Japanese soldier toying with him, like a cat with a mouse. He waits. Far longer than he needs to. Trying to keep stock-still, not to breathe so loudly. There's no movement, no sound other than the birds darting in and out, their short, husky *vit vit vit*. It's so quiet he can hear the chicks now, fuzzy, featherless things, moving around in their cupped nests, their faint chirrups, their mouths opening for the bugs their parents bring.

He steps forward and takes the Japanese food, stuffing it down into his own pack. A ration of rice, a tin of dried seaweed. Best of all, two ceramic bottles. Poor bugger, who hadn't come back for these.

If you're lucky, he tells the pilots, you'll get picked up by canoe. If you're lucky, you might find something better than coconut milk to live on. Yo ho ho and a bottle of sake. If you're lucky, you might see swiftlets, or even better, hear the gentle cooing of the superb, or the red-throated fruit dove.

If you're lucky, Helen will still be there when you get home.

Layla Island, Wanawana Lagoon, Solomon Islands, June 1943

They flew him in at night. It was dark, except for the thin sliver of a moon. The weather was fine and the pilot flew his plane at just fifteen feet, skimming the reefs. He wanted to see just how low he could take it, or maybe he was experimenting with the new airborne radar. Jim looked to either side for enemy boats. New Georgia was as yet behind Japanese lines.

It was a short noncombat mission. The plane freed of its usual payload. It isn't safe to land in the sea with two five-hundred-pound bombs lodged under your wings. But the crew had brought their own ammo: a cache of empty beer and Coca-Cola bottles to drop over Munda on their way home. The bottles make an eerie wailing sound as they fall, the gunners boasted—like she-cats in heat, enough to drive the Japs wild. They were excitable as a bunch of schoolboys with fireworks.

They called their plane a Black Cat because it was practically invisible at night, with its nonreflecting black paint. Officially, the plane was a patrol bomber, a PBY Catalina with a hull built to land at sea and four gunners, two lodged right up in the nose and two in blister capsules that bulged to either side.

"What a beauty," the pilot said. Jim wasn't sure if he was talking about the plane or the night or something else he dreamt of as he flew.

He landed skillfully, easing the plane's belly down in the water between two reefs. Jim could see the heads of coral marked by phosphorescence in the black lagoon. The pilot cocked open the hatch and Jim climbed out into a hot night, filled with stars.

He moved quickly, sliding down the nose of the plane. The rubber boat swayed beneath him as he reached up for his pack and guns, then for the cumbersome radio with its heavy battery pack and hand-cranked generator.

At that moment, he knew he was a perfect target. Any half-assed sniper on the island could pick him off. The Coastwatcher on the main island of New Georgia, Donald Kennedy, had sent scouts to patrol just days before. But who was to say a Jap hadn't landed since? He paddled from the bow with a single oar, his mind too primed by things he had seen in Guadalcanal. He could imagine exactly how his knees would buckle, his body jerk forward, how his blood would pump out to darken and thicken the already black water. If he was shot, he was to overturn the dinghy in order to wreck the radio. Those were his orders.

Behind him, the Black Cat's propellers whirred. The gunners were covering him, but he'd vowed early on in the war never to trust his life to anyone. Spooked, he leapt out too early, jumping into water up to his chest. It was warm and he felt protected there. Part of him longed to dive down and swim away. He waded in, pulling the boat up and over the beach, into the bush. Then turned and saluted and watched the plane back out and swing round, lifting itself heavily from the sea like an ungainly seabird, a pelican perhaps. Or a dragonfly with those strange bulbous blister hatches. Or a frigate bird.

It flew up, all black, just a shadow, and disappeared. Then he was alone, cradling his gun.

On those islands, tucked under the equator, there's a nightly cacophony of birds, lizards, insects. A full orchestra, but all its instruments strange and discordant. To Cadillac, who grew up there, these night noises would be the sounds of childhood, a jungle lullaby. But to the uninitiated, the unfamiliar sounds could drive men mad so that they jumped up and knifed each other in the dark. The jungle itself could seem to breathe.

He remembers once on Guadalcanal, a sudden scuffle in the undergrowth, the reverberating throaty cry of the large buff-headed coucal, *Centropus milo*. How he'd watched a whole patrol panic, mistaking the bird for a Japanese ambush. Men shooting in the dark, recklessly exposing their position.

It helped if you knew what you were hearing. It helped if you could hold your fire. That first night after being dropped off by the Black Cat, Jim heard the far-reaching whistle of the shining cuckoo, like a

boy calling for his dog. He heard the gentle hoots of a boobook owl, crescendoing into a louder, more tremulous braying.

There was rustling in the dry leaves at the edge of the beach. The Solomons—home to hundreds of lizard species and at least twenty species of rat, including rare giant pouched rats. Coconut crabs with powerful claws as big as a lobster's. On Guadalcanal, he'd met up with hairy fruit bats—their red eyes would stare at you in the dark—and the marsupial cuscus, both nocturnal. And everywhere, whining mosquitoes, any one of which might inject you with a potentially lethal shot of cerebral malaria.

What Jim listened for was more specific. The sound of a man's footstep, the clearing of a throat, the metallic *snack* of a rifle. In the dark, there was nothing he couldn't put a name to. Except just before dawn, when he heard a strange, wet smacking noise that made him clutch his gun tighter.

When the sun rose, he saw it was fish slapping and flipping all across the surface of the sea.

Fox Island, Penobscot Bay, Maine, July 1973

Sarah comes in the kitchen door with Cadillac. They've met on the road somewhere the other end of the island. The girl striding along in flip-flops and Sarah taking a good look in her rearview mirror before pulling over.

Saturday's her half day. She will have closed the post office. Most likely she's come to spend the afternoon rootling in the garden. She plants masses of vegetables and flowers for summer folk who aren't here in time to plant them, or are just too damn lazy to get down on their hands and knees in the dirt. She makes a good business of it too, no doubt, though Jim's not exactly sure what he needs flowers for. Maybe Cadillac intends to help. But no, here they are, with other ideas.

"We're thinking Cadillac might like to use Fergus's bike—the one down in the boathouse," Sarah says somewhat defiantly as she knows Jim's been peculiar about the place. Not letting her father open the boathouse even to air it. "I can clean it and pump up the wheels."

"Fair enough," Jim says, stubbing a newly lit cigarette in his empty tin mug and pushing his chair back from the table. He can tell she's surprised by his willingness. Even more so when he wheels down the hill with them, on the sloping path Stillman laid.

Hell, maybe it's to make amends for getting drunk. For not making contact with Tosca earlier, when it turned out it was so easy to do so. He'd like to make up for it now, to help Tosca's girl. Sarah's showing him a way.

Shoving the chair up against the shingles of the small house, he fumbles for the key in its hiding place, on a nail behind the wood soap dish of the outdoor shower. Then struggles to force the sticky lock.

Inside, it's dark and stuffy. Streaks of sun angle through closed shutters, falling across a large trestle table and upturned dinghy. There's an overpowering smell of mold and mildew. Stillman was right; they should have opened the place earlier. Now Sarah strides forward to lift a heavy latch and pushes open two large doors that swing out over the sea, letting in air and light and brown-green reflections of the water that play along the knots of the weathered pine walls. The doors wide enough to haul up a small boat and high enough to bring a boat round at low tide to fix the rigging.

"Here it is!" she says, finding the bike propped against the wall. She rolls it along, checking for rust and squeezing the brakes. It's right enough. They'll just have to clean the guano off.

Jim had felt too dispirited by the thought of all the things he can no longer do, to want to come down here. But now, he's caught off guard by a disquieting anticipation—the boyhood thrall the place still casts over him. He looks about at all the familiar things. The table where he'd spent hours clamping wood, fixing motors, plotting courses for his own small sailing journeys. The two cots built against the walls, where he and Cecil used to spend nights. The kitchenette. The black potbellied woodstove with its pipe going right up through the beams. The tools hanging from nails in the walls, with black outlines behind them to show where each goes. Jars of nails, screws, cleats, linchpins. A box of rolled-up charts. The fishing rods. An Aladdin's cave of treasure, shut up at the end of each summer, awaiting his return. Abracadabra.

Still other things: the ship-to-shore, the kerosene storm lanterns, the half-burnt green mosquito coils. A jar of wildflowers dried to their brittle skeletons so that they'd crumble and disintegrate if he touched them.

He glides the chair slowly across the room, wedges the wheels against the thick plank lying across the threshold of the sea doors. Leaning forward, he peers down into the green-brown water, watches a crab scuttle around the weedy cement blocks that hold up this end of the house. It's a place he and Cecil used to sit, pulling up mackerel on handheld lines. Legs dangling over the side.

Cadillac's interest is drawn to a black shape hanging from a hook, looking like a discarded skin or some sort of misshapen fishing trophy. Fergus's wet suit. As children, Jim and Cecil and their sister Ann would hold their breath and leap off the dock or out the boathouse doors. Whooping and plunging into the cold sea was a rite of summer. For this reason, Jim supposes, the wet suit rankled. He'd felt put out when his teenage son arrived with it years ago and spent the summer snorkeling round the cove. He'd thought it sissy. The same way he never liked the boy's plastic kayaks, unable to understand how Fergus could prefer that to sailing.

It's apparent the girl feels differently. She reaches out, fingering the mask and snorkel, eyeing the flippers as if to gauge their size.

"Go on, take it down if you like," Jim says, unintentionally gruff and dismissive. "Try it on."

She turns to him, beaming. Holding up the suit, like the Australian divers' skins in Munda. Hell, she can't be expected to get used to the temperature of the water here. He realizes he hasn't seen her swim.

"Jesus Christ, take anything." He spreads out his arms. "Just don't ask." The material's a little cracked and dry. It ought to have been oiled.

"Looks just about perfect," Sarah says. Fergus must have been seventeen when he brought it, and the girl's tall.

"Let's swim," Sarah says, "I've got my suit in the car."

Black skin over black skin, Cadillac steps into the cracked wet suit. The suit accentuates the broadness of her shoulders, the shape of her muscles. When she arches her back to pull the zip right up the back of her neck, Jim looks away as if it's a thing he shouldn't see.

She looks like a navy SEAL or a deep-sea creature, hooded, frog-stepping across the room in the awkward flippers, the mask strapped to the top of her head.

"We can go in right here." Sarah lifts the old wood boat ladder from where it hangs on the wall, fits the curved ends into two holes in the floor.

"What will I see?" the girl asks, looking at Jim.

"Kelp, I expect."

"Crabs," says Sarah. "You can swim down to take a look at my old man's pots. See if we caught any lobst'ah."

Cadillac lowers herself over the thick plank, stepping down the ladder one rung at a time. The cold presses against the legs of the wet suit, leaking in icy around her feet and ankles. Head level with the floorboards, she stops and spits into the mask, as she's seen the Australian divers do, then turns and launches herself. Whooping, Sarah jumps.

Hearing Cadillac's distorted voice through the snorkel, listening to the splash of her flippers, Jim feels a keen yearning, a regret for things he will never do. It puzzles him that he'd swum with a mask in the Solomons with Tosca, alert to every coral and colored fish, but here he has used one only to cut or untangle rope from boat propellers. He has no clear view of his own seabed.

Sarah climbs up the ladder again, to dive out the boathouse door this time.

Tosca traces a tall A in the sand, the shape of a New Georgian diving frame made from tall saplings. Trying to persuade Jim to let him build it, just for one day, a single morning. Then they can dismantle it. The boy eager to show how he can he can fly off the top, boasting that he can flip two or three times in the air—at least. "Swim 'long sky," he calls it. "Alsem bonito fish."

Jim shakes his head. Wait until after the war, he promises, not realizing how little time he'll have.

Hearing Sarah shout, Cadillac swivels and watches her splash in. Through the mask, she can see Sarah's pink legs treading water. She lifts her head and grins, her teeth biting into the mouthpiece of the snorkel. Then kicks out to see if she can warm herself.

The crawl, our greatest export. She recites to herself the patriotic boasts of Silas Wickham, a handsome boy who goes around with her brothers. *The Olympic stroke introduced to Australia by my grandfather!* he'd say—lest they forget.

Silas's grandfather Harry Wickham had gone to school in Australia and thrilled the Aussies with his Solomon Islands swimming stroke. Even more famously, his brother Alec broke the world record for high diving in 1918, by plunging off a two-hundred-foot cliff above the Yarra River—a feat that left him unconscious for days. It's an inheritance Silas loved to crow about, using the exact same words each time, so that Cadillac and her girlfriends would fall about laughing. Or, if they were already in the sea, they'd struggle to stay afloat.

Somehow his words come differently to her here, so far from home. As if he was pointing out something important and brave. As if he is cheering her on: here's a thing we can do as well as anyone else, maybe better.

Silas's father had come to the airport to see her off, part of a startlingly large delegation. *"Put the Solomons back on the map,"* he'd urged, slapping her arm as she stepped up the stairs onto the plane for Brisbane. They all knew she'd be swimming for the Yale team, as part of the way to repay the university for her scholarship.

She won't be able to practice her strokes in this constricting suit and cold water. But how fast the flippers make her go. And how clearly she can look down into the weeds, rocks, and mud with the mask, a thing she'd always coveted at home. She revels in the freedom, the release from gravity, the novelty of using the mask in Jim's cold, green Atlantic.

A little way out, just off the submerged beach, she looks down where rays of sunlight flicker through a tall forest of kelp, glittering off the sandy seabed and silvery halves of muscle shells.

When she climbs up the ladder, Sarah's waiting with a cup of hot, sugary tea.

Jim had opened the tall cupboard, turned on the pump from the well, and run the water clear. Along the shelves, Cadillac sees jars of tea bags and sugar and matches, their lids screwed on tight to keep the moisture out. Next to them, boxes of fishing tackle, bird shot, and a half-drunk bottle of whisky. To her surprise, two shotguns are lodged up on a high rack. Guns are illegal in the Solomons. After the war, the British had rounded up all guns and had thrown them into the sea. It was still a source of bitterness though Cadillac's mother insists it was a good thing. "We have enough trouble without those guns," she said.

Cadillac peels off the wet suit, wraps herself in the colored *laplap* she'd worn over her bathing suit, and takes the hot tea gratefully, laughing to find her hands shaking as wildly as Jim's. Her teeth chattering against the tin cup.

"I'll be swimming for the Yale team," she stutters, as if she needs some kind of excuse, a reason—though she's well aware she just wanted to try the wet suit and to swim. "At least in my first year." When she will be studying as a premedical undergraduate.

Lifting the mattress board off one of the cots, Jim leans forward and takes out a woolen blanket. She wraps it round herself, smelling a sharp scent of mildew.

"Th-thank you."

"For Christ's sake, you'd better go run yourself a hot bath," he says.

"Come on," Sarah says, putting her arm around Cadillac and walking her back up to the house.

Layla Island, Wanawana Lagoon, Solomon Islands, June 1943

Jim never found Guadalcanal beautiful. To him, *the Canal* would always be a dark, brooding place, with fetid swamps and lowering mountains. Where rotted, bloated faces and other body parts lay half-buried in the black sand of its volcanic beaches. In his mind, he would always associate it with the deafening air raids of Henderson Field, the mud, the stench of it.

Maybe that's why, the first morning after being dropped off by Black Cat, Layla revealed itself to him like an awakening. The sun rose hot and sudden. The sand was white and the beach strewn with orange flowers. He stepped out onto it like a boy. He picked up delicate spiraled cone shells with pale yellow markings and tiny sand dollars the size of dimes and held them in his palm.

Here the sea was clean and blue with great pools of paler blue over the shallows. A small white line of surf curled far away over the outer reef. He could hear the distant hum of it. All around, other small low-lying islands seemed to float like mirages, with small clumps of palm trees sticking out of the ocean.

It was as if the war had been erased by sleight of hand. He knew this wasn't true. He'd seen the supply dumps building up at Honiara. The bulldozers, heavy trucks, big guns. More than 50,000 tons of equipment and tens of thousands of fuel drums ready for the New Georgia campaign. He'd seen aerial photos of the Japanese airfields at Segi, Munda, and Kolombangara.

But from Layla, a tiny slip of a place in the Wanawana, the sharp outline of Kolombangara looked like a child's drawing of a volcano. A small, white, triangular sail of a dugout canoe passed innocently. A flock of shrieking parrots flew in like miniature squadrons, and from somewhere across the island he heard the plaintive cooing of doves. The palms stood tall and still.

He knew his sense of peace was illusory but he was happy to embrace it, and be embraced. He was alive. He'd survived the night. He'd survived *the Canal*. After the crowding on the aircraft carrier, the bunks that smelled like locker rooms, the rain and mud at Henderson Field, the terror of the bombing raids, he felt an ecstatic joy at being alone, in a place that wasn't immediately in the Japs' sights. A place of beauty. He'd grown up reading about explorers on islands like this.

He struggled to untie his boots, pulled off his clothes, then sprinted bent over across the beach, all the while holding a palm frond over his head to hide himself from enemy planes.

Schools of fish shimmered in the bright sun of the morning, as they flipped this way and that. The sea teemed with what seemed to him a biblical richness. He plunged in. The salt water stung his bites and rashes, the itchy fungus that had taken hold in the folds of skin between his toes and fingers, behind his knees and around his scrotum. The fish brushed his legs.

He felt so supremely happy, he shouted out loud. Startled by his own voice, he dove underwater and held his breath as long as he could in case a Jap soldier was still waiting to take him out. He felt like Tom Sawyer out on the Mississippi with Huck, after he'd run away from home.

The thing about war was you never felt so goddamn awful and then, all of a sudden, you never felt so goddamn good.

Fox Island, Penobscot Bay, Maine, July 1973

The others gone, Jim shuffles over to the cupboard and dislodges one of the guns with his crutch. A single-barreled 12-gauge, made in England. It feels good and solid in his hands. Opening the breech, he peers down the barrel, which is badly blackened. He really shouldn't have left the guns down here with the moisture and salt air. Bad as the tropics.

When Cadillac returns, she finds him sitting in a patch of sun, a bottle of gun oil on the table and several patches of blackened cloth. She watches as he shoves a clean patch down the open barrel with the ramrod, then screws a small metal brush onto the end and inserts that. His movements are quick and professional, his hands surprisingly steady.

In the bright sun, a deep shadow exaggerates the groove running up the back of his neck from the knobby line of his vertebrae. His left shoulder is hunched. She sees the way his ears stick out, the sun-spotted backs of his gnarled hands.

Something about the boathouse is familiar to her, its one room with doors opening out to the water, its roof curving like a Chinese hat. Something about Jim too, so thin his blue buttoned shirt hangs off him and his shoulder blades jut like fish fins beneath the thin cotton, his intensity. She stifles a grin, realizing what it is he reminds her of— Jim, like one of those Japanese soldiers still said to be hiding out on the islands. An MIA in his sea cave.

"No go walkabout way 'long bush," the old aunties call out after Cadillac and her brothers as they head back into the brush with their bush knives. "Suppos Japani him catchim you." The aunties sit under the big mango tree, their legs straight out in front of them. Their mouths are stained red from chewing betel and the ground around them is stained with blotches of red from their spit.

Cadillac's brothers roll their eyes. "Don't worry—we'll give him Cadillac," they tease, pinching her arm.

It's not that Jim scares her. The old women's stories of Japanese MIAs always intrigued rather than frightened her. It's that he fits the picture she'd formed of these men. Jim, alone here, cleaning his guns when there's no more war to fight, maybe no bullets left to fight with.

Some, the old aunties said, had gone *kranki*, or crazy. Others didn't know the war was over. Cadillac imagined there were others who'd just grown used to living in the bush and didn't want to go home anymore. It's not a comparison Jim would like.

Glancing over at the open cupboard, she sees something she hadn't noticed earlier. On one of the lower shelves, next to a damp unopened box of Triscuits and a can of Brasso: a canvas bag. She walks across, lifts it out, and unrolls it on the table, next to the gun oil. A skinning set, like the one her father has. The long sharp scissors, the scalpel with its sharp tip stuck into cork, the knife, the pair of tweezers, each in its individual pocket. The brush and block of arsenic for treating the skins. A pair of dividers for measuring, needles. A spool of Size 1 thread.

"That's for skinning birds," Jim explains without looking at her. Deep in his own thoughts, he doesn't notice the surprised, then amused expression that crosses her face.

III
Hunting Grounds

"Ah," says he, "this here is a sweet spot, this island—a sweet spot for a lad to get ashore on. You'll bathe, and you'll climb trees, and you'll hunt goats, you will; and you'll get aloft on them hills like a goat yourself."

—*Treasure Island*

Fox Island, Penobscot Bay, Maine, July 1913

As he wedges the cleaned guns back onto the rack, Jim looks up into the thick beams that run under the fish-tail roof and remembers how Pieter, his grandpa's Dutch boatman, would tie a rope there each summer with a fat knot called a monkey's paw at the end. How they'd climb onto the worktable, or scramble up a ladder, angle their feet onto the knot, then jump.

He remembers the feeling of it, grasping the rope and flying right out the big open doors over the sea, up and up until the rope swung taut, then dropping and flying back inside. Whirling over the worktable, the big storm anchor and its heavy chain, over the open cans of boat paint, brushing past sails hung up to dry like flags, the skiff turned up on its gunwales.

Pieter would go first, whooping and hollering to show how it was done.

He remembers walking down here early mornings, before the others woke, to help Pieter scrape weed and barnacles off the hull of the skiff, and later off the hull of Jim's own sailing dinghy. The dizzying smell of paint remover and fresh paint.

These islands were his early collecting grounds. First the Dumplings, which he could row out to: mere outcrops with a few stunted trees looking from the boathouse, in this clear light, like a scene from a Japanese wood-block print. Further out the Sugar Loaves. And past Goose Head, islands he can't see: Hurricane, Leadbetter, and the White Islands. Or eastward, out the other end of the Thoroughfare: Stimpsons, Calderwood, and Babbidge. All places he could sail to in the dinghy Pa gave him for his tenth birthday. A boat Pieter taught Jim to sail.

"Tell me when to haul up the centerboard," Pieter would say as Jim beached the boat. And Pieter showed him how to hitch the anchor around a tree or rock and drop a stern anchor in case the tide turned. And if he didn't secure the boat properly, Pieter would whistle and let Jim sort it out for himself.

Once ashore, Jim leapt from rock to rock. It was his habit to circumnavigate any small island. If he came across some obstacle, a cliff or thicket of prickly raspberry or *Rosa rugosa*, he'd strike inland. Ducking under prickly firs, he'd enter a hushed world of dappled light. Each step on the spongy bed of needles releasing clean, sappy smells of balsam, spruce, and pine. The high lisp of a cedar waxwing rang sharp in the muffled air. The forest floor was a garden of moss, ferns, and hooded mushrooms. In open meadows, dewy spiderwebs were cast like fishing nets in the wild grass.

Pieter, waiting on the beach, kept an eye on the tide and cast his fishing rod. Teaching Jim everything there was to know about his small boat until he learned to go alone.

Summertime, there were picnics with roast chicken and thermoses of clam chowder. Big jars of cold lemonade and iced tea brewed with peppermint that grew so thick in the garden you could grab handfuls of it.

The front porch was strewn with fishing rods and tackle and life jackets and folding deck chairs. There was a large sun umbrella from India, which opened up with tassels and brightly colored elephants marching across the top; and a wicker basket with padded pockets to hold a tin kettle and tin cups one nestled inside the other, for hot tea when the children got cold from swimming.

And Ma in her laced-up boots and petticoats and her large sun hat presided over the whole thing like a field marshal on a campaign.

Everything had to be transported out to Grandpa Murray's boat, an eighty-foot twin-masted schooner he sailed up from New York. Jim would slip away as soon as he could to help the boatman on the water.

"Well done!" Pieter exclaimed as Jim brought the tender neatly up to the big boat, thrusting the gears into reverse as the boatman had taught him. Then Pieter would jump aboard and Jim would throw the painter and stern line.

The boat smelled of warm teak and tar, oil, Brasso, and rope and, when Ma climbed aboard, of musk perfume.

Pieter was from a fishing village on the Waddenzee. He had served in the Koninklijke Marine, the Royal Netherlands Navy, and worked on four-masted cargo ships. He was quick and neat and wore a blue fisherman's cap pulled over his tight curly hair. He was always in motion: scurrying along the deck to drop anchor, leaning over the bulwarks to check the set of a sail, shinnying up the mast to un-jam the rigging.

Lively as the water rat in *The Wind in the Willows,* Jim thought, with his smart cap, his bristly mustache, his infectious enthusiasm.

Jim offered himself as swabbie, ever-willing to coil, polish, sew, grease, mop. In return, Pieter unfurled charts and introduced Jim to the art of navigation: how to plot a course; how to use the dividers, parallel ruler, and compass rose. Instructing him on how to make entries in the logbook: to set down weather conditions, direction of wind and tide, point of sail, and compass bearings. Things Jim would later teach pilots in the war.

If they set off for the day in Grandpa's schooner, they could go almost anywhere. Across the Penobscot to Brimstone with its black rocks and wild cliffs or to blue Isle au Haut. Out through the Merchant Row to Jericho Bay, or south to far-flung Matinicus and Matinicus Rock— where the lighthouse keeper doubled as a warden for the National Audubon Societies. There Jim would clamber ashore to watch the nesting birds and ask whether the Atlantic puffin had returned. The colony decimated by fishermen who ate them and took their feathers.

"The lad should be made to eat with the rest of us," Grandpa Murray objected.

But as soon as he turned away, Frau Leiber, the housekeeper, wrapped Jim's lunch in a linen napkin and slipped it into his hands, or into the small cotton satchel he carried over one shoulder. She'd never paid attention to anyone except Jim's ma and would later become more headstrong, hardened by anti-German prejudice stirred up by the First World War.

Then Jim would vanish for the rest of the long summer afternoon. So that years later, the Welds and Chandlers, the Bowditches and Gastons, all of whom summered on the island and had children Jim's age, would have trouble placing him. They'd remember Ann. They all knew Cecil—even then he was someone to take note of—but they'd have trouble putting a face to the older brother.

Never mind. Jim collected smoothed stones and rocks with flecks of mica and serpentine. He picked up sand dollars and dried sea urchins and the dry hollow pouches Ann and her friends called mermaids' purses, then tossed away when he pointed out they were egg cases of skates or whelks. He couldn't understand that—wanting to pretend something was other than it was.

Some of his finds couldn't be brought home. Iridescent jellyfish stranded on the beach, porpoises gamboling near shore, a young otter playing with a crab.

"Are you lost again, lad?" Grandpa Murray bellows. He strides with heavy splayed steps across the sand, grabbing Jim by the collar as if he's caught a vagrant urchin or stowaway. Even now Jim winces, reliving the old anger, his injured pride. Feels his heart race with stifled indignation.

He was never lost. He'd leave signs, a scratch on a tree, a pile of rocks, a twig pointing backward. It was a game for him, committing landmarks to memory: a boulder shaped like a dog, a tree scarred by lightning, an outlook where one island disappeared behind another. Like other boys, he imagined himself an Indian scout—one of the great Algonquin warriors or the Red Paint Indians who used to inhabit these islands in prehistoric times. He imagined himself one of Sanford's collectors.

"No sir," he answers.

Grandpa pulls him so close Jim can smell the soured sherry on his breath, and other lingering remnants of the picnic—crab, jellies, cigar smoke.

"Something the matter with your ears then?" Grandpa growls low. "That you dinn' ae hear the horn?" He sets Jim back down on his feet and smacks both his ears at once. And Jim's face grows hot, not so much from the pain as from the humiliation. He remembers the feeling. It was as if he'd run aground or smashed up against a very large rock.

"I'm in a right mind to leave you here and pick you up the next time we happen along," Grandpa threatens.

Good, Jim thinks. He'll be Robinson Crusoe. Or poor David Balfour in *Kidnapped*, who ate raw limpets until he got sick, not realizing he wasn't marooned at all but merely stranded on a tidal island from which he could walk to the mainland at low tide. *A sea bred boy would not have stayed a day on Earraid.* Jim considers himself *sea bred*. He'd like to prove he could survive.

He says nothing. Grandpa's a big man, not tall but broad-shouldered and powerful, and Jim doesn't want to be smacked again. He dares himself to look direct into his grandpa's eyes, which makes the old man grow redder.

In truth, he suspects Grandpa Murray's a coward. These incidents don't occur when Pa's around, and Pa's not big. He's tall and thin and bearded, but strong in a moral sense, like Abraham Lincoln. And if Pa's there, Grandpa doesn't treat Jim like a petty thief. Demanding that he turn out his pockets and satchel, Grandpa tosses Jim's hard-won treasures into the sea, crushes a small shell or a bird's egg under his shoe.

"Good God, lad, there's enough flotsam and jetsam without you having to carry the whole island home!" he guffaws, making the others laugh. All except Pieter, whose brow is furrowed. Jim's heart opens to him—this man who only laughs at joyful things.

After that, when he sees Grandpa's drunk too much, Pieter will help smuggle Jim's finds aboard.

"Let me see what you have, young Jamie," he'll say, leaping across the rocks to intercept. His fishing rod flailing in the air above.

"Why don't you let me take that for you?" Wrapping a bright yellow tree fungus or egg in his silk neck scarf, he'll stick it in his jacket pocket or nestle it in his fishing tackle box. It becomes a secret pact between them.

And later Pieter would bound up to the house to deliver the contraband goods, and admire Jim's room, with all his finds labeled and arranged along shelves and in glass cabinets, like a museum.

Summertime, there were uncles and aunts and cousins. Soon after their own arrival on the island, Mother's sister would come up from New York with her girls Harriet and Jane and baby Dod. Once or twice, Pa's brothers traveled from Tennessee with their boys who spoke funny and asked, "Where you'all going?" and got horribly seasick.

"That's 'cause there ain't no sea in Tennes-see," Jim's brother Cecil whispered to him, mimicking their cousins' twangy accent. There were other guests too, from New York and Long Island and Boston, many of whom had their own summerhouses on Fox Island or across the Thoroughfare on Carver's. And Grandpa Murray's friends from Pennsylvania: steel men and fellow Scots.

Mostly Jim kept to himself, avoiding the company and his grandpa's temper. Helping Pieter. Exploring the cove and reed beds with Stillman.

If he was lucky though, Pa would come sailing and bring Sanford, who was visiting from Connecticut. Both men worked as doctors at Yale. Sanford was chief surgeon to the football team but his greater love was birds, particularly seabirds, and his work as a trustee at the Museum of Natural History in New York. It was Sanford who first recognized Jim as a fellow enthusiast and presented him with books: Frank Chapman's *Handbook of Birds of Eastern North America* and Elliot Coues's two-volume *Key to North American Birds*, which was a bible for birders in those days. And later, he gave Jim his first skinning set.

When Pa brought Sanford, Jim would hover nearby. He remembers Sanford leaning back in one of the deck chairs on the foredeck, in front of the raised cabin, feet up, entertaining them all with the Indian names for birds. *O-du-na-mis-sug-ud-da-we-shi* or

making-big-noise-for-its-size, the Chippewa's improbably long name for the tiny house wren. *Nan a-mik-tcus* or rocks-its-rump, the Malecite name for the spotted sandpiper. And *uwes' la' oski*—lovesick—the name the eastern Cherokee warriors gave the red-tailed hawk.

As the great sails filled, all cleats and ropes straining—and Pieter shouted out their increasing speed in knots—Sanford would point out to Jim the rafts of eider ducks that floated in Jericho Bay, the males temporarily flightless after their postnuptial molt. The shearwaters, and scoters, which the Maine islanders called coots. Rarer Wilson's storm petrels, short and stubby with a distinctive white ring around their rump like the band of a cigar. Named for St. Peter for the way they patter the calm surface of the water with their tiny feet. And Arctic terns, almost driven from the Maine coast, Sanford explained, because of a craze for ladies' feathered hats.

He'd bring news of the museum's collectors. James Chapin in the Belgian Congo. Rollo Beck in Peru, later to sail to the south seas.

"And President Roosevelt?" Jim asked. Having lost the election, the Bull Moose candidate had set off to explore the River of Doubt, Rio da Duvida, in Brazil.

Sanford pulled up a chair next to him and Jim sat, intrigued by these stories of men and birds. He was beginning to imagine a life for himself, while the other children chased each other up and down the long, wide teak deck, or played French and English flags. Or, if it was the end of the day, wrapped themselves in towels and blankets. Then Jim's brother, Cecil, would lean his head up against Ma's knees.

Cecil was Ma's favorite. She called him her cherub, her Adonis, her Endymion, wishing she could keep him young forever. When he leant back against her knees, she'd stroke his golden hair, which she kept long and curly like a girl's.

Cecil, like their sister Ann, was all golden brown and voluptuous. He was charming and could make the adults laugh. While Jim was quiet, lean, and rangy. He turned a dark brown in summer. His hair, darker too like his pa's, was kept cropped, almost militarily short. When he looked at himself in the mirror, he could see the sharpness of his features, his ears protruding. A certain defiance in his eyes.

"Most of the lepers on Penikese are black and some are Chinese," Cecil informs them. "It's because they're immigrants." He pronounces the last word with a slight derogatory inflection he's likely picked up from Grandpa.

One late afternoon, they're down at the beach in front of the big house in Greenwich, savoring that last hour of freedom before Frau Leiber rings the big ship's bell outside the kitchen and they have to run up and get clean for dinner. Ann's arranging her porcelain dolls on beds and chairs sculptured from wet sand carried up from the surf. While Jim lies facedown, splayed like a sea turtle, nestling his brown arms and legs into the white sand's lingering warmth.

It's a topic that fascinates them—the fifteen or so infected patients banished to the wildest, most remote island in Buzzards Bay.

"What's im'grants?" Ann asks and Jim digs his elbows into the sand, hoping she won't see that he's not sure. He does know where Cape

Verde is, home of the Cape Verde sparrow and Alexander's swift. He traces the west coast of Africa in the sand.

"An immigrant is someone from another country who wants to live in America, because it's better here," Cecil explains. Sitting just a bit further up the beach, he wraps himself in the colorful sarong Ma gave him from Indonesia. Exuding in its bright colors the air of their tribal chief.

"That makes Grandpa an im'grant too," Ann points out. As youngest, she's stubbornly determined to set her brothers right.

"Yes but *he* doesn't have leprosy," Cecil retorts, as if this is the obvious distinction that separates good immigrants from bad. Jim has a vague notion that there may be more to it, like the color of people's skin even if they don't have leprosy. The fact that some people come from Africa or China, while others come from Scotland. But he doesn't care to interrupt. He feels too content, too drowsy, happy to listen to the chief.

Cecil's a year younger, ten to Jim's eleven. But more precocious and already more knowledgeable about the grown-up world. Jim doesn't mind. He sees the advantage of having a brother willing and able to decipher adult needs, leaving him free to concentrate on sand bugs and periwinkles. He doesn't covet the hours Cecil spends sitting through cocktails or lingering at the dinner table, well after they've been excused, when Jim's been itching to go.

Besides, Cecil tells Jim other things. That Grandpa's a cousin of Carnegie, the richest man in America. That he made his fortune working in the steel business but grew up as a grocer's boy in Dunfermline, Scotland. That he and Pieter once broke the world record for fastest crossing of the Atlantic, but that their boat didn't win the Kaiser's Cup a few years later. Although it turned out the cup was only gold-plated, not solid gold as the kaiser said, which just went to show about the Germans.

"But not Frau Leiber," Ann pipes up in defense of their housekeeper.

It's Cecil who confides in Jim that Pa's family fought on the Confederate side in the Civil War but that it didn't matter because Pa went to all the best schools on the East Coast and graduated summa cum laude from Yale.

Now he has news that a baby had been born at the leper colony on Penikese and shipped the day after to New Bedford.

Lucky baby, Jim muses, watching a sand bug tossing up grains of sand as it burrows, and is surprised when Ann objects.

"The baby would rather be with its mother," she says bossily, pouring a blanket of the hot, golden sand over her dolls.

"Don't be stupid," Cecil says. "The mother wouldn't even be able to hold her baby if she doesn't have hands. And if she sneezes her nose might fall off."

Ann snatches up a doll and clutches it to her as if Cecil might threaten to send it away. And Jim quietly wonders if she might be right. Whether being youngest, she is best placed to judge.

There's a boy on Penikese—Jim's age—with a knack for physics and electrics. The New Bedford Women's Association sends a kit radio, which he assembles and uses to communicate with fishermen and signalmen on passing ships. Pa shows Jim an article about it in the paper. And sometimes, Jim finds himself imagining how he might make friends with the boy, if Grandpa actually does set him ashore there, as he sometimes threatens to do.

On the island, he would keep track of the seabirds and migrants and the boy could report their sightings on his radio. When Pa tells him the boy died, of pneumonia and weakness due to the leprosy, Jim remembers going off to cry as if the boy really had been a friend.

Fox Island, Penobscot Bay, Maine, 1916

*P*lay nicely, Ma says. But the others don't want to search for sand wasps or the traps wolf spiders set for them. They aren't interested in dissecting owl pellets and trying to reassemble the tiny bones of a field mouse. The boys Jim's age are thirteen now and more interested in impressing girls.

There's one game Jim excels at: hide-and-seek. But he's too good. Even if there are six or seven other children looking for him, no one can find him.

He wriggles right into the hollowed middle of a juniper bush. Or climbs so high in a tree that they don't look far enough upward. He covers himself with seaweed, which they find too disgusting to imagine, though you can swim the smell off afterward. Bored, he changes the game to one of evasion rather than concealment. Running through thickets, crawling under the latticed wood along the front porch, swimming under the floating dock where he can see their feet stepping across the slats above him.

Frustrated, the others forfeit and wander off to other games, and Ann, cross at being beaten, runs to Mother in tears.

"Why can't you play nicely like other children?" she scolds. "They're all littler than you." Though some of them weren't.

He remembered those games years later, when Helen read him a book about some British children growing up near a river in Bengal. In the book, a boy named Bogey plays *Going-round-the-garden-without-being-seen*, which was just the right name for Jim's game. He remembered how invisible and powerful and magical he felt, but also frightened— as if he really might disappear if he tried hard enough.

"Bogey's just like you," Helen had said. Jim knew. At least Bogey was how he might have been, if allowed to run feral, to remain illiterate and practically mute. Helen loved him for that. She was more untamed than he, having grown up wild on her own island.

Once when Helen was angry—Jim was going to Indochina on another collecting trip and this time there was no chance she could join him because she was pregnant with Fergus—she'd stamped her foot and shouted, "I hope you get bitten by a cobra." Which was what happened to the boy in the book.

"In that case, would you mean the Asian spitting cobra or the Indian king cobra?" Jim replied. She'd attacked him with her bristle hairbrush and they fell on the bed laughing.

Summertime, Jim kept lists of seabirds: gulls, cormorants, and fish hawks that whistle and mewl and build their ungainly nests on the tops of dead trees.

Once he set off along a sand spit to collect a tern's egg. The birds swooped and dived like stunt pilots, so close he could hear the air whistling through their feathers; their shrill cries deafened him. And he could see why they raised such havoc because here's a thing that utterly surprised him: the way their eggs lay unprotected, unsheltered, exposed to all the elements, sun, wind, sea spray. Easy picking for predators. Some of the birds had lined their shallow scrapings in the sand with bits of seaweed or grass, but it wasn't any proper nest or bedding. Just some halfhearted attempt at decoration. Nestled in each hollow were two or three brown mottled eggs, smooth as river pebbles.

He remembers climbing to the edge of a cliff, lying in the wild grass and watching the adult gulls nudge their young off the rocky ledges, sending them reeling perilously down on untested wings, toward the rocks and sea foam. Herring gulls, laughing gulls, and great black-backed gulls. It was a seagull flying school. The air echoed with screeching and crying that reverberated off the cliff, and the sea crashing below. It's why he hadn't heard the ship's horn. The birds' cries were so loud, the sight of their first fledgling flights so mesmerizing.

It's how Jim feels sometimes—giddy, exhilarated, then falling dangerously fast.

"Row harder, boy. Row harder," Grandpa Murray shouts. But the wind is set dead against him and the oars are too heavy.

"When I was a lad, I could row across the Firth in better time than this," Grandpa boasts. On and on he makes Jim row until the skin of his hands splits and he can feel the blisters on his palms chafe wet against the wood.

Jim looks to his mother pleadingly. She's sitting next to Grandpa in the stern of the boat but she gazes right past Jim, out to sea.

Rat Catchers

As he grew older, Jim realized that the naturalists he met and worked with shared this childhood passion or preoccupation. Take Brewster, curator at the Museum of Comparative Zoology and cofounder of the American Ornithologists' Union. Brewster's boyhood scramblings won him a cache of eggs and nests that to this day form the heart of the Harvard museum's oology collection.

He thinks back a few years, to a lunch at The Dominican Place, around the corner from the museum in New York. All of them there: Delacour, Farrell, Laina, Griscom, whose book he'd given to Cadillac. After a few carafes of wine, the conversation turned to childhood. And Griscom bemoaned his teenage agony when his parents insisted he perform birdcalls as an after-dinner party trick. An acned city boy, Griscom had taught himself to recognize and mimic the chirrups and trills of every bird in Central Park.

Jim tries to imagine it: eminent New Yorkers and the bespectacled, knock-kneed boy. *Ah yes, a blue jay! A cardinal!* The guests clapped in wonder. *Incredible. Astounding! Doesn't that sound just like it? A Cape May warbler*—Griscom throwing that one in to thwart them.

He had *an ear* and his parents plied him with music lessons, and French, German, and Italian tutors. They hoped their son would become a concert pianist, or, failing that, a diplomat, and were dismayed when his oddball hobby led him to the study of birds.

And Delacour, Jim's great mentor after Sanford and closest friend. There he was reminiscing about his first pet: a small white downy Faverolle chick named Moumou, kept in a box by his bed to amuse and distract him as he suffered through a bout of scarlet fever. He was five and it was already clear what interested him. Christ, he'd raised chicks from his crib.

Aged ten, Delacour took charge of some disused aviaries at the farm attached to the family château near Villers, which he filled with local songbirds, then rarer birds he sought out in the Paris markets, like whydahs and Peking robins. *Les oiseaux méchants* as he liked to call the parrots and grosbeaks. It's why his knowledge was so extensive and so intimate. He grew up with these birds. He knew their habits, their petty eccentricities, the way another child might know a dog.

By the time he was a man, Delacour had built an extravagant park, its domed aviaries set along pathways of espaliered fruit trees. There were ponds and waterfalls for rare geese and ducks; fenced paddocks for rheas and ostriches, crowned cranes and pink flamingos; and indoor galleries populated by the rarest, most colorful exotics: hummingbirds, tanagers, sunbirds, birds of paradise. Birds you were lucky to see stuffed in a museum. Aviaries designed to make you feel you were walking through a library of rare books.

At its center, his own favorites, Lady Amherst's pheasant and Chinese painted quail with their tiny bumblebee broods.

He fashioned an ornithological Xanadu so fantastical that the French general Foch declared he'd like to be reincarnated as a bird there. Foch requisitioned the château and planned his advances along the Somme while sitting in Delacour's pheasantry. And Delacour, stationed nearby, would ride a bicycle over in the evening, entering by the back gate, and find the general there.

That was before the trenches ripped right through. Villers being the town where French soldiers fought off the German advance toward Amiens in 1918.

"The truth is we never grew up," Delacour declared. They all raised their glasses. Though Jim suspected Delacour must have grown up the day he walked around his park for the last time, listening to his birds. He was thirty-eight, the town was already evacuated, the first shells beginning to fall.

Delacour served at Champagne and Verdun. He lost a brother at Verdun. He told Jim once that another brother had committed suicide before the war began. War had ruthlessly upended his life, as it later would Jim's.

"We were supposed to get interested in girls and coming-out parties, then eventually our wives," Griscom said. "Or husbands," he adds, winking at Laina. "Only we never did. At least I didn't!"

"We were distracted," Farrell added.

"Stunted," someone else throws in. "Like some sort of tree gall."

Jim remembers Laina looking at him with concern, or was it affection? Christ, she's a schoolgirl; there are reasons he keeps quiet.

He was some paces behind, musing over Griscom's mention of piano lessons, considering how an interest in music or natural history might be fostered and nurtured, passed down from one generation to the next. Or how it might emerge on its own in the most unlikely family, unappreciated.

Even Darwin's father groused at his son, *You care for nothing but shooting, dogs, and rat-catching, and you will be a disgrace to yourself and all your family.* Darwin wrote it down in his autobiography and Jim laughed when he read it. He'd marked the passage in his book, scribbling in the margin—*a child's wanderings, the lodestar.* Birding, he realizes, offered him both a way to engage with the world and a means to escape it.

Worried that Laina might reach out and put her hand on his knee, he'd got up and left.

Greenwich, Long Island Sound, Connecticut, 1917

It's hot in his room at the top of the house. Jim lies on top of the sheets; his bare feet scratch against a thick wool blanket folded at the end of the bed. He feels hot. Other times, he pulls the blanket around him and shivers in a sweat. He has a fever from shock, Pa says.

From the tall bed, he can look out the dormer windows, through the tops of copper beech trees, out across the Sound, and watch the steam ferries crossing back and forth from Greenwich to Long Island. The lines of black smoke hang in the air behind and are blown into shapes by the wind. Though the sea and its boats are the last thing Jim wants to look at now. What he wants is to sink his face into the dark of his mattress and never show his face.

In the evening, the stairs creak. His hears his ma reading a bedtime story to Ann. The sound of her voice goes up and down. He'd like to hear the words; they might distract. But at age fifteen, he's too old for bedtime stories. Across the Sound, sparkly lights blink on, tracing the shore of Oyster Bay, where Roosevelt, back from the Amazon, agitates to raise a volunteer regiment for the war in Europe.

From downstairs, Jim hears rumblings of their own war. "You will not talk about the boy that way," he hears his pa say down in the front hall. His voice polite but frighteningly cold. Grandpa swears. A door slams. Jim hears his ma crying. And here is Ann, who's supposed to be asleep, leaning in over the side of Jim's bed, clambering up on the mattress, whispering to him that Pa's going to Washington to help run the Medical Corps. That Pa says he won't leave Jim to be *bullied* by Grandpa.

Frau Leiber brings a porcelain bowl and puts it beside Jim's bed in case he's sick again. She takes away the soup Jim hasn't drunk. Soon, she says, U.S. soldiers will be fighting her nephews in Germany.

When the fever rises, Jim feels the walls of the room swelling and pressing in on him until he feels in danger of being crushed. Or else his own body thickening, his arms and legs becoming grotesquely large. It's a hallucination he'll suffer again with malaria. He wraps himself in the blanket, shivering. Waiting for his pa to dose him with a spoonful of brandy and to sponge him with a cloth.

It's not Jim's fault, Pa says. Pieter knew better. Hadn't Pieter himself often told Jim to keep low? Jim had done exactly the right thing, helping take in the sails, helping to bring the boat in. Few other boys would have kept their head. Pieter, Pa tells him, would have been proud.

It's good to hear Pa's voice. It's good to feel him near, sitting on the edge of the bed. His doctor's hands wring out a washcloth over a bowl of water. He runs the cool cloth behind Jim's neck. Lifting Jim's head gently off the pillows, he runs the cloth across the boy's thin shoulders.

At night, the waves of the Sound lap the shore, the wind tousles the beech trees. The big grandfather clock on the landing strikes a deep, sonorous one, then two, echoed by the higher chime of the French mantel clock in the hall. Just before dawn, the raucous gulls start up, crying his name, *Jamie, Jamie, Jamie*. Until he finally falls asleep. Then wakes in a sweat.

Pieter had asked Jim to take the tiller while he rushed to the bow. He aimed to take in the jib or to reef the main, or both. They were out in Grandpa's day sailer, a twenty-foot Herreshoff, running in before a storm. The sky boiled up angry behind them and the boat was being badly hit by gusts.

"Hold the course," Pieter said gently. The trickier things got, the calmer he became. Jim nodded. Grandpa Murray had chosen that moment to push tobacco into his pipe; otherwise Pieter would have passed the tiller to him, and then how different everything would have been. Pa was there too, but he was no sailor.

Just as Pieter stepped away, the storm caught up to them, and a fierce wind, like a fist, grabbed the sail and lifted the boom up and over so that before Jim had time either to shout or to haul in the mainsheet, it swung across, smashing Pieter in the head and sweeping him into the sea. Jim heard the crack of wood against the boatman's skull. He saw the astonished look on Pieter's face.

The next thing he knew Grandpa Murray lunged for him and threw him across the cockpit, taking the boat round in a wide circle.

"Let out the sheet. Lower the goddamn sail," Grandpa shouted. The sails flapped all over the deck like funeral shrouds as they hauled Pieter back over the gunwales. Pa tore off the boatman's sweater and shirt and laid him facedown, trying to force water from his lungs. Flipping him over, he knelt astride Pieter's waist, drawing the boatman's arms up above his head, then back down to pump his chest, over and over. It was no use. All the pumping did was make seawater run out of the boatman's mouth. There was no air in him. The seawater ran between the boards into the bilge. The boatman's body lay limp and heavy like a great fish.

"Jim." Grandpa snarled up at him, from where he crouched in the cockpit, his hand thrust in Pieter's mouth to keep his tongue clear of his throat. "Lord Jim. You were ever a bad piece of work."

Then Pa, unfolding himself from Pieter's body, brought the boatman's arms down to his side and laid a gentle hand over his eyes. And the rain, battering down, splashed onto Pieter's face. So that Pa took off his jacket and laid it over him. Then the rain soaked Pa. It ran off the waxed jacket in rivulets. And Jim was sobbing and it seemed the whole world had drowned.

IV
Tosca's Story

"Wherever a man is, says I, a man can do for himself."
—*Treasure Island*

Fox Island, Penobscot Bay, Maine, July 1973

The day after they open the boathouse, Jim finds a small bird cradled on two large maple leaves in front of his typewriter. A green-brown bird with a black head and a deep yellow collar and chest.

She must have found the bird dead and brought it in. Or did she take one of his guns and shoot it? It doesn't look like any native. Too big to be a flycatcher or warbler. Its tail too stubby for an oriole. Now, he sees the cotton buds carefully pulled through the eye sockets, the wings pinched back, the small legs folded under the tail. He leans forward, his armpit pressing into the crutch, to pick it up. The specimen is light and dry in his hands. He turns over the small, handmade label attached to its leg.

Layla Island, Wanawana, New Georgia.
Pachycephala pectoralis centralis.
June 2, 1973. T. Baketi.

A golden whistler. Christ, it's Tosca's!

The skinning is beautifully executed. Jim couldn't have done it better, even in his best days. The feathers are clean and dry. No evidence of blood or fat stains, no broken or missing feathers, no sign of shot.

He turns the small bird belly up, pulls back the skin with his thumb to examine the neat spindle of cotton wool inside. An amateur will commonly overstuff and thereby stretch the specimen, but this is perfectly done. No need to sew the belly of anything smaller than a pigeon, Delacour instructed. The belly isn't sewn. Moreover, Jim sees the whistler's left leg crossed over its right, its head cocked left, which was exactly the way he fashioned his own bird skins.

"Cadillac!" he yells. Cupping the small bird in his hand, he swings across the room with the crutch and pushes open the screen door. She's sitting outside, along the flat balustrade of the porch, feet up, reading.

"Is this yours?" he demands, thrusting the small whistler forward. It occurs to him suddenly that maybe someone from the museum had snuck in and left the bird as a practical joke. No, only she would lay it out on his worktable like that, on leaves like an offering. And besides, here's Tosca's name.

"Where the hell did it come from?" he demands, waving the small bird at her.

"A gift from my father." She smiles, swinging her legs down the side of the balustrade. Then laughs, no doubt because he looks so bewildered.

"Mr. Jim, my father's a bird skinner. He learned it from you."

So it's true—Mr. Jim doesn't know anything at all about her father and their life after the war. Just as Tosca knew nothing of Jim's leg, or, most likely, of his bad temper and drunkenness, or he might not have sent her here.

Jim leans awkwardly on the crutch.

"When we were small, my father kept skins all about our place," she says. "Bird skins mostly but others too: a stuffed cuscus, a crocodile, a

wild pig." She tilts her head upward, drawing her hands through the air to show him the sweep of the pig's tusks, remembering how some of her school friends would run home when they saw that.

They'd kept live birds as well, parrots and cockatoos tame enough to eat pieces of fish or bits of cassava pudding out of their hands. And Tosca would lure honeyeaters and sunbirds in from the bush with red hibiscus planted in half coconut shells, and wild orchids tied to the house posts. Cadillac's favorite was the hornbill Tosca raised from a chick, until her mother complained it ate too much and made him row it back to Kohinggo.

"No one understood what he was doing and some people said he was a witch doctor." Her voice, low and easy, holds Jim, even if he's not sure he wants to hear too much, to think too closely or too far back to those islands. Perching on the edge of a rattan porch chair, he pats his breast pocket for his cigarette pack, which he seems to have left inside. She lets a brief silence fall between them.

"My father learned all the bird names," she continues. "Not only in Roviana but in English and also their Latin names. He learned these from the book you sent him. His favorites are the whistlers. He can whistle all their tunes: the whistler from Tetapare, the whistler from Kolombangara, this whistler he sends you from Wanawana." She leans forward, gently touches the bird he still holds in his palm.

"Some of my friends were scared of him. Because their parents told them stories that he was talking to our ancestors, or to dead Americans."

Adaptive radiation. It makes sense of course that birdsong changes and evolves, just like bill shape and plumage. Slow but inevitable variations that take place after a parent species disperses and adapts to different islands. Darwin discovered this studying his finches from the Galápagos. Wallace came to the same idea, marveling over his birds of paradise in Papua. It's what Jim and Bryan had been looking for in Hawaii—adaptations in the tongues of honeycreepers. And now Tosca, mapping the evolution of birdsong. He'd have a knack for it, the ability to mimic the subtle variations. He was already skilled at that when Jim knew him in the war. Jim doubts any Westerner could match the islanders' fine-tuned hearing, or eyesight. Even Griscom with his musical ear. Jesus Christ, how would you account for the evolutionary advantage of a new tune?

Stroking the bright feathers of the whistler, Jim's startled by the shaking in his hand. He draws it back and tugs self-consciously at his earlobe. He'd like to massage the stump, which is beginning to cramp, but won't do it in front of the girl.

He feels unnerved by her, sitting so close. This girl with Tosca's skin, his height, his eyes. His forthrightness too. Unraveling Tosca's story of bird skins, wild boar, and children.

Jim feels suddenly suffocated, unable to breathe.

He rolls up his canvas skinning kit and carries it down to the blue sea, wedging it under the rough-hewn seat of Tosca's canoe.

"Belong you," he says, using pidgin. Trying to explain to the boy he's going back on one of the big ships. That he's been ordered by Admiral Halsey to stop collecting.

Tosca grins and takes his hand. "Tankyou tumas."

It's the kit Sanford had given Jim years before and he wonders what Sanford would make of it. The jet-black boy in his British military shorts, bare-chested. The war that rages all around them, among these islands where Sanford had sent his collectors. The corruption of Jim's skills as a bird skinner.

He puts his hand on Tosca's shoulder and leaves it there a minute. The boy's skin is hot from the sun.

"My father never learned to write," Cadillac's saying, seemingly unaware of Jim's discomfort. "He can read but it was my mother who copied out the names onto labels. Then, after I went to school, it was my job."

At first, Tosca's enthusiasm had intrigued Cadillac's mother. His whistling was a good way to put the children to sleep at night. But then, as the children grew older and the huts began to fill with stuffed specimens, when Tosca didn't get a job, she started to complain. She wondered, as others had, whether there might be something wrong with her husband. Whether he'd gone slightly *kranki* in the war.

Cadillac remembers a day when her mother declared she'd had enough. She wasn't going to write one more label, ever. Tosca should go find a proper job. At least he should spend his time fishing or helping to clear the bush for the garden—like other men. Tosca glanced over at Cadillac, his girl, and she'd immediately raised her hand as if she were in school and promised to write all labels for him. Her mother glared but Cadillac was too proud of her writing skill not to offer. She was ten and already the smartest in her school.

When Cadillac pauses, Jim stands. Even this minimal movement offers some relief. The clenched muscles of the stump stretch and relax.

"Hold on a moment," he says, lurching to the screen door. Putting some space between them.

Inside, Jim lays the whistler gently back down on the leaves and glances at his watch. Safely past one. Christ, he's due a drink. He makes his way to the kitchen for ice, then to the drinks table in the big room where the bottles line up against the dark wood paneling. It'd be a good deal easier if he kept the gin by the fridge but he sticks to the ritual of the cocktail hour, which gives a veneer of respectability, an illusion of restraint.

So, Tosca kept the skinning set and put it to some use. Also the book Jim sent, Mann's *Birds of New Guinea and the Solomon Islands*. It was a wartime publication hastily printed to satisfy the sudden demand for all and any information on the Pacific. The names Guadalcanal, the Coral Sea, New Georgia, momentarily on everyone's lips. Mann, who'd collected on these islands before the war, had kindly sent a copy to Jim in the Philippines, and he'd sent it directly to Tosca, scrawling *Baketi* on the envelope and entrusting it to a pilot flying the supply run. It was as much a punishment to himself as any act of generosity, because he believed then that his birding days were over. He was beginning to lose hope of ever going home.

Jesus Christ, he never knew if Tosca received the book or cared to. Frankly, he hoped the boy's interest may already have been diverted. New Georgia by this time was safely behind the front. Munda rebuilt with piers and Quonset huts and supply depots and jeeps careening along the road from shore to airfield, he'd heard. And weekly movie pictures.

Tosca had been at a Methodist school in Munda, before the Japanese came to build their airfield. As war approached, the missionaries sent the boys home, Jim remembers. Aged sixteen, looking for excitement, Tosca had sought out the former district officer Donald Kennedy. A barrel-chested, hotheaded New Zealander, Kennedy was one of the key Coastwatchers. Known for his brutality as well as his bravery, for his tight-knit group of local scouts and his willingness to ambush, rather than simply spy on, the Japanese.

Jim pours the gin slowly, watching the clear, viscous liquid splash into the cold glass and crack the frosted ice. Breathing in the good, sharp tannin of the juniper, he swirls the glass deliberately, lovingly—allowing the gin to chill before he adds the tonic water. Each act offers its own distinct pleasure, a promise of relief he's eager to prolong. The smell of quinine in the tonic. The fresh tang of lime.

He lifts the glass and drinks. Gin and tonic: the staple of colonial officers, who believed the quinine helped hold off malaria. He pours himself a second glass, knowing his own infection could still recur.

The last time Jim had seen Munda, it was a blackened wasteland, gray with ash, pockmarked by bomb craters. Its broken palm trees jutted from the wreckage like jagged crosses. He remembers watching Tosca paddle away toward the Roviana Lagoon. He'd felt a great sadness then, and a distinct envy. A small measure of the grief, the abandonment, he'd suffer later when he came home.

Easing himself down in the wheelchair, he rolls back out onto the porch, grabbing the cigarettes off his worktable as he passes.

Jesus Christ, why does he need to be so wary after all this time? Even with this girl whom he hardly knows, who will disappear again in just a few weeks, who means nothing to him?

"When I was twelve, everything changed," Cadillac begins, then stops, waiting perhaps to see if Jim wants to hear the rest.

If not, she'd be happy enough to sit back with her book or go down to the boathouse to swim in Fergus's wet suit again. She's a good storyteller, he'll give her that. Like Cecil, telling him things he suspects he should already know. He rests the glass on the balustrade, pulls out a cigarette. Thus armed, he looks straight at her.

"What happened then?" he asks, sucking in the good tobacco smoke.

She lifts her legs onto the balustrade and leans back against the shingles of the house. "That was the time a motorboat came across the gulf from Gizo Island." It was a plastic boat with a three-horsepower outboard. "In it were three people: Chief Sunga, we knew him; a second man in a suit; and a white woman."

It was the woman who interested her most. She'd seen white women before but this one was different. She wasn't wearing a bathing suit or sarong like the Australian girls at Munda, but was formally dressed in a skirt and jacket and heeled shoes. Her black curly hair was tied up on top of her head and she wore big, heavy necklaces made of rings from clamshells and beads of ebony. To Cadillac and her brothers, it was clear this woman was some sort of chief from the way she walked, the respect the others showed her. She spoke in pidgin too, not in English, and also could speak some Roviana.

Cadillac looks at Jim. She's grinning. "You probably guessed who she was, right?"

"No." He shakes his head. How could he know?

"She was Ms. Sethie, Ms. Sethie Bloom. The one who helped me apply for a scholarship. The one who wrote to you."

Jim frowns, remembering with distaste the bossy letter on the State Department paper, reading like a summons or command rather than any sort of request. He realizes with surprise he'd assumed Sethie was a man. Cadillac sits beaming, apparently holding a much more favorable impression than he has.

"Word had got around about the skins," she explains. "Are you the bird man?" they asked Tosca. "The man in the suit was a zoology professor from the University of the South Pacific in Fiji. He and Ms. Sethie had helped build the Solomon Island Museum in Honiara. They wanted to exhibit my father's bird skins. Once they met him, they asked him to take charge of the natural history displays."

It was because of the skins Tosca got a job, because of the job, Cadillac went to school in Honiara. It was because of her success at school, Ms. Sethie encouraged her to study in the United States—to come to Jim.

"Ms. Sethie always has many projects," Cadillac adds proudly after a short silence. Jim nods. Cadillac's apparently one of them, and he too by extension.

He finishes off the last drops of gin, slightly dazed by how all the pieces fit together. Like iron filings attracted to a magnet, spinning round and colliding into each other. The war, the girl's scientific upbringing, the golden whistler, the interference of a bossy American woman. It might have been a damned sight easier for him if Ms. Sethie had just minded her own business and left the girl well enough where she was.

Jim swivels the wheels of the chair, turns away to look out over the sea. Trying to keep hold of the things he'd kept to himself for so long. Trying to fend off his past and the presumption of Ms. Sethie Bloom.

Layla Island, Wanawana Lagoon, Solomon Islands, June 1943

"I met your father June 6, 1943, on Layla Island in the Wanawana Lagoon," Jim says.

It was mid-morning, the first day after the Black Cat dropped him on the reef, when Tosca appeared from nowhere. A tall, slim boy whose arms and shoulders were just beginning to fill out, with hawkish eyes like hers, slightly hooded, which made him look oddly scholarly.

He whistled like a small bird and when Jim turned, there he was, squatting. Just a few feet away—as close to Jim as the girl is now.

"Me come 'long Kennedy," he said, explaining the Coastwatcher had sent him. He was sixteen, six years younger than Cadillac. And he grinned, pleased to have snuck up on Jim.

"And it's a damn good thing I didn't shoot him," Jim adds.

She stares, watches Jim run his tongue wolfishly over his teeth. She wouldn't put it past him. With his drink finished, his cigarette stubbed out, he seems vulnerable and unpredictable.

"What I mean is, I didn't see him arrive. I didn't even hear him." More likely, it was Tosca who could have killed Jim if he'd needed to. Shot him with the Jap gun the Coastwatcher had given him, or just knocked him over the head, which was the way of headhunters. He was that stealthy.

June 6—they had a month before D-day of the New Georgia campaign. Jesus Christ, it seemed a lifetime. They'd handed Jim too much freedom maybe. Time enough for him to create a whole other world.

"I know Layla," she says. "It's a place my father takes us to cook fish on the beach and look for fruit doves."

"Here's a coincidence," Jim says, turning to face her again. "He brought me a fish, just like you." It was a reef fish hanging from a reed hook. They cooked the fish over a fire, which was Jim's second breach of regulations. The first was swimming in broad daylight. It was a time of day, Tosca assured Jim, that Jap planes didn't fly over. The fire was a risk but the fish tasted like heaven. Though the boy was more interested in Jim's canned rations of ham and beans.

He wore a pair of British khaki shorts. There were small raised scars on his chest, some sort of tribal marking. A woven band of dyed leaf around his upper arm.

Layla was Tosca's name for the island. The Americans didn't have a name for it though Halsey and Kennedy agreed to call it Bird's Eye.

There were few accurate maps at the start of the war. They'd relied on British, Dutch, and, ironically, German charts and pilots, filling in details with local knowledge. Later they had their own aerial photographs and sent patrols to reconnoiter.

Layla was a slip of a place, three miles across by six miles long, flat with few places to hide. You could walk right round it, though going through the middle was tougher because of the brush.

The reefs of the Wanawana prevented anything larger than a transport boat from coming close. But Admiral "Bull" Halsey chose it because of its perfect sight lines: southeast to Rendova, east to Munda, northwest, up through the Wanawana, toward Kolombangara. Just as he singled out Jim as a loner and nonconformist. Someone who, as he put it, *didn't fit comfortably* in the military structure.

The war was about to move here for a time and Jim's mission was to keep watch and report on Japanese ship movements. In particular, he was to warn of any Jap reinforcement of Rendova, which was to be one of the key landing sites in the forthcoming invasion.

The Coastwatchers were already in place. Hiding out on mountaintops and in the thick bush with their cumbersome radios. Protected and helped by Solomon Islanders who acted as their guides, guards, runners, and scouts. Halsey pointed to small flags on his map. Josselyn on Vella Lavella, Harry Wickham (of swimming fame) in the Roviana, Dick Horton on Rendova, Evans on Kolombangara, and Donald Kennedy of course at Segi Point.

But the Bull wanted a few of his own men too. Jim remembers standing awkwardly in the admiral's Quonset hut listening to Halsey outline the four-prong invasion plan. Operation Toenails they called it, because although they'd secured Guadalcanal as a foothold, they were still just hanging in.

Jim suggested Sitting Duck as his own code name. Halsey chuckled, glancing around at the others, as if this confirmed the lieutenant's credentials. Halsey was only half-joking when he said he'd been looking for some godforsaken outpost to stick his maverick, Jungle Jim. The island would be perfect.

Here's what Tosca owns. A spear. A bush knife. A pair of shorts. A captured Japanese rifle. Fishing line made from hibiscus bark. A cooking pot. A canoe hewn from the trunk of a qoliti tree.

He watches with eager curiosity as Jim turns out his pack. Squatting back on his heels, he picks up Jim's things one by one to examine them. Jim's tin plate and fork and knife, his razor, his helmet. Holding up a small mirror, he smiles sheepishly into it and mimes brushing his teeth, pulling up his lip to inspect his gums.

More intriguing is Jim's field book. He leafs through it thoughtfully, the list of skins Jim collected on Guadalcanal.

Hemiprocne mystacea, female. Lunga River. April 15, 1943. The whiskered tree swift.

Aplonis metallicus, male. Koli Point. May 21, 1943. The colonial starling. Jim had come across a colony of thirty or so pendulous nests hanging from a single tree, like the nests of weaver birds but scruffier. He'd drawn a quick sketch, which Tosca recognizes.

And here, down at the bottom of the pack, something the boy's never seen before—the skinning set. He extracts each sharp, shiny tool, running his thumb against the blade of the small scalpel to test its sharpness, looking up at Jim with new respect.

"You alsem kastom man?" he asks, wondering if these instruments are for some sort of magic or medical use.

Jim shakes his head.

"Birds," he says, lifting his hands, looking skyward, not knowing how to explain himself.

That evening, after hours spent tuning the radio, Jim bushwhacks to the middle of the island and shoots a whistler with his .410. The report of the gun is louder than he expected, out here on the lagoon without the muffle of true jungle. Flocks of coconut lorries rise from the trees squawking. A solitary Brahminy kite flaps up on vast wings. He'll have to be more cautious.

Squatting side by side with Tosca, Jim demonstrates the use of his tools, skinning and stuffing the small whistler in minutes.

Once the boy knows of Jim's interest, he can't help showing off. Jim watches the elusive green pygmy parrot scuttling down a coconut palm headfirst like a nuthatch—the boy snares one in a small trap made of reeds. Then shows Jim where the tiny parrots have excavated a nest in a large termite mound on the side of a tree.

After a day spent helping Jim construct a lookout at the top of a tall canarium tree, weaving sago palm and creepers, cleverly concealing footholds inside epiphytes, Tosca takes Jim by the hand, and leads him to the burrow of a boobook owl. There, in a small cavity at the base of a tree, two tiny fledglings with great yellow eyes blink in the unfamiliar light of his torch. Jim switches it off and lets them be.

Later the boy ties ferns under the platform so that no Jap could ever see them.

"Sitting Duck to Marine Headquarters, come in," Jim says over and over, fiddling with the dials of the radio, twirling them back and forth while Tosca shinnies up a tree to position the antennae. The radio's bulky, weighing thirty pounds, with an equally heavy battery and generator. They've built a waterproof shelter for it, hidden away from their own campsite. If Japs come, it's the first thing they have to destroy.

Finally, a crackly whine. "Come in, Sitting Duck. Read you loud and clear."

The call of doves is ever-present on the island, like the wash of the reef, the rustling of palms. The soft *coo-oo-coo-who* of the red-throated fruit dove. The more guttural roll of the *Ptilinopus superbus*. Still the fruit doves prove most elusive to track. Jim perches on a fallen trunk, his neck cramping as he looks up. Until Tosca, bare feet tucked under him, cups his hands to his lips to imitate their call. A moment later, a gorgeous dove flaps out, followed by two others. Olive green and scarlet materializing from the thick foliage of a ficus tree.

It's then Jim decides to have the boy help him collect. Hell, they have a month. Between watching for Jap ships and making their radio reports, they have time to acquire as complete a series as possible of the birds of Layla Island. It'd be a waste not to. The boy's a natural, snaring or bringing down a bird with a small arrow cut from the midrib of a palm, or a slingshot, as easily as he can spear a fish. So that Jim need hardly use his shotgun.

While patrolling and keeping watch from their tree, Jim explains as much as he can about museum work and the study of ornithology, taxonomy, and labeling. He draws a small map in the sand to explain something of the Wallace line: the sharp division that separates the flora and fauna of Asia from Australia. He tells Tosca about the New York museum's South Sea Expedition, which sent collectors to these islands, even to the Wanawana.

Then, before it gets dark—the night comes down quickly here—he sends the boy back to their campsite. They take turns sleeping and keeping watch.

In the morning, after he's made his radio report, before the Jap planes can make it down from Rabaul or Buin, Jim teaches the boy to skin. They swim in the blue shallows.

If he ever gets off this island, he'll send their skins to the museum and make sure Tosca gets credit for all the birds he's trapped and prepared. Christ, they might find something new to add to Mann's study of dispersal and speciation. A new species or subspecies, a new endemic or a bird that hadn't been found in the Wanawana before.

Radio report: *Sitting Duck to Marine Headquarters. Come in. Come in. This is Sitting Duck. June 18, 0700. Cloud and rain at present over the Wanawana. Visibility to Kolombangara and Rendova poor. Looks set to stay that way. Ninety degrees at present and heating up. Surface craft busy throughout the night. Three destroyers sighted heading southeast around Kolombangara. Six cargo ships and two oilers steaming south toward the Blanche Channel. Three troop barges moving eastward toward the west coast of New Georgia. No landings observed last night on Rendova.*

Field notes: *Zosterops. June 18, 1943. Snared two white-eyes. Both male. Let one go. Forehead and eye black, bill yellow, belly yellow, sides of breast olive, white eye ring. 4½ inches.*

Radio report: *Sitting Duck to Marine Headquaters. Come in. Come in. This is Sitting Duck. June 22, 1100 hours. A squadron of thirty bombers, twenty-two fighters just passed over heading your way, south-southwest over Munda, toward Guadalcanal.*

Field notes: *Ptilinopus viridis. June 22, 1943. Red-throated fruit dove. High in ficus tree, SE side of Layla. 8½ inches. Head and chin, dark gray green and olive. Wings and tail, olive green with pale gray shoulder patch and gray spots on the tertials. Lower breast and abdomen deeper green. Under tail-coverts yellow. Throat, crimson. Iris, orange. Bill, yellow. Feet, red. Crop full of fig seeds. Gonads enlarged.*

So beautiful you almost regret shooting it.

Fox Island, Penobscot Bay, Maine, July 1973

Jim has a pilot's map he kept from the war. Elongated, thin, designed to fit in the instrument panel of a Grumman Wildcat or a Douglas bomber. He extracts the paper from a stained, battered envelope and unfolds it along the kitchen counter.

It's strange for Cadillac to see her home this way—from the bird's-eye view of a bomber or fighter pilot. The familiar green shapes of her island overlaid with red circles and arcs that spread from Munda airfield like ripples. Fifty miles to Vella Lavella, one hundred fifty to Bougainville, further up the island chain where the Americans went after New Georgia.

There by Jim's knobbed index finger, she can see her mother's place. A cluster of huts set back in the shade of pawpaw, and the broad, thick leaves of a mango tree. A platform of woven sago palm between them. The separate hut for cooking. She shuts her eyes and hears the sound of the rain thudding on the thatch roof, thwacking the thick leaves of the mango tree. So heavy it digs red rivulets in the ground that run down toward the sea. Behind her, her brothers argue. She hears her mother chatting with some aunties who've stopped by. They chew betel and spit the red juice onto green leaves. Someone's rolled a cigarette. She can smell the rough smoke of tobacco.

When it stops raining, her mother will call her to go to their garden, where they will hoe neat lines in the dirt and shape small hummocks with their hands for planting taro, yams, and cassava; train tendrils of peanuts onto bamboo sticks; and tend to the small stands of sugarcane and betel. Her mother's hands and knees red from the earth.

"We live here, at Enogai, near the village of Bairoko." She points to the place on the map.

Bairoko: a major Jap encampment. The main staging ground and resupply route for reinforcements from Kolombangara. It was one of the marines' first objectives, a place they hoped to take in a matter of days. But the Japs managed to keep it right through August. Holding the Americans down in the jungle—hungry, injured, sick, pounded by machine guns and mortar fire. Though they at least managed to capture the two 140-millimeter coastal guns at Enogai.

Jim remembers a vast explosion, July 6, the night after the landings to the north of Enogai. The whole sky over Kohinggo lit up with flames and smoke. Later he learned it was the cruiser *Helena*, hit by torpedoes; that six hundred men had been rescued at sea, pulled up onto the decks of destroyers slick with oil. While two hundred others, clinging together in a flotilla of life jackets and life rafts, had swept north to the coast of Vella Lavella to be rescued by Coastwatchers.

She stands next to him, the map spread out before them on the table. Jim peers down through half-rimmed reading glasses, which make him look gentler, almost scholarly. She notices that he lets her stand closer than usual, on the left side with the stump. He lays Tosca's skinned whistler on the windowsill above the sink.

Can he see her mother's place? The sweet ginger and spicy turmeric planted near the huts to ward off bad spirits? The heady smell of *Evodia* flowers drifting across from the reef islands? She'd heard the stories of how the saltwater people moved into the bush when the war came, erecting makeshift shelters, moving on when they had to. How they shied away from lighting fires in case they attracted planes, and sent their boys to sneak back to their gardens at night. Cadillac's own mother had been ten. She'd had to forage in the bush for wild yams and taros, fern hearts, and spinach, wild plants she still calls *hunger food.*

By the time Jim got there, all coastal villages would have been abandoned. No women would have been working their gardens. No children jumping into the sea.

Cadillac remembers her grandmother twirling her wrinkled hands in the air to describe the swoops of airplanes flying overhead, diving, somersaulting, and plunging into the sea. Blowing out her cheeks to mimic the crashing of planes and bombs. Still astonished, thirty years later, by the strange figures of pilots falling through the air with parachutes. The great gray ships that bombarded the shore. Teasing her sister, who she said had thrown herself on the ground each time a plane flew over.

They were warned and threatened too. If anyone was caught rescuing or aiding the invaders, Donald Kennedy and his boys would strip them, stretch them over a barrel, and whip them with a cane made of rattan. If you neglected to salute, Kennedy would strike you with his walking stick. Once he'd hit a Japanese prisoner across the face with the butt of his rifle. Tosca had been one of Kennedy's boys. He spoke of these incidents openly, without embarrassment, so Cadillac couldn't tell if he approved or not.

As a girl, Cadillac swung off the great Japanese guns near her mother's place, which by then had rusted into place with their long barrels pointing out to sea. She slid down bomb craters in the bush nearby. Swam out to the rusty transport boats that lay on their sides in the bay with great holes ripped through them.

The wreckage of Jim's war lay all around. They grew up in it. Rolls of barbed wire rusting in the jungle, dented canteens that washed up on the beach, medicine jars still full of antimalarials, knives, bullets.

If they found any of these things, they'd bring them to a man in Munda, who'd give them a piece of chewing gum or candy or a Solomon Islands cent. He had a whole collection and built a big thatched hut to keep it in. American helmets, canteens, eyeglasses, baseball mitts on one side. Japanese swords, knives, sake jugs on the other. Strange as Tosca's birds.

Inside the wrecked transport boats, reefs grew in the rusted hulls. Cadillac and her brothers could swim out and catch colorful fish gliding in and around the twisted metal. In Jim's day, the sea around the sunken ships would have been thick with oil and sharks.

Ready to fold up the map and put it away, Jim glances at Cadillac and sees her eyes are closed as if she's in some trance or clutch of homesickness. Maybe it isn't such a good idea to remember the war, these islands. He's not sure it would be at all right to burden the girl with his past, or Tosca's, for that matter.

She sits cross-legged in the bow of Tosca's canoe, her brothers just behind, all three of them grinning with anticipation. It's stopped raining and he paddles out into the blue of the Kula Gulf, south toward the narrow Diamond Passage. He knows the place, and finds it by aligning the canoe precisely between a hut on Kohinggo and a tall palm at Enogai. They peer over the sides to see the unfocused outline of a fighter plane shimmering down some twenty feet underwater.

"The famous Wildcat," Tosca crows. He watches them leap in, his three children swimming down through the warm blue sea, their bodies becoming wriggly and fishlike the deeper they go.

Down, down, until the shimmery mirage, this ghost wreck, becomes real. Cadillac clutches the metal wing to hold herself down while her brothers silently dare each other to swim into the cockpit, positioning themselves before the rusted control stick. Kicking over to the nose, she runs her fingers along the blades of the propellers, searching for nicks where bullets hit, then runs her hands along the side to the hole where a bullet had pierced the fuel tank.

She stays down as long as she can, holding her breath until she feels her lungs will burst.

Papuan hornbill, Rhyticeros plicatus

The hornbill hops around the cooking hut, braying like a mischievous half-wit.

"Shu, shu." Her mother waves him away with a wooden spoon, throws a hot stone from the fire. But the pesky bird only flies up to the top of the cooking hut, still deafening her with his loud protests.

"Aie, aie, disfella bird makim ears bilong me sore tumas," she complains.

"Owee, you lookim alsem devil devil bird," her brothers scoff, marveling at the bird's huge horny beak with its serrated casque, the naked pale blue skin around his eyes, his preposterously flirtatious eyelashes.

The bird likes to throw things up in the air. He tosses his food up, catches and swallows it whole, later regurgitating anything he can't digest, the hard pips of fruit and fish bones. They teach him to catch sticks, rewarding him with a lizard or piece of fish. Like a dog, except he's cleverer than a dog and soon starts to toss a stick and catch it all by himself. Mistaking their laughter and applause maybe for the croaking

of other hornbills. Then pesters and honks boisterously for the food he expects as a reward.

"Shu, shu. Go way 'long bush." He's becoming a pest, although to Cadillac a lovable one. Then, the final insult—he starts trying to mate her mother's shin in a brazen attempt to win her over or to subdue the person who likes him least. And Tosca's forced to take the bird back to the wild, back to Kohinggo, where he found it. All three of them go with him in the canoe because they love this bird. He's become another sibling or playmate to them. Cadillac's brothers sit on either side, chatting away to keep him calm. The hornbill's feet tied down so he doesn't fly back.

There are flocks of hornbills on Kohinggo. Cadillac can hear them across the water, braying and grunting. Their own bird grows excited by the noise and begins to flap his huge wings. And when Tosca unties his feet, he flies greedily, unceremoniously away. Up to the top of a tall ficus tree as if he'd never cared for them in the first place.

They've come a long way, fifteen miles or so. Tosca paddles to shore to cook some food. After they've eaten, he leads them into the bush to show them where he found the fledgling bird. The hornbill nest is in a hollow halfway up the side of a tree, plastered up with a cement made of mud, spit, and feces which has hardened like brick.

The female's inside, Tosca tells them, walled up in that dark, tight space with only a narrow slit open to the world outside. In there, she will have molted and shed her tail feathers for bedding and to give herself more room to maneuver. And she'll stay cooped up for a full two months until her eggs hatch and her babies are half-grown. Then smash her way out with her big beak.

They wait huddled together in the bush close enough to get a good view, keep silent and still until the male arrives. Clutching the bark with his feet, using his frayed tail to hold himself in place near the small hole, he bobs his great head back and forth to bring up his food. Then they see the female—at least her beak—emerging through the slit in the plaster as the male passes her his regurgitated figs. The tips of their huge ungainly beaks meet almost delicately, click tenderly one against the other.

When he mated their mother's shin, did their hornbill imagine this? That he could thereafter get their mother to climb into a small hole where she would wall herself in and he would feed her regurgitated fruit?

At the bottom of the tree is a small pile of pips and fish bones, a pyramid of guano. It's what alerted Tosca to the nest in the first place. And now he makes them wait longer until one of the birds inside the tree squirts a small projectile through the narrow slit. A sight that makes her brothers collapse with laughter.

Tosca corrects, explaining that the hornbill in this way is a good housekeeper, not polluting her own nest with *pekpek* like other birds. "Disfella, he no buggerup house belonghim," he says.

Hornbills, he tells them, mate for life and, like humans, will go to this extraordinary length to protect their young. It's what Cadillac's thought all along, the hornbill like another child, another brother, only a smaller, sillier one.

And their own hornbill does care. He flies out, following the canoe when they leave, but Tosca shoos him off with his paddle, not allowing the bird to land. "Go bek. Go bek. Mi Mari she say you eat tumas."

"And shit tumas," her brothers add, waving their arms.

The hornbill croaks forlornly, tries to approach from the other side. Finally, he gives up and turns back with a loud swooshing of wings they can hear for some distance.

"Go now, go 'long home belongyou," Tosca's saying.

A week or so later, Cadillac insists her father take her back. Once again, they hear the flock honking, tooting, grunting from across the sea. And she sees her own bird brother there hopping along the shore. She can tell it's him by the way he turns and eyes her with a huffy nonchalance. Then flicks a lizard into the air and swallows it whole.

Delacour, New York, July 1973

"Jim skinned like an Annamite," Delacour says. He uses the old colonial term for the people of central Vietnam, intending it as a compliment to both Jim and the Vietnamese, particularly his head boy Nhi, who showed the greatest mastery of all for the intricate work.

"Jim could squat too," he adds. Michael has seen that. Jim, in his seventies, inspecting the mist nets on Great Gull Island, his sharp knees pointing up around his protruding ears.

They sit at a table near the window of The Dominican Place, a family-run restaurant around the corner from the museum. Where the slow ceiling fans with rattan blades make you feel you are back in the tropics.

It was Jim's favorite and Delacour suggested it when Michael called. Looking across the red-and-white-checked oil cloth, Michael envisions Delacour's camp in Indochina. A younger version of Jim squats by the edge of the fire, sharing hand-rolled cigarettes with the native skinners. While Delacour and his great friend Jabouille, the rotund, monocled resident superior of Hue, lean back on folding camp chairs outside the tents smoking their pipes or Gauloises cigarettes. There was something distinctly indigenous or primitive about Jim that set him apart.

"Huevos rancheros. Señor Delacour?" the proprietress asks. She's pleased to see the Frenchman and remembers his usual order. "Will Señor Kennoway be joining?"

"Solamente en pensamiento," Delacour replies. Multilingual, he slips easily into Spanish.

He and Jim like this place for its home cooking. Also for the brightly colored mural depicting a forest in the Dominican Republic, complete with an African gray parrot. The artist was from Zimbabwe, the owner had apologized, much to their delight.

"Jim was a good shot, *un bon tireur.*" Delacour nods as the proprietress refills their glasses from a half carafe of red. "He could shoot a leaf warbler from fifty yards. But when he wasn't shooting—always so impatient."

He's thinking back thirty-five years to their 1939 expedition to Laos. Traveling up the Mekong in their pirogue, they were beset each morning by thick river mist. He and Lowe and Jabouille would sit back in the boat's long cabin smoking, waiting for it to lift, reading old issues of *Paris Match.* He'd brought a stack of the magazines to wrap the skins in, and they must have read every one.

But the mists drove Jim crazy. He couldn't sit still and was forever jumping on and off the boat, fiddling with the motor—which was new to the boatmen of the river. Sometimes, bursting with impatience, he'd rush off with his gun, returning with nothing but a bad temper, because you really couldn't see anything in that mist, let alone shoot.

He remembers how Jim helped the boatmen pull the long pirogues across rapids and over shallow rocks, while Delacour and the others followed a walking path to meet the boats upstream.

"He was ten years younger than the rest of us. He never passed an opportunity to show off."

Michael smiles. It's somewhat of a relief to think of Jim prey to youthful vanity and prowess. It makes the man seem more human.

"And what about Jim's wife?" he asks. They've finished their huevos and have ordered *flan casero*. He doesn't want to miss the chance to fill in that piece of the puzzle.

"Ah yes, we mustn't forget, Jim was in love."

And with his wife too!" Delacour adds as an afterthought, raising his glass and taking an appreciative sip of the wine.

Michael waits for him to elaborate.

"The lovely Helen. She came to Indochina on our 1935 expedition. It was the year they married and a sort of honeymoon for them. Jim picked her up in Saigon and drove her up to our camp above the hill station of Dalat, one of the most enchanting places on earth."

They'd had a small cabin on the edge of a forest of pines, with a bed, a table, three cooking pots hanging from the wall, and a nail to hang your hat. When Helen came, Delacour gave up the bed and moved into Lowe's tent.

"We had a lemur, one Lowe brought from Madagascar," Delacour says. "Helen was very fond of it. She could get it to sleep on her lap like a baby.

"I remember once it was hanging by its tail from a tree. And Jim went and hung upside down by his knees right next to it. I have a photo of that. It made us all laugh. You can see how he was showing off, especially for her."

"And what happened to her?" Michael probes, trying to steer Delacour gently down this path, to establish the minimal facts. Instead the older man falls silent, shaking his head.

"*Alors,*" he responds, resorting to French. "*Cela arrive à tout le monde, n'est-ce pas?*"

He sighs. And Michael is too polite to persist, remembering how Delacour's family home was destroyed in the First World War, then his own château in Normandy overrun by the Nazis. Not to mention his beloved Indochina, invaded by the Japanese and now savaged in this brutal American war. After that last trip up the Mekong with Jim, Delacour had never returned.

"Here's a thing you might not know," Delacour offers, wanting to help out, even if it's not the exact information Michael is looking for. "Jim helped me leave France. Back in 1940, when the Germans took my house in Normandy I fled to Lisbon. It was Jim who arranged my papers and paid for my passage on an export liner to New York.

"Back then I was a refugee, *sans le sou.*" He laughs, comforting himself with the flan, then offering a toast to Indochina, to old friends, to Jim.

Perhaps it's why they continue to be friends, why Delcaour puts up with Jim's irascibility, his poor behavior, Michael thinks. He owes.

Walking back to the museum after lunch, Michael considers how different the two men are. Delacour—short and stocky with rounded shoulders and that big bald head. Ten years Jim's senior, though you wouldn't know it. So lively, so full of stories, that having lunch with him makes you feel you've lived through a piece of history, that you've been invited in.

While Jim's angular, sharp, and craggy. He'd lived through a good part of history too but was closed up and secretive. If you went to lunch with him, he might choose not to talk at all. Once he'd had a drink or two, he might turn unpleasant or abusive. Or his statements might be so coded and elliptical, you'd need a seer to decipher what he meant.

An ass, Jim had called him.

Looking at the black-and-white snapshot Laina had taken of Jim, Michael can see the small field station of Great Gull Island in the background, some rocks. The sky overcast and hazy. It must have been that same day.

Jim, he remembers, had set himself to skin a bird. Nothing exotic, a small warbler or a sparrow, one that had got tangled in one of the mist nets and broken a wing maybe or died of shock. But his hands shook awfully, most likely a side effect of the alcohol he was consuming. His gnarled fingers would no longer do as he asked. This man who, as Delacour said, had turned out particularly fine specimens, who'd been known for his dexterity and speed.

The old man worked alone at a trestle table set against the wall, so that Michael could have ignored him. They all could have. But somehow the intensity of his frustration drew everyone's attention. And even if you happened to glance over, you could see the mess Jim was making of it. The bird's feathers all askew and stuck together, the skin stretched and elongated, the cotton stuffing loosely wound. Jim's brow furrowed not just with frustration but with some deeper despair. They could hear him muttering obscenities under his breath.

Michael had only meant to be helpful, to puncture the tension that was building up in that small, hot hut. Just why he took this upon himself, he can't imagine. Walking over to the table, he'd delivered a homily about all specimens being important to science no matter how executed, the need to value each bird's life. Assurances, he sees now, that would have been better directed at a student, someone who was just learning and would only improve—not at the master, who was careening downhill fast. Still, it was no reason for the old man to turn on him like that.

"You're a monkey's ass," Jim had said. Cruelly. Distinctly. With a searing contempt that was even more humiliating than his words. Everyone fell silent and looked away. It pains him to think Laina had been there.

He remembers Jim stuffed the sorry specimen in the pocket of his jacket and didn't say another word.

Iron Bottom Sound, Off Guadalcanal,
En Route to the Solomon Islands, October 1942

The problem was that he saw those islands differently. To the other men, the Solomons were savage and inhospitable. The Cannibal Isles. The land of headhunters. A fetid equatorial swamp. Wet, hot, febrile. A place where dysentery or malaria would get you if the Japs didn't. Where you might slowly decay if you weren't shot straight off, from foot rot, skin infections, pustules, and tropical ulcers that could bore right down to the bone. They all suffered in some form and treated themselves with sulfa powder. The islanders fared better going barefoot.

Subhuman, some called it. The uncivilized bowels of the earth. Belowdecks they sounded out the unfamiliar names: Guadalcanal, Tulagi, Savo. The names of rivers they would have to cross once they secured a beachhead: the Ilu, Tenaru, and Alligator Creek. Cursing their friends or brothers, anyone they knew who'd been sent to Italy, France, or even North Africa—anywhere but these godforsaken islands.

The jungle spooked American boys. They didn't like the thick vines or serpentine woody lianas, the pulpy herbs, the flagrant orchids, the thick sweet smell of ginger. Everything close and cloying. They'd stick to the coast when they could and traverse high ridges of grassland to avoid this jungle, even if the grass was high and razor-edged.

Jim came with different eyes. He'd dreamed of these archipelagoes. He knew their names, their history, their birds. He delighted in the wild tangle and disorder of these forests. The great nutmegs soaring up to 150 feet or more. The banyans with their buttresses smooth and gray like the flanks of elephants. The aerial roots, hairy and twisted, dropping down to suck water right out of the air itself. To him, it was familiar and intriguing, like the landscape of his own mind.

It's not that he wasn't scared. Jesus, he was scared as the next guy. He'd heard the stories too from Nanking, Malaya, and Bataan. He'd seen the grisly photos that circulated the ship, of pilots mutilated at Wake. Later, he'd see for himself what could happen. A man's genitals hacked off and stuffed in his mouth. His corpse lashed to a tree and left as a warning. It made you sick at first, then it made you thirsty for revenge.

You didn't want to get caught. That was the main thing. There were no prisoner-of-war camps in the Solomons: American or Japanese.

Jim didn't panic in the jungle. He didn't fire at the slightest scuffle. He knew how to use noises to hide. It was other men's fears and their friendly fire that worried him. He volunteered to work alone—to scout. What the others mistook for foolhardy bravado, bravery, or even for his own death wish, Jim knew to be selfish.

No dying for the men beside him. He didn't want to get blown up because someone pulled the pin but forgot to throw the grenade. Nor did he relish the thought of anyone witnessing his own mistakes, or his own disintegration if it came to that. They all saw men fall apart. Turning tail, shitting in their pants, lowering their heads between their hands and sniveling like babies, or worse, becoming too cruel.

To him, the Solomons were the land of colored fruit doves; flightless rails; the Melanesian megapode, which leaves its eggs to incubate in the hot volcanic sand; Meek's extinct crested ground pigeon, *Microgoura meeki*, with its headdress of blue feathers and purple tail, never to be found again. The many species of white-eyes, Zosteropidae, Mann sent back from New Georgia and which became crucial to his groundbreaking theories of dispersal and evolution. These were the islands where Meek and Beck and Mann had all collected, first for Lord Rothschild, later for the museum in New York.

As a child, Jim lay on the beach reading Meek's autobiography, one of the many books Sanford brought him. And there was Cecil kneeling in the sand next to him, a hot hand resting on Jim's back, peering over his shoulder at the black-and-white photographs—of these same coastlines fringed with palms, men in loincloths, thatched houses high on stilts, canoes with sails made of bark. There was one particular image that held their interest longer than the others, a photograph of bare-breasted girls smoking tobacco in long bamboo pipes.

At the back of the book was a map you could fold out, showing the South Pacific scattered with islands, coral atolls, reefs, as if someone had stood in Asia and tossed out a handful of pebbles and debris. From kangaroo-shaped New Guinea, down the long double chain that made up the Solomons, to the tiny Pitcairns in the east. Running above them all—the equator! Even then, Jim sympathized with Meek's dismay at city life, at nearly getting run down by a cab in London. His conclusion that *civilization has also its perils*; how it seemed he'd feel safer, more at ease, more himself, as soon as he could return to *collecting in the wild country*.

It was how Jim felt too, preferring his own small archipelagoes in Maine and Connecticut to the hazards of the dining or drawing room. The habits of birds were predictable and orderly. A thing you could count on.

October 11, 1942. The night before Helen's birthday. He stood out on the deck all night waiting for his first glimpse of Guadalcanal. The rain spat down, the sky was a murky black, which was what you wanted—cloud cover, dark.

Then the sun rose, lighting the huge clouds over Florida and Tulagi a bright red, so it looked as if the islands were under fire already. In that sudden light, the ship felt huge and exposed. A giant bull's-eye gliding across the vast ocean. They were in reach now of the Japanese planes and subs based at Buin and Rabaul. Torpedo Junction, Iron Bottom Sound were the nicknames given to this stretch of water.

At 0700, the fleet of sixteen Wildcats all ready for takeoff. Their propellers deafened as he climbed up into the cockpit next to a grinning pilot. Then the plane sped off, down the long, top-heavy deck of the USS Copahee and up over the water. One by one, the other planes appeared on either side, all flying in formation to Henderson Field. Halfway between Tulagi and Guadalcanal, the pilot dipped a wing so that Jim could see a pod of porpoises streaming along just ahead of them, racing the shadows of the planes.

He wished Helen a happy birthday. Somewhat ashamed of his exhilaration and expectation because he'd longed for these islands. He'd chosen to go there, rather than stay with her.

V
Wantoks

Fox Island, Penobscot Bay, Maine, August 1973

After hunkering down at both ends of the Thoroughfare the day before, the fog had pushed its way in during the night. He'd been aware of it in his sleep, half-woken by the mournful horn at Goose Head. Now the garden and cove are wreathed in a whitish gray, the whole bay cloistered in a thick wet blanket. Erased.

Somewhere off the point, the gong's heavy iron pendulum clangs discordantly as it swings back and forth on the wash. He wonders what the girl makes of it.

In this muffled hush, the phone rings like a shot going off and Jim stumps into the kitchen to pick it up.

"Hello Pappy."

"Hold on." Jim pulls up a chair.

It's Fergus, calling to warn his father that he'll be arriving for his summer visit a few days early. Jim glances at the calendar next to the phone. Mid-August already.

"Do you need any supplies? Any food from New York?" Fergus asks. "For your guest?"

He's heard about the girl then, from Sarah, and will be put out that Jim hadn't mentioned her. Though he's far too polite to say.

"No need," Jim says. "We're fine."

He can read his son's thoughts on the other end of the line. A silence as the word *we* strikes the wrong way, a stifled impatience at Jim's reticence. He doesn't intend to be curt. It's just—they are fine.

"She's not my long-lost sister?" Fergus asks. Jim doesn't bother to reply. Although, to be fair, those things did happen.

"OK then, Pappy."

Jim puts the phone down, strikes the leg of the kitchen table with his stick. That's that then. Fergus will come whether Jim wants him to or not. He'll cook his elaborate meals. *The chef,* Stillman calls him.

Perhaps Jim should have stayed in Greenwich. At least there, no one bothered to foist themselves on him. Interrupting his solitude. His apartment over the stable was too tight for company. If guests came, there was the big house at the end of the drive with its palatial rooms. To hell with that. He would have been even more of an invalid there, even more watched over. Besides, he needs this place now. The fish hawks, the swallows that nest up the road in Stillman's barn and swoop over in the evening feeding on mosquitoes. The sea, even if the fog's swallowed it all up at present.

He crumples some newspaper and stuffs it in the big cast-iron stove, then lowers himself onto the chair to gather a lapful of wood from Stillman's stack. Once it gets going, the stove'll burn off the wetness in the air, and make the place warm for Cadillac. Putting a match to the paper, he puzzles over why he ever stayed so long in Greenwich, calcifying and pickling himself with drink. Commuting into the city to work. Perhaps he'd fooled himself with an illusion of mobility, not realizing how stuck he was. Home to Greenwich was just where he went after the war. Helen was in the hospital nearby, their boy was there. The museum in New York offered work. It seems he'd been too crushed to ever get himself out.

Fire blazing, he closes the stove's heavy door and makes his way out to the porch, stepping carefully so as not to let the crutch slip on the wet boards. He peers into the gray, watches it swirl through the garden and up the porch steps, wrapping itself around the balustrade. He catches glimpses of things: a corner of the boathouse, the end of the dock, a tree branch. Everything unmoored and insubstantial, like ghosts drifting past.

Through the fog, certain sounds come loud and distinct as if the mind, deprived of sight, casts out for other navigational markers. A heron shrieks. A door slams. A dog barks. He listens to the gentle wash of the waves, the raspy grating of a crow.

Now he hears something else—a splashing of flippers in the sea. A forced breath of air through a snorkel that makes him think of the hushed exhalation of a whale. Jesus Christ, the girl's swimming!

Without thinking, he hollers her name, worried she might lose her way or become disoriented. It happens easily. She might swim out instead of in, then get caught in the colder water of the Thoroughfare. His voice is alarmingly loud, croaky as the crow. A moment later, Cadillac hoots back through the snorkel, cold but safe, and he swivels around, angry at himself for fussing.

Christ, she made it here, all the way across the globe, on her own. No doubt she can find her way to the dock. It's not his fault if she insists on swimming in this soup. At least there aren't many boats out to run her over, as any mariners in their right mind would stay ashore today. Fog so thick, as Mainers say, even birds walk.

She'll be happy for some diversion, he thinks, blowing into the fire and putting the kettle on top to warm. He worries she's swimming because she has so little else to do. She's bored. As Fergus suggests, Jim's no sort of company for her, for anyone really. He certainly falls short as a goddamn introduction to the United States, or whatever it is he's supposed to be.

"My son's on his way," he says when Cadillac comes in cold and shivery. She'll go upstairs to run a hot bath but first she comes over to warm herself in front of the stove's open door, and gratefully takes the coffee he offers.

"He wants to meet you. He's worried I'm only feeding you whisky and cigarettes."

He lights the end of a cigarette with a stick from the fire. Sees the imprint of the mask around her eyes, her skin a frighteningly purple color. She looks delighted. Christ, maybe it's a good thing Fergus is coming after all. He doesn't want to care.

Fergus lifts two heavy canvas sail bags from the trunk of the car, walks toward the house. Before reaching the kitchen door, he pauses to tuck his hair behind his ears and takes a deep breath.

He's felt baffled ever since Sarah happened to mention a *houseguest.* Not just any guest either, but a young woman from the Pacific Islands on her way to study medicine at Yale. A medic who's been fishing and swimming in his old wet suit. He can't remember Jim ever having a guest. His old friend Delacour or the Japanese bird expert Iggy Austin, might have slept on Jim's sofa once or twice, but that's all. Is he jealous at his age? Is that why he feels suspicious and usurped?

Picking up the bags again, he pushes the screen door open with his shoulder, then catches it with the back of his heel to keep it from banging. He smells the smoke of frying fish.

"Good morning, Pappy!" he says, reaching for a cheerfulness he's not sure he feels. Beset already by the undercurrent of disapproval and disappointment that always lie in wait for him in his father's house.

Jim grunts and leans forward to fiddle with some lock on the wheelchair.

Why is it that his father can never manage to say hello? Why is it that he looks so startled, as if Fergus had taken him by surprise and is not quite welcome? Jim knows the ferry time; he must have heard the car pull in. Surely he could have unlocked the chair before, even wheeled himself to the door?

At the same time, Fergus suffers a sharp pang of sadness and guilt to see Jim in the wheelchair. His pa, thin, hard-set, pitched forward over the missing leg—an amputation he knows Jim partially blames him for. The cutoff stump juts forward accusingly, the khaki trouser leg tied off in a makeshift knot.

He strides over and lays a hand on his father's shoulder. Then turns to see the young woman, who is standing at the stove. She's tall and barefoot and blacker than anyone he's ever met. Not at all like any doctor he knows, she wears a bright flowered skirt and ironed shirt.

He stares awkwardly, waits for the old man to introduce them. But Jim keeps stubbornly silent as if it's no business of his if they speak, and maybe he'd rather they didn't. Now, to Fergus's embarrassment, it's the girl who steps forward and greets him with a cheerful openness that catches him off guard.

"Hello, I'm Cadillac Baketi," she says. "You are Fergus." When he puts out his hand, she takes it earnestly between both of hers, holds on for longer than he expects. It makes him feel a certain astonished joy—as if she were his long-lost sister after all.

She sees him glance around the room, taking stock: Stillman's stack of wood, the pile of old newspapers, Jim's stubbed-out cigarettes, the book by Hemingway Jim's been reading, the jar of feathers and a small yellow stuffed bird laid out along the windowsill, two flounder frying in the pan.

"I hope you've been using my fishing rods," he says. And hears Jim snort behind him.

He's taller than his father. In his early thirties—she'd asked Jim that—with thick, sun-streaked brown hair that reaches to his shoulders. He wears blue jeans, a neat T-shirt, a pair of sunglasses tucked in at the neckline. The sort of man who'd have raised eyebrows among her girlfriends at King George VI School. Who they'd giggle about later, sitting on each other's bunks in the girls' dormitory.

Is he a bit too carefully groomed, her girlfriends might ask? Was that a sign of conceit? Or if you asked that, were you one who looked for faults? He's good-looking, but is he also slightly knock-kneed?

You'd have to wait to see him in a bathing suit or pair of shorts to be sure. The prospect of ogling a man's legs would set them all laughing again. If he was black, that is. She can't remember ever discussing a white man that way.

Holding this imaginary conversation with herself, Cadillac misses the company of her friends and people her age.

"I've brought some food," Fergus says, hoisting one of the heavy canvas bags up onto the kitchen table. Reaching in like a magician, he pulls out ripe pawpaws, a breadfruit, a whole box of yellow mangoes. The island's one grocery store is short on fruit, or anything much past the basics.

"Whee!" she exclaims, clapping her hands. She'd begun to wonder if Americans ate most of their food from cans, as she knew they had during the war. He looks at her, smiling at her unabashed pleasure. Happy he'd made the effort to walk up to Chinatown from Wall Street.

And she sees his eyes are an unusual light color, yellow and flecked with green and brown speckles.

With Fergus here, the kitchen suddenly feels alive and busy. He clatters in the cupboards, extracting plates and teacups she didn't know existed, and lays out muffins he brought from a place in Rockland. Then halves and squeezes oranges to make fresh juice.

She's pleased there's at least one *wantok*, or relative, to care for Jim, to cook for him. That he's not entirely alone. Though she's not at all sure Jim feels the same way.

The day before she'd helped Jim move down to the boathouse.

"Fergus will need my room," he'd said gruffly, wheeling himself up and down from the shore. Though she's not at all sure why; there are more than enough bedrooms upstairs. She's counted six in all.

She'd made a quiet inventory of Jim's belongings. First, his clothes: a stack of nearly identical blue button-down shirts, laundered and ironed in Rockland; several pairs of khaki trousers. Second, a myriad of bandages and creams for his leg—she knows better than to touch any of those. Finally, his papers, notes, letters, books, the typewriter, his binoculars. He'd let her help with all that, reorganizing his papers along the big table in the boathouse.

"Fergus will want the sitting room," he'd muttered.

Cadillac had insisted on carrying down fresh sheets and blankets. She'd laid the small cot mattress out in the sun for a few hours to air out the smell of mold and mildew. While Jim arranged his things along a shelf in the cupboard underneath the guns and skinning set. She didn't see what he did with the photo of the woman twirling on the beach.

"If you want to be useful, you could bring down a couple of bottles of gin," he'd groused.

She looks over at Jim now, balancing awkwardly on the crutch as if unsure whether to sit with them or flee. She suspects he'd like to do the latter. Instead, he swings forward and picks up one of the newspapers Fergus has brought, then sits back down on the chair, spreading it across his lap as a sort of defensive barricade. Protective of his stump.

"Would you like some fish or juice, Pappy?" Fergus asks.

"No. Not hungry," Jim replies.

We had run up the trades to get the wind of the island we were after—I am not allowed to be more plain, the boy Hawkins narrates as the *Hispaniola* nears Treasure Island. Just why Stevenson needs to be so coy, with most of the treasure lifted, is anyone's guess.

It's Jim's task to be more plain. He scrolls a fresh piece of paper into the portable Corona, casts a quick glance out the doors to the cove, and types: *Just where is this island that Stevenson wrote about and where Sir Edward Seaward was shipwrecked?*

Already, he makes a slip which he has to X out and type over. Sometimes there are so many mistakes, he has to rip out a page and start again. Sometimes, fed up, he retypes a single paragraph or half page and will stick the pieces together with Scotch tape.

Old Providence, an island in the western Caribbean, is about 140 miles from the coast of Nicaragua. British and U.S. navies put the settled or northeast point at 13° 19' 13". Seaward, in his diary, writes 14°. This difference of one degree is not anything to write home about, considering that latitude was a pretty hit-or-miss affair in 1732, the year of Seaward's shipwreck. Jim sits back, then adds: *Even today captains of small boats in far places think themselves lucky to arrive within ten miles of their intended destinations.*

What baffles Jim is how Seaward, writing his voluminous account, could have neglected to include a chart or even a simple sketch of his island. It's an oversight that's caused Jim considerable aggravation as he's painstakingly collated all Seaward's geographic descriptions to draw up his own map.

For a man who claimed to have been a gunner in England, Seaward proved obtusely unobservant. Ever more concerned with food and the safety of his wife and dog, who were both cast ashore with him, than with any proper exploration or mapping. Instead of topographic observations or notes on coastal markers, tides, and the location of fresh water, Seaward gushes over the puddings his clever Eliza made from flour and raisins salvaged from the wreck, their lobster and iguana stews. The antics of his dog, Fidele.

Jim looks up, out the open doors of the boathouse, where upside-down trees and the muted color of the sky are reflected in the green-brown shallows of the cove. It occurs to him that maybe Seaward and Stevenson left the exact location out intentionally, not necessarily to protect treasure, or even because they loved the place. *Oxen and wain-ropes would not bring me back again to that accursed island*, young Hawkins says. But because the island had become a linchpin. So elemental, so crucial to their own sense of identity, that it was important to hold something back, to keep it close. Jim recognizes that instinct—not to give everything away.

He's glad he moved into the boathouse. It's what he liked as a child too—to be down here working long hours on some piece of wood or engine, splicing rope or mending a torn sail. Relieved to be able to reenter this other world of pirates, charts, and shipwrecks, to be close to the sea. Now that he's alone, he regrets his hostility to Fergus. He could have been more welcoming. He should have eaten the food, drunk the goddamn juice his son offered.

But why does the boy have to move so fast? Rushing here and there, too quick, too eager to please. Shaking fresh orange juice and ice too vigorously in Jim's drink mixer.

"You might improve it with a little vodka," Jim had interjected unhelpfully. He could see Fergus wince. Even his son's kindness irritates him. He'd fingered the pack of cigarettes in his breast pocket, drawing one out, as if to purposefully annoy the boy.

Jesus Christ, he's already craving a drink—not a good sign.

It's a physical pain sometimes for Jim to have Fergus so near. His clean smell; his neat, laundered clothes; his precise, careful manner. A fastidiousness Jim can't help feel as a rebuke, as if the boy perfected it over the years as a bulwark against parental chaos.

If only he'd cut his hair, as Jim's suggested many times, maybe he'd look less like Helen. But then there are his eyes.

"What color are my eyes?" Helen asks, lifting her face to Jim but holding her palms over her closed eyelids.

"Green?"

She grins and asks again.

"Brown?" He casts about with desperation. How can he not know? "Blue?"

"No, not blue, brown, green," she taunts. "Yellow."

She lifts her hands and stares straight at him. Her eyes all green yellow, olive, flecked with brown. He'd been right each time.

She reaches out and her fingers feel cool as she places them over his own eyes. His brown eyes.

"Kiss me."

They slide the kayaks down from the beams in the boathouse, drag them under the outdoor shower to wash away a year of dust, guano, and cobwebs. Then float them off the dock.

Fergus fetches two life jackets they must wear because of the cold water. "You do swim?" he asks.

Cadillac nods vigorously. "I love to."

She picks up the knack of the double-ended paddle easily, the way you lean back in the boat, legs stretched in front. And wishes Tosca could see it. The boats, so light and quick, draw angles and hypotenuses between bright lobster pots, and leave shallow wakes like water bugs. Resting her paddle for a moment, she imagines herself back in Tosca's canoe: the small triangular sail lies furled around its mast beside her; the dented tin kettle he keeps by his seat; his fishing line; the waterproof flashlight they can use for spearfishing at night; his basket of nests and eggs. Her father's bare knees stick up on either side.

If she shuts her eyes, letting the sea lap and push against the side of the boat, she's back in the bright blue of the Wanawana. Canoes pass by as men paddle between islands, carrying *Trochus* shells to sell to the Japanese at Noro, to be made into buttons. Or maybe someone's caught a great shark with thick, silvery blue skin and glazed deep-sea eyes. She remembers their excitement a few years back when Tosca returned from Honiara with a kerosene lamp and transistor radio, which meant she had a good light to read by and they could tune in to the Solomon Islands' News Roundup in pidgin and the BBC World Service. Whereas before had been the orange glow of palm oil lamps and fires, the screeching of birds and cicadas, the chirrups of frogs and lizards.

Fergus draws alongside, reminds her of the names of Jim's Atlantic islands. Fox Island on one side, Carver's on the other, known for its stonecutters, with the Thoroughfare running between. Behind them, the rocky outcrops that stretch from Jim's cove are called the Dumplings. And the Sugar Loaves: two bigger islets, which looked small and insignificant from the ferry but now rise steep and lumpy above them. One sprouts thin spiky trees like the hair on the back of a wild boar.

He dips his paddle, swiveling the kayak, and points to a spit called Widow's Neck, to Goose Head Light. Good names—she'll have to write them down for Tosca.

He takes off his shirt. His chest and back are whiter than his arms, evidence of a summer spent in the office. But by the end of the afternoon, she notices his shoulders are turning a reddish brown.

The next day Fergus shows Cadillac a place she can swim without the wet suit.

"Do you mind mud?" he asks as they grab towels and climb into his car.

Starting the engine, he remembers stories of mud, incessant rain, and foot rot at Guadalcanal and feels a bit foolish. He takes the Middle Road, following the course of a tidal river that runs up the center of the island. Then turns onto a badly eroded track, through a grove of birch trees, over the top of a dam, which cuts off the end of the river and traps a large, brackish pond.

"Owee, it's warm!" Cadillac exclaims, stepping down the steep bank into the water. Her toes squelching into the bottom send up thick clouds of gray mud just as Fergus warned.

"Launch yourself out," he instructs. "Keep your feet up." There was a saw mill here once but it's long gone. Shutting down and sold off at the end of the century, along with most of the island farms and fish wharfs. Now only the dike remains, with a large steel pipe embedded in it, through which the tide rushes in and out.

Across the pond, a dilapidated farmhouse belonging to an ancient uncle of Stillman's. White paint peels off in strips and there's newspaper stuck in the windows to keep out drafts. The uncut field running down to the pond is a tangle of Queen Anne's lace, wild snapdragon, and blue peas. The tall grass gives off a musty smell in the midday heat.

He peels off his jeans and T-shirt and executes a neat, shallow dive to avoid the mud. Thinking he'll catch up with Cadillac but by the time he surfaces, she's streamed ahead.

By God, he thinks, Yale's got something coming. He's not sure what to make of her, this tall woman from the Pacific going to medical school. He doesn't mean to be prejudiced but Cadillac doesn't look one bit like anyone he knows who went to Yale or Harvard. Clean-cut men mostly, who wear loafers and oxford shirts after work, women who tie their hair up in ponytails. Then again, she's not like anyone he's met before.

She should slow down, wait for Fergus, be careful not to show off, but she's too taken by the sheer pleasure of it: the thrill of her muscles working again, her limbs stretching, her pulse quickening. Real swimming, free from the cold and the restriction of the tight suit.

The pond must be about sixty meters across, longer than an Olympic swimming pool, though she's never swum in one. She races across. Reaching the far shore, she floats into a small inlet and finds herself eye level with a squelchy forest bed of moss and lichens. Through the low branches of pines that overhang the edge of the water, a rivulet runs down from the wood, and black water bugs dart across the shady surface.

Turning back, she dives down. Underneath, the pond's a brown-orange color with a slight taste of rotting leaves. It's cooler but not cold, soft, more freshwater than salt. She turns a somersault then floats some feet below the surface, blows out air, and watches the bubbles rise up and burst against the bright sky.

She feels a hand clasp her ankle and bolts up to the surface.

They laugh, blowing out pond water.

"OK, I guess I'm not going to ask you to race," Fergus concedes somewhat breathlessly.

"Aaii, I thought you were a crocodile."

He dips his head back to get the hair out of his face, while Cadillac, he notices, can shake her hair practically dry. He'd like to reach out to touch it. They laugh again, their heads and shoulders bob at the surface, their bodies disappear under the murky water.

A heron starts up and glides away from the pond on huge wings.

Living down in the boathouse, Jim finds he takes to certain routines. Each morning, he'll turn on the ship-to-shore radio, tune in to weather updates and shipping forecasts. In the evening, he'll listen to mariners: captains of yachts and fishing boats being put through to shore by Camden Marine, checking home with wives and boatyards.

At night, he lights the kerosene storm lamps and the mosquito coils so that he can leave the big doors open over the sea as long as possible. Finding some mosquito net rolled up in the closet, he rigs it above the cot; and after that, on clear nights, he doesn't shut the doors at all. When he lies on the cot, the large doorway frames the sky like a star map.

He finds cleaning the guns calming. The smell of the gun oil, the catch of the breech as soothing to him as mixing a drink. He wheels his bottles down from the house and lines them up on the kitchen counter between the sink and the small fridge: scotch, gin, martini, rum. He drinks liberally, more than before. After all, Fergus is here to look after the girl now.

On cooler nights, he lights the potbellied stove and stokes it in the morning. He brews a strong pot of sugary tea or coffee and has it ready for Cadillac when she climbs out of the sea. She swims each morning, briefly because of the cold, to the other side of the cove or out toward the Thoroughfare.

Some mornings he hears Stillman, fitting his oars into oarlocks at the far end of the cove, shout a good morning to her. When she climbs up the ladder, her feet leave wet prints in the dry wood floor. He works. He rereads Hemingway.

"Mr. Jim!" Cadillac crows, bursting into the house. "Fergus has shown me a warm place to swim and to practice my strokes."

The millpond. A place he used to go look for great blue herons and swamp sparrows, belted kingfishers and yellow warblers. Greater and lesser yellowlegs pecking in the mud along the drained bed of the tidal stream. Christ, he could have told her about it if she'd asked. Of course it'd be a hell of a lot warmer.

So what rankles then? He takes a good sip of the gin he's treated himself to—a martini, now that the boy's brought olives.

The next morning, he finds himself waiting, listening, and curses his own heart for the way it leaps when he hears Cadillac humming as she walks down from the house. He tries hard not to smile when she comes in for the wet suit, busies himself with his work as if it's no matter to him.

In the Solomons, there's the stinging tree, which can give you a blistery, itchy rash if you stand under it in the rain and its sap splashes onto you. The blind-your-eye tree, found in the mangrove swamps, full of milky, poisonous sap. The vomiting tree. There are centipedes that can drop down on you and whose bite will make you break out in fever and convulsions. Deadly rockfish and lionfish and fire corals you have to be careful not to step on, or brush against when you swim.

When she was small, she learned to avoid these dangers. Just as she learned to harvest yams and cassava with her mother in the garden, and to find wild fern hearts and cabbage in the bush. How to split the stems of pandanus, of sago and bamboo, for house making. How to grate coconut kernels to make soap, and which vines and flowers you can boil to perfume it.

She's eager to learn the names and uses of plants here. To be able to identify the birds, fish, and animals, and know their habits. The familiar fish hawk she knows from home. The way it will swoop down in front of her and grab a fish out of the sea with its talons, turning its prey forward to lower wind resistance. The orangey seaweeds and kelp that wash along Jim's seabed.

It's a way of orienting herself, of understanding the place. Just as another might study a map or read a guidebook, or a sailor would consult the chart and coastal pilot.

At the same time, she wants to know more. What's in the stinging tree that makes you itch? What's in juniper that repels bugs? Each plant and poison potentially used for a cure or antidote, or at least a balm. The way her mother uses betel to settle an upset stomach or take the pain out of a bad tooth, the juice of ginger to disinfect, or a guava thorn to lance a boil.

Walking up to Jim's house, she feels eager for her medical training to begin. Her initiation into the invisible, microscopic world of cells, bacteria, germs, and medicine. It's a knowledge still associated in the Pacific with the spiritual power of *kastom men*. Cadillac's well aware of the opposition she will face, not only as a Western-trained doctor but as a woman.

Still, she knows the importance of good doctoring. She remembers, age ten, watching her newborn sister die. Her mother's growing desperation as she tried to nurse the tiny baby between violent seizures and frightening bouts of rigidity. Most likely, her sister died of neonatal tetanus, Cadillac had learned at the Fiji School of Medicine. The bacteria all too easily introduced if the umbilical cord was cut with a dirty knife or mothers followed the traditional practice of wrapping it in soothing leaves. A disease now almost eradicated, thanks to a simple course of tetanus toxoids offered to pregnant women.

Cadillac's uncle too, her mother's brother: she remembers the time he was horribly burned after a World War II mortar exploded under him. He'd been trying to extract explosives to use for flares in night fishing. She and Tosca had paddled him as fast as they could to the hospital in Munda. After the panicked canoe ride, the calm proficiency of the Methodist sisters in their ironed uniforms had made a lasting impression.

Even more miraculous were the surgeons, particularly the Irish surgeon Dr. Tony Cross. She remembers Dr. Cross's patients gathering outside Central Hospital near George VI School. It was a terrible sight. Many were victims of a polio outbreak in 1952 and had been reduced to dragging themselves along the ground like crabs. Others had withered, useless arms that hung down.

Dr. Cross could see up to a hundred patients a day, curing cripples and helping men walk again. Some he operated on, cutting and lengthening the tendons. Others he fitted with splints and calipers. Once on a school visit to the hospital, he'd showed the students around the new rehabilitation center and enthusiastically pushed them in a wheelchair he'd built, welding a hospital chair to large bicycle wheels—sturdy enough to run across rough coral.

Jim would have liked to see that.

The boy's laid a full, cooked breakfast out on the picnic table under one of the apple trees: bacon, sliced papaya, a pot of hot coffee, and formal place settings.

Jim wheels over, positioning his chair downwind so the smoke from his cigarette won't bother them. Looking out to sea, he listens as Fergus talks to the girl about getting to Yale, about going to see some of the other islands.

"Do you drive?" he asks.

Cadillac shakes her head, not sure how to explain that if you had a car in Munda, you'd only be able to go a few hundred yards to the end of town, where the road stops abruptly, ending at a thick wall of brush.

"There are so many islands, we go about in canoes." Jim senses she's worried about sounding backward.

Like gondoliers in Venice, Fergus thinks, though he knows better.

She could mention the small fleet of plastic outboards with their five-horsepower engines at the Munda guesthouse, the ones used to take Australian divers. But after seeing the massive engines here, forty times more powerful, she thinks she won't.

Or the overnight ferry from Honiara, the one she and a handful of other New Georgia kids would ride home at the end of each school term. The women sitting out on the deck with baskets of scrawny chickens and bushels of onions and ginger, chatting loudly, laughing, spitting betel, and shelling peanuts they'd bought from the market at Honiara. Or chewing ginger if the seas got rough. The men carrying home sacks of rice or spare engine parts. The children getting seasick over the side. Pigs. Dogs.

At night, they'd spread their woven mats along the deck if the sky was clear, or huddle near the cabin if it rained. The boat trailing its fishing lines behind. And if someone had a transistor radio, they might tune in, sing along to Solomon Dakei's Bamboo Band.

"We have planes, of course." Megapode Airways, named for a flightless bird, had recently been rebranded Solair.

"We have the runways built by your Seabees during the war," she says, turning to Jim, hoping he'll back her up. "At Munda, Gizo, and Henderson Field." Wondering if he remembers the names, the geography. It worries her the way he retreats into himself, even more withdrawn and silent since Fergus came.

Damn right, Jim thinks. The runways laid with crushed coral and Marston mats, watered down with rain, sweat, and blood. He remembers the goddamn geography all right. The switchbacks and steep ravines, the coral outcrops, the streams that turned into flooded rivers, tangles of rattan. Topographic details that aerial photos couldn't pick up.

The men of the 169th and 172nd Infantry were green and untested. Guided in by native canoes and scouts, they were dropped off in a jungle so thick they could hardly see more than a yard ahead. Unseen snipers camouflaged in trees picked them off. In the dark, Japanese soldiers shouted out and fired rounds. Those first nights, failing to lay trip wire or to dig in properly, the men of the 169th began to panic. Imagining Japanese all around, they mistook rotting phosphorescence for Jap signals, the thick unfamiliar smell of decay for poison gas. When land crabs scuttled through the brush, they imagined Jap soldiers inching forward on elbows and knees. They jumped up, firing indiscriminately into the dark, threw hand grenades that bounced back at them from coconut and nutmeg trees, then mistook the rebounding shrapnel for enemy ambush. They knifed each other.

On the second day, they ran into their first Japanese trail block with machine-gun emplacements dug into the ridges above, and riflemen pouring down fire. It took them three days to reach the Barike River, only a few miles away, which was officially the regiment's point of departure.

The Munda Trail was a major thoroughfare for native islanders, passing as they did singly, quietly, barefoot. But beneath the boots of companies and platoons, of soldiers carrying mortars, cables, machine guns, it quickly churned into a muddy morass.

Jim was on Layla. From their lookout in the canarium tree, he and Tosca watched the destroyers and transport ships slip by in the early hours.

June 30, D-day. The dawn landings went largely unhindered but by eleven hundred hours, Jap and American planes tussled it out in the air. The flagship *McCawley* was struck. Two days later, bad weather from the south held the American planes down in Guadalcanal, and Jim radioed frantically, as more than fifty Jap planes flew in, circling like sharks behind Rendova peak before diving in for the attack. The Americans hadn't had the chance to set up their radar or antiaircraft guns and Jim saw the great blasts of the fuel drums exploding, the fires, the smoke. Early morning July 6, the USS *Helena* burst into flames in the blackest part of the night.

He saw the casualties at the end of the campaign. The physical and mental carnage. Men missing legs or arms, or both. Men with their faces bandaged. And other men, uninjured, who dragged themselves along slumped over, mumbling, staring out with vacant eyes. Jesus Christ, as if they were dead already.

He remembers why he hadn't wanted the girl to come. The last thing he needs is the past and its ghosts rising up, unbidden. It's hard enough coping with the goddamn present.

Seventeenth Division Field Hospital, Rendova Lagoon, Solomon Islands, August 1943

Colonel Harding, slim with thick glasses, ushers Jim into his tent marked Surgeon's Headquarters and pulls up a chair.

Jim worries the doctor might be overly impressed by his background, that Harding won't treat him squarely as a patient. Already he'd pressed for details of Jim's work at the Harvard museum, confessing that a trip there with his mother had been a highlight of his boyhood.

Harding's tent is an outpost of rationality, orderly and quiet, amid the scenes of lunacy outside. There's a straight row of three army-issue desks piled with neat stacks of folders and charts. A pretty nurse in a clean uniform who, to Jim's regret, gets up to give them privacy, placing a file on the surgeon's desk as she leaves. It's the end of Operation Toenails; the troops now will move on to Bougainville.

"We've had an epidemic up here," Harding says. "Unlike anything we saw on Guadalcanal. Some fifty to a hundred mental cases a day."

Panic, fear, and collapse had swept through the troops as virulently as malaria or dysentery, he explains. Hundreds of men had simply broken down, refusing or unable to do their work. They'd climbed out of foxholes, stood up behind sandbags, and simply walked away. In the middle of firefights sometimes. They'd screamed out in the night, putting other men's lives in danger. Or they'd just given up.

Some must have been shot, Jim imagines, by the Japs or by their own comrades desperate for them to keep silent. He imagines men wandering lost in the jungle. They can't lose their way here because the hospital's on a small island in the Rendova Lagoon.

"War neurosis is the current diagnosis," the doctor continues. "And these men are lucky," he adds with empathy. "In past wars, it was called desertion."

He jumps up and produces a bottle of bourbon from one of the filing cabinets, riffles around for two glasses, and fills them generously, as if realizing all of a sudden what the older man might want. Damn right. It doesn't seem to Jim that Harding's any kind of drinker. He exudes a high-strung, intellectual excitability, so that Jim's not sure how he'd hold up under fire himself, or under too much bourbon. He looks far too young for his responsibilities, though Jim doesn't doubt he's a damn good doctor.

He sees the way the men relax and grow saner in Harding's presence. The ones who cower and whimper if you come near, calm when he talks to them. The ones who look right through you, focus as the surgeon quietly persuades them to change the trousers they've wet or to shave. Even the man who crouches all day behind the empty supply boxes wringing his hands, looking like a goddamn beetle searching out a place to hide, will emerge, take hold of Harding's proffered hand.

"Kentucky Straight Bourbon Whiskey," Harding reads from the label. He himself is from Chicago, he tells Jim. He'd not yet finished his medical degree when war broke out but his interest was already in psychiatry.

"Damn nice of you," Jim mutters. He doesn't deserve this special treatment but senses the doctor's starved for half-sane conversation, for anyone to talk to with at least a smattering of scientific knowledge. Or maybe it's just because Jim's older. Everyone else here is so goddamn young.

The war presents Harding with an opportunity. As a doctor, he might never again be handed such a vast array of raw material and data. It's the same chance Mann had collecting his white-eyes, each species endemic to its particular island. Jim stands to examine a large chart behind Harding's desk with names of patients, their division, and date of arrival, all arranged according to diagnoses—subspecies of illness.

He sees a short list of names under the heading "Atabrine-induced psychosis." Even their antimalarial pill could drive men mad. It was a drug many men refused to take anyhow, because it turned your skin and eyes yellow. "Alsem Japani," as Tosca put it.

One of his findings, Harding explains, is that men with a borderline defect, even a squint or a lisp, bad teeth or flat feet—men who in the past might have been disqualified from war—are far less likely to break down.

"It's not what you'd expect, is it?" Harding asks animatedly. The war's thrown so goddamn much at him. "But a disability can spur men to overcompensate, to prove themselves, it seems."

A more predictable conclusion is the role of experience. "Men like you who saw action on Guadalcanal simply didn't suffer the same way," he says with admiration. "It's why your work in jungle training is so crucial." Which is one of the reasons he'll recommend Jim be put back to work.

Harding's method—simple but effective—has been to separate his patients into two groups. To distinguish between those suffering from physical exhaustion—men who could be bathed, fed, rested, and sent back to fight—from those he calls "psychoneurotics": men who'd suffered true mental breakdown and who were now useless, if not det-rimental, to the war and needed to be sent home. Already he'd been commended for conserving resources.

"Which am I?" Jim asks, tipping back the last of the oak-aged whisky.

Harding laughs. Jim's not mad. He's an ornithologist, a museum man. He's happy to be reminded of that.

"As far as I'm concerned, you can go back to fight tomorrow," Hard-ing says, pouring Jim another shot. "From what you've told me, it seems you've had plenty of rest, too much perhaps. Unless of course you want to stay here for a bit. I can arrange that too."

Normalized abnormality is how Harding diagnoses Jim. He writes it up in a report to be sent to Naval Headquarters and shows it to Jim for his own approval. It's about how ideas and perceptions of nor-mality and acceptable behavior break down when men are faced with the brutality of the battlefield. Actions that seem abhorrent and even criminal to those still living a civilized life become the norm in war. If Harding wonders whether a certain callousness or savagery is actually a prerogative—what a man needs to survive here—he does not put this down in writing.

Jim thought of the broken men when he came home and went to Helen in the hospital. How it seemed to him then that the war hadn't ended at all but had spread its long, vengeful fingers all the way across the world, reaching deep into the heart of his home. Infecting her with its disease, its terrors.

Fox Island, Penobscot Bay, Maine,
August 1973

Fergus watches his father. Jim's expression is so hard, ferocious almost, as if the world's set against him. What harm would it do to respond to Cadillac's mention of those runways when he's been there and seen those islands?

Oppressed by his father's truculent silence, Fergus swings his legs over the small bench, seizes the excuse of clearing breakfast to retreat to the house.

"I taught boys from Brooklyn not to chew gum in the jungle," is about all Jim's ever told his son about the war. If he questions further, his father grows so forbidding and threatening that he backs off.

He sets the tray of dishes next to the sink. They can wait. Only one week here and he, age thirty-five, with a hugely successful career, already feels as frustrated as a small child. Grabbing a pack of cigarettes Jim's left on the table, he crumples it angrily, stuffs it into his pocket, walks out the kitchen door and down the road.

Before the war and after the war is how Fergus sees his childhood. Split into two irreconcilable halves.

Before the war, only a few impressions stand out. His mother's hair falling across his face and tickling as she leans down to kiss him good night. His father's sharp bones as he lifts Fergus high in the air to lower him onto his shoulders.

He was four. They lived in Cambridge, Massachusetts, where Jim worked at the Museum of Comparative Zoology. He was riding Jim's shoulders to his first day of school. When they reached the schoolhouse, he'd refused to get down, clutching wildly at Jim's hair, stiffening his small legs round Jim's neck. He can't remember the room or the teacher, just his gratitude when Jim sat down, not saying a word, not even tugging his leg or trying to extract Fergus's hands from his hair.

Striding down the road through the piney wood, Fergus imagines his young father perching on a child-sized chair. He's wearing his navy uniform and maybe that's why the teacher doesn't say anything. Just lets him stay there, sitting at the miniature desk, listening to her read a story. Until Fergus, tempted by paper and crayons, decides for himself it's safe to come down.

Two crows call raucously from the trees beside him. He stops at a stone wall where the wood ends abruptly and a plowed field opens up with a sweeping view of the Thoroughfare. To his left, the drive to Stillman's place forks sharply back through the trees.

Of Jim's work at the Harvard museum, Fergus remembers fanciful rooms with steaming radiators, musty-smelling cabinets full of strange stuffed birds, drawers lined with eggs. He remembers being shown the great beak of a hornbill intricately carved with a mountainous landscape dotted with pagodas and Chinamen working in the fields below. There was a dusty, wooden attic he could climb to, up a ladder that pulled down from the ceiling. There the ribs of a blue whale pressed up against sloped rafters among boxes of old papers. And pigeons cooed and rutted outside arched brick windows.

Then the war. And while Jim was away, his wife, Fergus's mother, had been taken to a hospital. Fergus was only five. He doesn't remember it well. He remembers his mother kneeling down to him. The thick, white-stockinged legs of two nurses standing on either side. He remembers taking his mother's hands and not wanting to look in her face.

He climbs over the wall and down through the field. Better to leave the road in case he runs into someone he knows. V-J Day and the war was over! It was August and Fergus clung to the back of the Fox Island fire engine with the other boys as it roared through town, honking, its bells pealing. Everyone was rushing out of their houses, waving, cheering, and some weeping.

When Jim came home that spring, Fergus was living with his grandparents and uncle in the big house in Greenwich. He'd been broken-hearted to find that Jim wouldn't be staying with him there but would move into the coach house, with its groomsman's apartment above the stables, which Jim had decided to fix up.

After school and on weekends, Fergus would walk down the long drive. The coach house was in bad repair, having been neglected during the war. Everything needing fixing. And Jim was rebuilding the stairs, cutting and fitting new windowsills, laying new slates on the roof. His pa didn't say much but he was happy enough to let eight-year-old Fergus help. From the roof, you could see the sharp tip of the Empire State Building. The city seemed surprisingly close, though the house was surrounded by woods and pasture and the sea. Some days Jim would put down his tools and take Fergus fishing.

Those afternoons were good. Fergus was proud, like other boys were, to have a war veteran father. Even though he could never be sure when Jim might turn mean, when his pa might suddenly throw down a hammer and tell Fergus to get the hell out.

His father's sudden transformations frightened him. He treaded carefully, thoughtfully. Fergus had already seen how fast a person could fall apart. His mother shining too bright, then burning up like a shooting star. He didn't want his whole universe imploding. Sometimes, while sawing or hammering, or laying tiles in the kitchen, or painting, or holding the leveling line for Jim, or sitting on the roof, he allowed himself to believe that his mother would come back to live with them. Just as soon as they'd fixed the whole place up. That's why they were fixing it. He let himself imagine that sometimes, even after she died.

From the Thoroughfare, he hears some kids shouting as they glide past in two sailing dinghies. Turning into the wind as if to confer about some point, a girl stands and throws a wet sponge across into the other boat, then pulls in her sails and races off. He walks down to the water, rolls up his trouser legs, and steps into the cold.

After the war, he remembers Jim reading to him. First *Treasure Island* and *Kidnapped*, then Stevenson's other stories, such as *The Bottle Imp*, until Fergus began to identify Jim with those characters. His father—a washed-up pirate, a South Seas adventurer, which was as good a way as any to explain his roughness. When they'd exhausted Stevenson—Hemingway. Hemingway's stories were too old for Fergus. He didn't understand them. Though he recognized Jim in these books too, in the noble bullfighters, the sinewy jockeys, the war veterans who were hard and drunk, better at fishing and camping and shooting than at being with people.

He remembers Jim swearing at the critics of *Across the River and into the Trees,* saying they *didn't know their ass from a hole in the ground.*

He searches the shore for a flat stone and sends it skipping across the water. He needs to get away, just for a day. He should take the ferry across to the mainland, just for an afternoon.

Back at the house, Fergus thrusts his hands in his pockets and finds his father's crumpled pack of cigarettes. Not quite ready to go in, he leans against his car, draws out a broken fag, and is startled when Cadillac appears from nowhere and takes it from him matter-of-factly.

"At the Fiji School of Medicine, they showed us a smoker's lung," she says, pausing to give him time to imagine what it looked like. "You don't want one of those." Before he's had a chance to take a first tentative drag.

"OK then." He hands over the whole pack like an obedient schoolboy. Grinning at her bossiness.

"If it rains tomorrow, do you think you'd like to go over to Rockland?" he asks.

"Yes." She smiles.

And Fergus remembers his mother dancing with him for no reason, telling him she loved him so much.

VI
Long John's Earrings

Still more strange was it to see him in the heaviest of weather cross the deck. He had a line or two rigged up to help him across the widest spaces—Long John's earrings, they were called.

—*Treasure Island*

Fox Island, Penobscot Bay, Maine, August 1973

There's a rumble of thunder and wind tousles the trees. Jim looks up from his work. A large bumblebee floats through the open door. Now he sees that several other insects have come in as well. A monarch sips a drop of coffee on the edge of his tin mug. Three bluebottles buzz angrily against the small kitchen window pestering to get out. The humidity's almost tropical, so that his paper feels sodden and the type smudges easily.

Out across the cove, a curtain of rain splits the sea in two: the water in the Thoroughfare lies flat and gray while the bay, a mile or so out, is churned into frothy crests. White horses, his father called them.

Fergus and Cadillac have gone to Rockland for the day on the ferry, taken advantage of the bad weather to get supplies. So Jim has the place to himself—the whole afternoon, until six.

Chewing the butt end of a cigarette, he tries to concentrate on the chart he's drawing, and sees how the shakes in his hands make his outlines quiver like waves upon a rocky shore. Never mind, he's managed to put the islands down, to moor them on a single piece of paper. He feeds the page into the Corona, types the words *Caribbean Sea* toward the bottom, then the name of each island and its corresponding islet—*Treasure Island and Skeleton, Seaward and Edward, Old Providence and Catalina.*

Taking a sharpened pencil, he draws the key landmarks described in all three accounts—Stevenson's, Seaward's, and the Royal Navy survey. Triangular squiggles to mark each island's sugarloaf and distinct twin-peaked hill. Anchors in the three anchorages, described by all as pond-shaped or like a lake. A sort of prow or quarter-note rest to mark the limestone headlands, also a prominent feature in all three descriptions. This headland is the outcrop of white rock beneath which Ben Gunn kept his boat. In reality, it's called Morgan's Head after another infamous buccaneer. He marks the cave where Ben Gunn hid his treasure. Seaward too wrote of finding treasure in a cave.

With the islands set together like this, you can't help but see the similarities. Except for one glaring anomaly of course—that Treasure Island is upside down. Stevenson's harbor and little Skeleton islet, sketched by the author himself, lie to the southeast, whereas the actual anchorage and islet off Old Providence lie to the northwest. But this is the crux of Jim's argument—his epiphany. That Stevenson used Old Providence as a template but flipped the chart to make the place his own.

Jim feels a certain joy in this, as if Stevenson left a puzzle just for him. A narrative sleight of hand. A bluff to confound future readers or treasure hunters, which only he has managed to see through. Now all he needs to do is to use a straightedge to draw in compass points, and an arrow to show the prevailing northeast trade winds.

A great clap of thunder this time. A flock of ducks fly past, low and silent in their eagerness to avoid the storm. A streak of lightning cuts through the darkened sky. It's good to see such wildness, God's fiery wrath. The others in Rockland must be in the thick of it. He wheels around the side of the table to get a better view of the tall clouds piling up over the bay and feels the wind drop. There's a brief moment of still, like a drawing of breath, then, before you would think it possible, the rain plummets down in a torrent and he has to throw a book on top of his papers before his whole argument blows away across the cove.

Behind him, the small door bangs open. Jim crutches over, the shooting pain in his leg reminding him of the exercises and stretches he's forgone. He means to shut the door but instead finds himself looking out at the heaviness of the rain, the force with which the drops pummel grass and sea, sending up fresh smells of dirt, grass, seaweed, and hot shingle. Splashing up onto his trouser leg and across the wood floor. Rain so full, you can hardly tell if it's falling up or down. So that an umbrella wouldn't do you any good. And if you were swimming, you'd see pockmarks shooting up all around—as if you were in the pattern of a Japanese wood-block print. And the sea would taste soft and less salty.

He remembers dancing naked in summer storms with Cecil when they were boys. Taunting the lightning that streaked above them. He thinks of Helen twirling across the wide, white beach, the way she is in the photograph he tries not to look at.

The wind catches the door again, slams it into his shoulder. He shoves a chair up against it. Then, his trouser leg already wet, he steps out, hunched over. Out from under the eave of the boathouse, the rain pounds down the back of his head and neck, soaking his hair and shirt, weighing down the cotton and khaki. He lifts his face to the dark sky, letting the big swollen raindrops smack heavy against his lips and eyelids.

It was the way her hair felt, falling down into his face, across his eyes and into his mouth. Like absolution, like forgiveness.

Cumberland Island, Georgia, 1917

A train to Savannah, a change at Yulee to San Fernandina, then a boat to her island. Pa took him as far as Washington, D.C., where he was to help run the Medical Corps, then sent Jim on alone.

Jim doesn't remember much about his journey south. Looking out the window, he only saw his own reflection. Everyone was talking about American troops being sent to France, the German advance through Belgium. Jim was secretly glad. It took attention away from him.

He remembers his dread of the motor launch. It was the first time he'd been on a boat since Pieter died and he felt marked. Almost as if he should declare himself. Here I am—Little Lord Jim, an unlucky talisman, a bad piece of work. He felt embarrassed that Pa's friend, waiting for him on the island, would know what had happened, and why he was being sent away from home. Banished at fifteen. A pariah.

Great ungainly brown pelicans floated right next to the pier. He stared down at their huge beaks and grotesque pouches that sagged like the chins of old men, their round sharp eyes. Pelicans—even he couldn't be uglier than that. But as the boat pulled away, he watched

in wonder as they flapped their huge wings, struggling out of the sea. Once airborne, they tucked their heads back and flew with surprising grace—gliding long distances, low over the waves.

He remembers the tall white ibis as the boat approached the island, roosting up at the very top of the trees, stepping along the highest branches on their long, spindly red legs.

Jim stepped off the boat, walked up the dry slats of the pier and up onto the soft sand, stepping over large pieces of driftwood with his own spindly legs—as if he too were performing some sort of precarious balancing act.

Pa's best friend Uncle Fergo waits, his open-top Ford pulled up in the sharp dune grass and palmetto palms. He wears a broad-brimmed bark-cloth hat that he picked up on a hunting safari in Uganda. When he sees Jim, he flicks his cigarette into the grass and strides forward. Behind him, a girl swings down from the branch of a tree, where she'd been sitting to watch the boat.

No one had warned Jim about Helen. Perhaps they forgot. Perhaps they thought she'd be away, at summer camp. Perhaps someone had mentioned a girl and he'd simply assumed she was little, like his sister Ann. But there she is, almost exactly his own height, with long dirty-blond hair that falls like a mane over her shoulders. She wears a blue cotton dress with a simple braided belt of rope he thinks she might have made herself. Her bare feet and ankles are sandy and caked with bits of shell.

He feels confused and resentful, unsure he's ready to contend with a girl—this girl. He shakes her hand formally and looks down. Painfully aware of his pallid complexion, his awkward city shoes and suitcase.

"Jump in," Uncle Fergo says. He tosses Jim's suitcase over onto the backseat and gives him a collegial thump on the shoulder as if nothing's wrong in all the world, as if Jim might believe that too. "Young Jim, my favorite and only daughter, Helen." This by way of introduction.

Best thing to do is ignore her, pretend she doesn't exist, which isn't going to be easy as she steps up onto the fender, slides along the hood of the car, and leans back against the windshield. Looking ahead as they drive off with an intent expectancy of pleasure Jim at first mistakes for arrogance. She ties her hair down with a red bandana but the ends lash out in the wind. Red and yellow, like hand-painted photographs Jim's seen of Tibetan prayer flags left at the tops of high mountains. One hand pins down her cotton dress, the other spreads along the hood of the car for balance. She has elegant long fingers.

He wishes his uncle had come alone. He wishes she at least didn't have to sit right in front where he can't help but see her. But then he turns and feels the island's steamy air, blowing round the windshield, tousling his hair, tugging his shirtsleeves, caressing him. The warm, salty air, redolent with the smells of sea and swamp, the hot road, the sun, the mossy bark of live oaks that line the edge of the beach, stunted and windblown.

The car bounces along a white road made of sand and crushed sea-shell, imprinted with tire tracks, perhaps its own from the trip down. Uncle Fergo drives casually, one hand loose on the wheel, his elbow jutting out the side. His other arm, stretching along the back of the seat, seems to reach out to Jim, strong, protective, and welcoming. So that he feels a sudden, unexpected lightening of spirit. His grief and anguish begin to lift. And in their place, a sharp desire and eagerness, and anticipation he's almost ashamed to feel.

He swivels further round in his seat, away from the girl and his uncle. Resting his arms up on the open side of the car, he leans out, trying to hold on to this fragile sense of pleasure. The thick oaks arched overhead make the road flicker, light and dark, like a movie reel, and the car casts a stunted shadow in the sand. He breathes in the hot moist air. A smell of sulfur that can make his heart ache even now. The openings between the trees offer sudden glimpses of dunes. Further on, they pass wild ponies, an alligator basking in a weedy swamp. Turkey vultures tearing at rotten carrion lift their ugly bald heads to meet his eye.

He sees now how this lush barrier island, just a few miles off the coast of Georgia, unveiled itself to him as a place of exploration and discovery—his own Treasure Island. It's part of the reason Helen disturbs him, sitting up on the front of the car. He felt like Crusoe finding a man's footprint in the sand, or young Jim Hawkins coming across Ben Gunn. It sits uncomfortably that this uncharted wildness is already hers, her home.

He tries not to look at her, her long fingers spread over the tan paint of the car, her thin wrist bent sharply. The white dust from the road collects in the fine line of hair along her arm.

"Young Jim," Uncle Fergo calls from the garden the next evening, which isn't any formal garden at all. Just grass and big flowerpots with ferns and sweet-smelling gardenias.

Jim's lying flat across his bed, watching the ceiling fan circle round in a lazy, halfhearted way. His uncle's voice reaches up through the shutters, drawn to keep out the heat, along with the smell of his cigar smoke that wreathes up the side of the house. Jim can hear the scuttling of the two hunting dogs as they bound up the porch steps. Helen greeting them. A tail thumping.

"Yes, what?" he calls back, his voice cracking. Trying to shake himself free of the damp, smothering gloom that threatens to settle down on him again, to emerge from it, which is what he wants most.

"Your pa tells me you're a good shot," his uncle calls up.

"Yes," he says.

"Then come on down, boy. I'd like to see that."

He throws on a clean shirt, splashes water on his face from the washbasin on the dresser. Relieved to be told what to do, he tumbles down the big staircase, his face still wet.

Helen sits on the top step of the porch, cleaning a shotgun. One of the dogs thrusts its head between her legs, angling to have its ears scratched. That would be nice, Jim thinks, without intending to. He looks guiltily at his uncle but can't see his face under the wide brim of the bark-cloth hat. Just the tip of his cigar moving in circles as he chews it. Foot up on the balustrade, he polishes his boot with the gun cloth, then spits out a piece of loose tobacco.

Helen hands Jim the gun then follows, slinging her own gun over her shoulder. She hunts in what she's wearing—her dress and sandals. The dogs lope about her.

"Bet I can shoot that plum right out of your mouth," she boasts.

He plucks the fruit quickly from his mouth in case she means it. Holds it at arm's length, offering her the chance to shoot his hand off but not to blow out his brains. They've been target shooting or plinking, lining up bottles on the low branch of a live oak.

She lifts the rifle and peers carefully down the sight. He should have taken the plum with his left hand. Too late now. He misses his pa with a sudden intensity, realizing how reassuring it was to have a doctor at home. He watches her and concentrates on keeping completely still when the gun goes off. Her shot lifts the plum neatly off his out-stretched palm.

She walks forward with solemnity, pushing his shoulder down with the gun barrel. He can see she's shaking. He kneels.

"You've passed the test of gallantry," she says. "I dub thee Sir Jim of the Plum Pit." He bows his head, the heat of the gun barrel burns his skin through his thin shirt as she lowers it on each shoulder like a sword.

When he looks up, he sees her eyes widen, as if she realizes all of a sudden what she's done, or what she might have done.

"Poor Jim." She drops down on her knees in front of him, laying the gun on the grass. Her arms hang limply by her sides. Her eyes, level with his, are green, blue, and yellow and flecked with brown. "Don't ever let me do that again."

"I won't."

"I'll kiss you now to make up for it." She places her lips lightly on his. Is this what she wanted all along? To kiss him, or to blow his ear off? He doesn't know. Still he'd have her kiss him every day. He's fifteen. He's never been kissed before. Her lips are warm and moist. He closes his eyes and he can smell her skin.

Fox Island, Penobscot Bay, Maine, August 1973

Soaked, Jim turns and goes back into the boathouse. The rain on his face mixes with the salt of his skin and tears. He can taste it, fresh and salty. Like rain in the sea. He sits and peels off his clothes, pulling the wet shirt off over his head, then leans up against the weathered planks to pull his trousers down over his stump. Wet and cold, he hops to the counter and pours a neat Scotch to warm him. He feels a strange euphoria, naked, with the Scotch burning inside. As if he'd like to whoop out loud.

From the cupboard, he takes a threadbare cloth, an old picnic blanket Helen used to like, and wraps it around his waist like a sarong in case the others arrive. He pours himself a second shot of Scotch, then thinking better of it, picks up the bottle. Wheels it over to the potbellied stove.

The fire burning well, the rain still pouring down out the big open doors, speckling the sea, he flips through his old copy of *Treasure Island*.

206

Given to Jim by his pa on his eighth birthday. He reads the inscription in the front. It was the first edition to include the now familiar, well-loved illustrations of N. C. Wyeth, and he admires these anew.

Long John Silver sitting back in the galley, arms crossed, smoking a pipe—his one leg with a buckled shoe stretched out before him. The boat's keel cleverly shown by the way the parrot's cage lurches overhead. *It was something to see him wedge the foot of the crutch against a bulkhead, and . . . get on with his cooking, like someone safe ashore,* Jim reads.

Or Silver pulling the boy Hawkins along by a rope. *For all the world, I was led like a dancing bear,* Hawkins says. Wyeth paints the pirate's stocking half down, as if to show he's coming undone. Yet, at the same time, he celebrates the pirate's strength: Silver's muscular calf bulges above the sock as if it might have burst the button itself, a large hand clutches the rope, the other clasps the crutch as Silver rushes forward. The parrot squawks from his shoulder. His gun is strung across his back.

Wyeth doesn't paint in a peg leg, only cliff and rock and empty space where the pirate's leg should be. In the book, Silver bemoans *my timber leg* once or twice, but all other times it's just *his left leg cut off close by the hip* or *he and his crutch.*

Jim turns the dog-eared pages, searching for Stevenson's first description of the pirate navigating his way between the tables of the Spy Glass Tavern—hopping upon his crutch *like a bird.* A little later, Hawkins marvels at his ease up on deck: *He had a line or two rigged up to help him across the widest spaces—Long John's earrings, they were called; and he would hand himself from one place to another, now using the crutch, now trailing it alongside by the lanyard, as quickly as another man could walk.*

Is this what draws him back to the book after so many years? Is it what truly interests him—Silver's missing leg? More than the identity of the island?

He was twice the man the rest were, Hawkins says, still awed by the pirate even after foiling him at his own game. Still impressed by the sea cook–crook, despite having seen Silver hurl his crutch and strike the honest Tom between the shoulder blades, then drive his knife twice into the defenseless seaman's back.

Reaching down for the Scotch, Jim finds he's finished the bottle. Whisky bringing its own specific form of intoxication: a sharp clarity that cuts through the haze. Like the sun now peering out under the dark clouds, dazzling on the sea.

As they flee the island, Hawkins describes Silver *leaping on his crutch till the muscles of his chest were fit to burst.* How he was *set to an oar, like the rest of us* although *almost killed already with fatigue.*

Silver, the murderous, duplicitous, one-legged sea cook. Named for his silver tongue, like a double-edged sword. Buttering up young Hawkins with his grotesque, obsequious banter, all the while ready to slit his throat if it pleased him. Which was all part of the fascination, the horror. Or Silver, so called for his insolent, bloodthirsty pursuit of one thing only—treasure. *He had still a foot in either camp,* Hawkins says, although he only had one.

Silver: two-faced, one-legged. Foiled but not broken. *He was brave, and no mistake.* You had to admire him. He was the real hero of Stevenson's book. Jim would not have read the tale this way as a boy. Then, he would have put himself in the shoes of the boy Hawkins.

But it's Silver you grow into.

When Cadillac returns from Rockland, she walks down to the boathouse to bring Jim the cigarettes and typewriter ribbon he'd asked for and is surprised to find he's rigged the place with ropes. Ropes tied to eyeholes screwed right into the wall. One strung across from the door to the kitchen, so she'll either have to duck under it, or jump, like a child in a game of skip rope.

"Come aboard, me matey," Jim cries, pulling himself up by one of the ropes to show her how they work. He's wearing a cloth wrapped round him like a *laplap,* his wet clothes drying by the burning stove.

"Long John's earrings," he explains enigmatically, relieved the boy isn't with her.

She's impressed by his high mood as usually he lapses into silence or anger when he drinks too much. She looks round at the empty bottle by the chair, the discarded crutch, the doors open over the sea. And wonders if it's quite safe for him.

"Come aboard," he repeats. Then whistles with admiration when she jumps the first rope.

"Mind the parrot," Jim says, as she leaps over the second rope. He veers precariously close to the open doors and sea as he pulls himself along the rope. "Yo ho ho and a bottle of sake."

Cadillac laughs.

She hands him the ribbon and cigarettes.

On the ferry to Rockland, Cadillac had described a diving frame Tosca used to make at home from tall, straight saplings of bamboo. Passing a timber store on Main Street, he'd taken her in to buy some wood. That's just before the wind whipped through, swinging shop signs on their hinges and blowing over sidewalk displays.

When the shopkeeper opened the door again, wood shavings flew all about the store. And they'd raced across the street to the Rockland Diner to get out of the rain. Inside, there was a brisk business in coffee and syrupy pancakes, and a happy crush of locals and visitors. Even Cadillac could distinguish the two by clothing and accent, though the drama of the storm momentarily broke through any barriers. The glances folks gave Cadillac too, looking up as she walked in, were friendly if curious. Fergus felt he'd like to protect her from people's stares though he suspects she'd laugh it off.

The rain reminded her of home. She'd thought of how her brothers would cut wild banana leaves to hold over their heads to keep dry. Huge crashes of thunder were followed by excited laughter and through the back windows of the diner, which hung over a breakwater and muddy flats, she could see great bolts of lightning sizzle from the dark sky into the gray sea.

Sitting at a Formica table, they'd ordered hot chocolates and a single helping of the pancakes, which could have fed five.

The following morning, they lay the plywood down along the grass: four twenty-five-foot slats, which were as long as they could get. They come into the boathouse for tools and rope. Jim hears them outside, discussing some plan.

To start, they must tie two slats together at the top, Cadillac instructs. She pulls them apart to form a tall A-frame. Then they must cut struts to build a tapered ladder. Fergus lays a third piece of wood across and marks off lengths with a soft pencil. Balancing the slat of wood across the picnic table, he saws the measured pieces, then watches while Cadillac ties them to the frame knotting figure eights at each end. She moves easily, used to working on the ground, and he admires her straight back and broad shoulders.

"When we were small," she says, kneeling back on her heels and looking up, "we couldn't imagine countries without sea. We'd heard of places far away: America, England, Germany. But we believed each was an island like our own. Maybe they were bigger, with taller hills, like Papua New Guinea or Bougainville, but not so different."

There's an English word for that, for countries without any coast. She struggles to think of it. "Countries like Switzerland, states like Idaho?"

"Landlocked?" he suggests.

"Yes, that's the one!" It's how she'd feel—locked in. She'd miss the smell of sea, the way Rockland smelled of its mudflats and fish cannery. She'd miss being able to rest her eyes on the wide blue line of the horizon. The feeling, however misplaced, that she could jump in a boat and paddle home if she needed to, or swim. Besides, how could you ever tell where your own place ended and where another's began? How would you know where you belonged, if you couldn't row out in a canoe or kayak, or even ride out on the ferry to take a good look?

It'd be nice to see the world as one great palm-fringed archipelago, Fergus thinks. Comforting for a child to assume all countries were like your own. To see yourself at the center of the world, which technically she was: the Solomons being tucked right up under the equator. From the age of four, he'd been aware of other places that were far away and frightening—where the war was. He kneels down beside her, clutching a handful of small nails.

"When I was at school, we had two games," he tells her. "Americans versus Nazis and Americans against Japs. If you were one of the older boys, you got to be a GI, or even better a marine. The younger boys, like me, had to be goose-stepping Nazis or buzz around the playground like kamikazes."

Strange that he'd imagined himself flying around the Pacific. Even now, he remembers the names of battles they'd fought and refought, racing around the climbing frame, swinging hand over hand along the bar of the swing set, ducking under low branches or behind the trunks of oaks and beech trees. Midway, Guadalcanal, the Coral Sea, Saipan, Iwo Jima. Not New Georgia. He doesn't remember the name of her island, though Jim evidently fought there. He doesn't remember Jim ever speaking of it.

"We often pretended to be American Wildcats," she says eagerly.

Whenever Cadillac talks of her childhood, he notices she uses the word *we*. It makes him imagine her amid a band of children running about together: black, curly-haired, barefoot. Swimmers. Canoers. Tree climbers. She'd be one of the ringleaders. Also one of the smartest and most good-natured. He admires her open manner and wonders if her ease and poise come from a sense of place. Whether she carries an equatorial balance within her. By comparison, his own upbringing, on the slanted northern curve of the globe, has left him feeling unmoored and adrift.

He leans forward to hammer the nails through the ends of each strut: to reinforce the knots and keep them from slipping. Probably a good idea, Cadillac agrees. Unlike tree saplings, the plywood has no natural grooves to hold the steps. She slips an unused piece of wood under the frame to absorb the force of the hammer and he feels her arm against his. Warm and strong.

He keeps his shoulder steady as he finishes hammering in the nails, then tugs each strut to test its strength.

Cumberland Island, Georgia, 1917

He was sick and they sent him away and it changed him forever. That hot steamy air, the oaks dripping with Spanish moss, the cry of strange birds waiting for him to discover them, armadillos that unfurled and scuttled away under palmetto palms.

He sees now how his life followed a distinct trajectory, veering ever south from the islands of the Penobscot, down to Georgia, out into the Caribbean, across to Indochina, finally landing him on the shores of the equatorial Pacific. As if he'd succumbed to some gravitational force or instinct.

His uncle's house off the coast of Georgia, with its great porch, slatted shutters, and wide steps running down to the grounds, prefigured the resident superior's verandaed house in Hue. The live oaks and gatored swamps drew him in toward the muggy, tangled wildness of the Solomons.

It was here, on this barrier island off Georgia, Jim learned that the study of birds was no longer a hobby but a necessity. Offering purpose. It was here he fell in love.

"You know why this is called resurrection fern?" Uncle Fergo asks. He leans against the low branch of an oak, chewing a cigar, and gently runs his fingers along the bark, covered with what looks like dried scabby lichen. "It's because during a period of drought, it dries up and looks completely dead. But as soon as it rains, it unfurls and is green again."

Uncle Fergo is a congressman. But he only stays in Washington, he says, to protect Teddy Roosevelt's national parks. There's no real hunting on this island. Scavenging, he calls it. But he heads off anyhow, in the evening usually to avoid the heat, taking Jim and Helen with him on foot with their guns, or sometimes in the open-top Ford he's teaching Jim to drive. They go right to either end of the island or to the swamps in the middle. They shoot deer and rabbits and quail. They catch an armadillo, and a snapping turtle, which Aunt Susu makes into a soup. Uncle Fergo lets Jim shoot an alligator, a twelve-foot male. They skin it, dry and cure the leather for Jim to take home with him. Aunt Susu makes gator steaks.

A silent competition grows up between Jim and Helen over who can shoot first, who can get the cleanest shot. Until Jim lets her win. Because he's more interested in the birds. Warblers, tanagers, and buntings. A tiny Carolina wren he finds in a tree bore. He wanders off to locate the source of a particular chattering, sits quietly in a clearing to see what will come. Until the others call for him, or one of the hunting dogs bounds up.

He starts going off on his own.

He writes home asking for his skinning set to be sent. Uncle Fergo's tools will do for game but not songbirds. *I think the boy's improving,* Fergo scribbles in a greeting at the bottom of Jim's letter.

Now Aunt Susu gives Jim a room for his birds. It's a study lined with books at the far end of the house, with two sets of French doors opening to the long wraparound porch. There's a big desk with a leather top Aunt Susu clears off and covers with oilcloth. There's a pool table, covered by a dust sheet, where he can lay out his specimens.

She's not persnickety. If she were, she couldn't be married to Uncle Fergo. But she can't abide dead animals in a bedroom. She doesn't reckon that arsenic and mothballs are healthful for sleep.

Helen walks into the room without knocking or asking. She carries a large sketch pad and a clutch of pencils.

"I need to practice drawing," she declares. "I don't know why you want to skin *all* these tiny birds. We can't eat them." But since he has, she'll draw them. It's harder of course to draw them live.

Jim doesn't respond. He believes he's collecting for the good of science but worries he'll sound pompous if he lectures her. His goal: to collect a representation of all birdlife on the island, two of each species, male and female. Later, he'll see it differently, wondering if he just liked to shoot birds and steal their eggs.

Having interrupted Jim once, she now comes and goes as she pleases; she leans her drawing pad back on the fat leather sofa as if staking out territory. Sometimes when Jim comes in with his birds, she's already there, working alone.

She sits on the back of the sofa, astride as if riding a horse, or cross-legged on the floor with her drawing pad before her. She rearranges Jim's skins on the dust sheet to please herself. Taking a bird not yet skinned, she'll spread its wing and copy the exact detail of the feather patterning. She draws the same bird over from different perspectives: wing spread out, wing folded, on its back with its feet curled up, or propped up to look alive. Studying each until she knows it so well she can draw it from memory. She claims this will help her sketch birds in the wild, where she may be able to catch only a quick glimpse.

One day, Jim feels her gaze turn away from the bird she's drawing, toward him. He tries not to look up, to concentrate on the pine warbler he's skinning.

He parts the downy feathers along the breast and cuts a straight line down from the collar to the vent, careful not to pierce the membrane of the belly, and gently starts to pull away the skin. If he pushes down with the flat side of the scalpel, it comes away easily. There's little fat. Taking a pair of sharp scissors, he snips the bird's tiny legs at each knee and pushes the shinbones out from the skin to scrape them clean. He severs the tail, careful not to cut through the end of the quills.

In seconds, he pulls the skin up to the wings, and after snipping the shoulder bones, right up to the neck. The skin peels away as easily as an orange rind, folding over itself like a glove as Elliot Coues wrote in the book Sanford gave him. Supporting the skin in his hand, careful not to stretch the neck, he eases it off up to the ears. Then laying the bird down on the table, he dabs a small piece of cotton along the inside of the skin to absorb any blood or body fluid. Sprinkles some fine sawdust to keep it dry.

Now comes the trickier part. He detaches the delicate membrane of the ear with his thumbnail, uses the smallest scalpel to cut around the eye sockets, then tweezers to extract the eyeballs without damaging the bird's thin eyelids. He worries Helen might find this disgusting. For all the time she's spent in the room with him, she's never watched so carefully. He hears her pencil scratch the textured paper and tries to shut her out, to think only of the songbird and not make a mess of it. He cuts through the jaw muscle, and up past the eye socket to pull out the muscle and brain. He leaves the skullcap in place to retain the shape of the head.

The bird's now skinned. Its pink, featherless body lies on the newspaper before him. He dips a brush into the jar of arsenic and applies a generous coating, careful to get the powder into all the cavities, then dusts it off. The arsenic will prevent any fly or beetle infestation. He coaxes the skin right side round, draws out the wings and tail feathers, gently stroking them back into place. He feels her eyes on him, all over him; it's excruciating.

Finally, when he's finished stuffing eyes, neck, and body and is writing up the label to tie on the warbler's crossed leg—*Dendroica pinus, male*—he hears her rip the page from her pad. She brings it to him.

A drawing of Jim. He is young, lean, intent, his eyes fierce and focused. His dark thick hair, cropped short, juts up in almost military fashion. He leans over the tiny bird, wielding a scalpel. The pair of scissors, the brush, and the arsenic jar lie on the table near him.

She's drawn in other birds. A northern bobwhite, mounted in a glass cabinet behind him. The stuffed short-eared owl in the bookshelf under its bell-shaped dome of glass. Jim's own birds laid out across the pool table on the dust sheet. Transforming the study in her drawing into a laboratory, or museum.

He likes her drawing. It makes him look like a scientist. The kind of man he would want to be. He smiles at her. Grateful to be looked at. Grateful to be seen this way—the way he is.

The Eggs of Incubator Birds, American Museum of Natural History, New York, August 1973

Laina's come in early to read through the final correspondence from the South Sea Expedition collectors, checking for any mention of the type specimens she's been cataloging for Jim. She lays her papers across the wide table in the library. Enjoying the musty quiet before the others arrive.

She looks over a list: the banded rail and white-faced heron, the last birds sent back to the museum from New Caledonia. A bill of sale for the museum boat the *France*, dated 1932, from Rabaul. Then picks up a letter from the Expedition's last collector Lindsay Macmillan, her Australian compatriot, dated 1939—just as war broke out in Europe. In the letter, Macmillan expresses his shock to find that the formerly peaceable, *louche* colony of New Caledonia had turned Vichy overnight.

With typical Australian swagger, he mocks the French officials, *the resident superiors, clicking their heels and saluting the Führer*. And goes on to describe how a former drinking companion, a Bêche-de-Mer fisherman, had come to him in the night to warn him he might be arrested as an enemy spy.

If it comes to that, I'll be bloody well forced to tell them everything, about the roosting of swamp hens, where to find the eggs of incubator birds. I suppose that might save a man's life.

The island's pro-Vichy governor had been thrown out by the Free French colonials and sent packing to Indochina, Laina recalls. Its capital, Nouméa, had served as U.S. military headquarters during the war. Macmillan had gone home to be drafted into war.

This letter marks the end of the line of her research for Jim, work that has taken a good part of two years. She should feel elated to finish, or at least relieved. It's perfect timing, before her trip to New Caledonia. When the others come in, she should invite them to lunch, celebrate with a few bottles of wine. Instead, looking up through the row of windows to the leafy treetops of Central Park, listening to the steady swish of traffic from the street below, the occasional horn, she feels let down. It's Jim she'd like to go to lunch with. It's Jim's praise she'd want.

Crossing to the secretary's office to make a copy, she glances down toward the end of the hall. Imagines the gray elevator shuddering to life and Jim emerging from the creaky, folding door, fierce and disheveled, badly hungover. And if he did happen to appear just now, she'd ask him about the war. And the *France* too: the seventy-five-ton, cockroach-infested, former copra-trading sailing schooner. Home to a generation of museum collectors, it had crisscrossed the archipelagoes of the South Pacific for ten years. It might take his mind off whatever it is that ravages him.

Waiting while the copy machine warms up, she raises her arms over her head and brings them down in a slow stretch. And wonders whether the *France* went on to play any role in the war. Evacuating colonial settlers, rescuing far-flung traders or missionaries, repatriating copra workers to their native islands. Or dropping off Coastwatchers. Whether she might have been commandeered by revved-up GIs, risking their lives to salvage caches of scotch left behind by fleeing traders. Michener had written of that in his *Tales of the South Seas*. After reading through the field notes and journals of each collector, Laina feels close to the *France* and somehow responsible. She'd seen those schooners pottering around the coast of New Guinea, when she was a child.

She shakes her hair free of its tortoiseshell clip. Envisioning a whole new line of research she and Jim might pursue together. But no, she should stop. Besides, Jim's not here.

It's when she's refiling the letter, slipping it back in a filing cabinet of museum correspondence, that Laina sees another folder marked *Jim Kennoway—Urgent,* and inside it two letters with their envelopes paper-clipped to the front. One letter is stamped with the official seal of U.S. Naval Headquarters; the other is a carbon copy of a response from the museum. She lifts them out.

1943. By this time, the war was in high gear. In the Solomons, the marines had pushed the Japanese from Guadalcanal and were slowly working their way up the island chain. While a joint U.S.-Australian force, under General MacArthur, was fighting the brutal front in New Guinea.

Pending Court-Martial, she sees emblazoned across the top as she slips off the paper clip and runs her hand over the yellowed paper. It's one thing to read letters relevant to your research, another to read potentially incriminating information about a colleague, which probably should not be here.

She feels unprofessional, suspect. As if she's snooping in a child's diary. As if she's stumbled upon Jim's doctor's report or is reading his love letters.

Fox Island, Penobscot Bay, Maine,
August 1973

Jim doesn't attempt to finish the *Treasure Island* piece when drunk. Instead he trails through his scribbled notes, trying to list the flora and fauna, which he might later type up as an addendum—*The Natural History of Treasure Island*.

Sitting at the table in the boathouse, his whisky flask lodged in the side pocket of the wheelchair, he reads through what he's written so far.

1. *Ben Gunn's goats.* Most likely there were goats there. The Spaniards left goats to breed on far-flung islands to feed shipwrecked sailors.
2. *A rattlesnake?* Put that down to poetic license. Young Hawkins stumbles on one after giving the pirates the slip but there are no rattlers on the island. The beast no doubt lifted from Stevenson's California days.

3. *Shore and marsh birds. Wild ducks. If ducks, the West Indies tree duck and the Bahaman pintail are likely.* Stevenson describes *a great cloud, a whole troop of marsh birds, darkening heaven.* Unaccustomed to man, the birds on Treasure Island startle easily. *Wheeling and crying* at the plunge of the *Hispaniola's* anchor, then again when Alan, the first honest seaman, is shot.

He draws a line across the paper, scribbles in a new heading, and underlines it: _Seaward's Animals._

1. *A herd of peccaries, the small South and Central American pig.* If true, the pigs would also have been introduced. Or perhaps Seaward mistook feral goats for peccaries, though this was unlikely—even for the unobservant gunner.
2. *Iguanas.* Certainly. The lizards provided a staple diet for Seaward and his wife, no doubt for his dog too, faithful Fidele.
3. *Northern lobster.* The crustacean Seaward describes at great length, with its *spinous projections, two large horns, and two great claws*—a creature that terrifies Fidele—belongs to the family Nephropidae, the lobster fished right here off the coast of Maine. Seaward couldn't possibly have found one on Old Providence. The West Indies spiny lobster hails from a different family altogether, Palinuridae, with no claws to speak of.

Seaward must have added the northern lobster later for effect, or perhaps it was stuck in by his editor, Miss Jane Porter, who might have read of Nephropidae elsewhere. Mariners were known for spinning tales, and for their wild exaggerations. They had time on their hands. In Seaward's day, sailors would stitch together skins—a primate's body to a fish's tail, for instance—to sell to gullible collectors as mermaids.

Jim takes another swig of the Scotch, jots down a new heading— _Seaward's Birds._

1. *Parroquets.* The small or miniature parrots, ubiquitous throughout Central America.
2. *A brown pigeon. Zenaida,* most likely. A common bird still found there. Jim had seen plenty.
3. *A bird "with a sweet voice like a nightingale."* A mockingbird perhaps? Jim had come across one on the island of Saint Andrews, about thirty miles south. He'd checked his own field notes.

He looks up and out the door, where he can hear Fergus and Cadillac hammering wood, and thinks of another beast he'd forgotten—a sea turtle coming to lay its eggs. Seaward and his wife were too kindhearted to shoot it, moved by its human eye. Later though, after establishing their small colony, they corral hundreds to sell in Kingston. Hawksbills, green turtles, loggerheads, and leatherbacks. The birth of a trade that's made the sea turtle a rare and endangered beast. In his description of Old Providence a hundred years later, the naval surveyor Collett recorded 170 pounds of turtle shell shipped from the island each year.

There's another animal not mentioned in any of the accounts, though no doubt present—the dreaded rat, which follows man to any island he visits. Rats would have been on Treasure Island when the first pirate hauled his ship for cleaning. More of them would have no doubt jumped ashore when Seaward's boat banked on the sands, bringing with it a store of flour, eggs, and sugar for his wife to make puddings. A threat to birdlife as well as to turtle eggs.

Draining the last drops from his flask, Jim scribbles *Sea turtle. Rat.*

Love Letters, New York, August 1973

Michael's delight to find he's Laina's only guest at lunch and that she's ordered a bottle of ice-cold chablis is dashed when she produces a letter with Jim's name on it. He looks down with resignation. In her eagerness, she doesn't seem to register the dampening of his spirits

August 25, 1943. Sent from U.S. Naval Headquarters in Annapolis. *Pertaining to the recommended court-martial of Lieutenant James Kennoway.*

It has been brought to the attention of U.S. Navy Headquarters that during the New Georgia campaign, in July 1943, Lieutenant Kennoway defiled remains of Japanese servicemen. He peers at her through his reading glasses; her face is slightly blurry.

It has also been established that Lieutenant Kennoway attempted to send said remains to Dr. Gerhard Mann at the American Museum of Natural History. Such conduct stands in direct defiance of rules pertaining to the respectful treatment of war dead, particularly in regards to Articles 15 and 17 of the First Geneva Convention, as well as being contrary to the moral code and standards expected of all U.S. servicemen. In addition, it stands in violation of U.S. military postal regulations

She leans eagerly across the table. "What do you think?"

Frankly, Michael's not at all surprised to learn Jim committed a war crime. He wouldn't be at all shocked to learn that the man committed some atrocity in the department elevator. Before he has a chance to say anything though, she produces a second letter. A carbon copy of a response, written by Mann and cosigned by the department chair, Robert Cushman Murphy.

I can assure you that the Ornithology Department of the American Museum has never solicited, nor received, human remains of any kind, from either the Pacific or the European war fronts. Nor would our department have any interest in such remains, our work being solely dedicated to the study of birds.

Instead, may we point out to you that it is the U.S. government's own Smithsonian Institution, not our museum, that has shown a particular interest in the physiology and phrenology of the Japanese skull.

"Seems like Mann and Murphy went to bat for Jim," Laina says. He looks confused. She's far ahead of him here. "I've looked it up. At the start of the war, the Smithsonian conducted a study of Japanese skulls, looking at whether the bone structure reflected inherent racial aggression. Scientists there recommended that this trait be watered down through interbreeding with other Asiatics, presumably with more peaceably shaped skulls."

"Eugenics." Michael nods. "It was more acceptable at the time."

"Mann's letter reads to me like a veiled threat. If you go after our man Jim, we'll make a fuss, a big public fuss about government-sponsored research at the Smithsonian."

Yes, he supposes she's right. Secretly, he thinks it's too bad Mann interfered. It might have been good if the navy had been able to take on Jim. It might have taken him down a notch, helped civilize him. He feels slightly in awe of Laina. Her terrier-like ability to unearth facts, whether they have to do with type specimens or Jim. Her astonishing memory. He wonders what she might have become as a lawyer or politician.

"What do you think Jim did?" she asks. He shrugs, shakes his head. She wears him out. The wine at lunch doesn't help.

Back at the museum, it's sweltering. Michael strides across to the window and throws it open, only to be met by an even hotter, stuffier wall of city air.

He looks across the green copper dome of the Planetarium to the windows of the Ichthyology Department, then down at the North Entrance, where a group of children, part of a summer science camp, gather under the shade of plane trees.

How had he not seen it before? Laina's infatuation with Jim—and not just professional. A monkey's ass, Jim called him. It seems that's exactly what he is.

Looking down, he sees a small girl standing slightly apart from the others. A girl with dark hair, pulled back in braids, who reminds him painfully of his wife Nita—what she must have looked like. He lingers, watching as a boy turns a cartwheel, then kicks his legs up into a show-off handstand walking hand over hand along one of the benches. Impressive and quite wonderful, until a counselor rushes over to scold.

So why doesn't the counselor take charge of the dark-haired girl, who now sits down at the end of a bench, opening her afternoon snack all by herself, ignored by the others?

He wonders when it was that things started to go wrong between himself and Nita. Just when it was he'd stopped seeing her as one of his greatest discoveries, and instead looked on her as a stranger he'd brought back from Argentina, almost mistakenly, along with his crates of skins and field notes.

He looks down at the girl. Wonders if he folds a paper airplane and throws it out the window, whether it would float down to her.

Cumberland Island, Georgia, 1917

Helen's wild, unbridled, proud, naive. Jim might have seen a recklessness, a certain imbalance in her then, if he'd chosen to look for it. He did not. What he sees is that she's the only child of an outdoorsman politician who's away from home much of the time, a singular-minded mother who loves horses and believes strongly in letting children be. It's an existence he envies.

She knows every part of the island and leads him to dunes where they sift the hot, dry sand through their fingers, searching for sharks' teeth until they each have a fistful of the sharp, serrated, blackened fossils, thousands of years old.

She can call alligators too, cupping her hands and making a strange whistling noise, a trick she learned from her mother's blacksmith. She warns Jim that alligators will come right down on the beach, swim in the surf, following the coast until a burst of brackish water alerts them to the mouth of a creek. He thinks she's trying to scare him until he sees one, a small four- or five-footer, slinking out of the trees along the sand. She dares Jim to get close enough to touch its tail with a long stick and laughs heartily when he leaps back. The creature flips round like a highly wound spring.

What does she do the rest of the year? He can't imagine her at her boarding school in Virginia, obeying the unspoken and sometimes baffling rules of other girls, spending long, cold winter evenings indoors.

One night, she comes into his bedroom, the same way she comes into the room where he skins, unannounced, without knocking. She walks across to the bed and shines a flashlight right onto his pillow and over his face.

"Wake up," she demands. It's a full moon, they should go swim. Outside, she wants him to take the Ford and drive down to the beach. It's a hot night and the moon bathes the flat sandy road and the gnarled moss-covered oaks on either side, turning it to moonscape. He turns off the road, along two slats of wood Uncle Fergo has laid across the soft sand, down to the high-water mark, then veers along the shore away from the house. The waves of the Atlantic boom around him.

"Stop!" Helen says and points. There in the headlights, two lines like tire tracks, as if someone else is already here. He looks at her quizzically and she smiles and climbs out.

In the moonlight, they walk back up the beach until Jim sees what looks like an enormous rock heaving itself along. A sea turtle, a loggerhead, hoisting her huge shell, paddling the sand with muscular flippers.

When they catch up, she pauses and rolls back her great doleful eye with turtley resignation. Here, after her long journey across the Atlantic, her laborious trek up the sand—intruders, potential predators. It's too late now to turn back; she's halfway up the beach.

Slowly, the turtle drags herself above the high-tide line where the sand is soft and retains some heat from the day. Jim and Helen move off to a considerate distance. They sit up in the dunes at the back of the beach, wait in silence as she digs her hole, then shudders her huge body over it, depositing her clutch of a hundred or so eggs. Listening to the turtle's soft moaning, her sad, choked lullaby to the unborn, the eggs she will leave here, the tiny loggerheads that will hatch months from now and, without any guidance from her, make their own treacherous rush down to the sea. Easy prey for seabirds and gators. The ones that make it will ride the ocean currents hundreds of miles, following some secret instinct that will take them all the way to the feeding grounds of the Sargasso.

Helen touches Jim's arm. And when he turns to her, she unbuttons her dress and lets it slip down her back. She leans toward him and kisses his mouth and he draws his hand across her shoulder, along her neck behind her hair.

She stands up completely naked. "Let's swim." Leaving her dress on the dry sand, she runs down into the waves. Her skin is white and smooth, and all around the moon-bleached sand and dune grass. He remembers the firmness of the dunes beneath his back, the sharp grass, her hair falling down into his face, into his mouth like rain. Soft and young.

By the end of summer, when he has to return to Greenwich and they both have to go back to school, he's in love. It's a wonder to him now that he'd ever loved anyone.

VII
Japanese Bones

Fox Island, Penobscot Bay, Maine, August 1973

He's drunk too much. He shouldn't be here. He should have excused himself. Jesus, he can always blame the leg.

He came to the island to be alone, his desires simple. Now here they all are, jabbering and getting in his way. Cadillac, Fergus, Sarah too and Stillman at Fergus's summer dinner party. Though Stillman, Jim suspects, is about as keen on socializing as he is.

He's helped himself to several martinis, even before they arrived. The effect of the drink is an opaque, muffled haze, hard as glass. An irritability roused by sudden sound or movement. By Fergus at his side, serving a plate of crabmeat laid out on endive leaves as if they were at a goddamn New York restaurant.

"For Christ's sake, sit down," Jim snaps. Half aware of a silence that falls over the table, as if this is all happening somewhere else, to other people. He feels himself slipping away, somewhere beyond his control. He sips his martini, having dispensed years ago with wine at dinner.

Though the boy makes a fuss over some bottles of rosé he's brought from New York. He misses standing up to eat where and when he likes, washing his own tin plate, his cans of corned beef. He misses not eating. At last the boy sits down.

Jim's not deaf. His hearing's keen even when it comes to kinglets and waxwings. He can hear the chicks in the fish hawk nest, can't he? But here, with the clatter of plates and cutlery and talk, sounds are muddied and unreliable. Worse still, the undercurrents, not the words themselves but the desires underneath, the needs, demands, hurts. Even more treacherous, his own.

They're talking about their trip to Rockland and the storm, the rain that sent them running into the Rockland Diner.

Now Fergus turns to Jim. "A colleague of yours at the museum called me, just before I left New York," he says. "A man named Michael." Jim glares. "Did you know he's assembling a retrospective of your work?"

"Michael writes obituaries," Jim snaps. Well really, did the boy expect to get very far talking about that fool?

Fergus takes another tack, struggling to draw his father out with a persistence Jim finds demeaning. Saying something about repairs to the house, a cracked windowpane, blown fuses, all things Jim used to look after. Yes, he'd noticed. He'd noticed the broken banister on the veranda, wood rot in the latticework under the porch. Jesus Christ, no need to consult him anymore. Nothing he can do about it. Goddamn cripple. Besides, he'd just as soon let the house be, let it grow old around and with him. Let it crack, disintegrate, rot. Be a home to mice.

"When do they need you back in New York?" he asks. Sarah almost chokes on her food.

Jesus, he's wheeled himself up from the boathouse. Isn't that enough? Do they have to expect him to join in? And yes, he'd like Fergus to go away, the girl too.

Stillman leans forward to fill the glasses, for everyone except Cadillac, who doesn't drink, good girl. Jim sees him wink at the boy. They need a drink to cope with me, he thinks. Christ, he needs one too.

It's always been this way. Jim, rude, aggressive, bullying. Especially to his son. His brother Cecil had been a better father to the boy than him. Jim resents that too, though he'd be the first to admit he'd relinquished his place, forfeited. Just another example of his inadequacy, his failure. Jim, the drunk, the misfit. He'd been unable even to care for Helen.

Suddenly, he can bear it no longer. He feels claustrophobic and trapped. He feels the room swelling and pressing in on him, the hallucination he'd suffered as a feverish boy. As if all the things that matter to him have been smashed, destroyed, or just whisked away. Tosca, a name, a lead character in an opera, not the sixteen-year-old Solomon Islands boy Jim once knew. Cadillac, a girl his son likes, not a ghost from his past sent to free him. His son, not his son. Unable to stifle this growing despair, he declares too loudly, he's going out for a smoke.

Even then it's not easy. There's a god-awful commotion as they move back, out of the way of his wheelchair. Cadillac jumps up to move a sail bag, a pair of flip-flops. Even these ordinary things become major obstacles and he has to back up and swivel the chair to get round them. Goddamn it, it's not even easy for him to stumble out drunk anymore, or to slip quietly away.

Outside it's warm and still, with only the thinnest sliver of a moon, like the glint off the blade of a knife or sickle. The dark exaggerates the stars, making them appear closer and far more numerous. The sky swathed in the gauzy filament of the Milky Way.

He wheels himself around the side of the house, listens to the quiet jangling of boat shrouds and stays, the sea sucking quietly at the rocks and around the dock, and feels so grateful for it, he could weep.

The others must be breathing a sigh of relief too, to be rid of him.

He lights a cigarette and inhales the sharp smoke and soft sea air. The small flame illuminates his palms and face as he leans into it. Down in the shallows along the shore and dock, phosphorescence flickers where the water stirs and he imagines a silent communion between the stars and the tiny luminous protozoa, the tip of his cigarette glowing red each time he sucks in. Each light follows a particular pattern, a quiet rationale that can be deciphered and relied on. Like the light at Goose Head, the rhythm of his breathing.

He won't go back in. He's too drunk. He'll go down to the boathouse, divert himself reading Hemingway or tuning in to the ship-to-shore where he can listen to people who expect nothing from him.

He bends down to unstick the brake, jerks the wheels forward, and feels a fresh surge of anger at being stuck in this goddamn chair, one-legged and unable to ever walk properly again. When what he'd like to do is run. Run down the hill. Plunge off the dock into the phosphorescent sea.

Clamping the cigarette between his teeth, he spins the wheels hard with both hands. Even when he reaches the slight slope, where he should be holding back, he pushes forward furiously, recklessly. Until the chair veers off the path and hits a rock or a hard hummock of grass, and he feels himself lifting, rising up on one wheel. Swinging the weight of his upper body to counterbalance, he tries to bring it back down but it's too late—past the tipping point. The chair topples slowly. Then his shoulder hits the ground hard and there's a sharp, painful bang along the tender edge of the stump.

Stunned, he listens to the upturned wheel spin in the air above him, looks up to see its spiked silhouette against the black sky. The stump throbs violently and he feels confused and disoriented by the ninety-degree shift in perspective. The metal arm of the chair beneath him digs into his ribs.

Goddamn, this is a fine predicament! A goddamn poor piece of luck to fall on this side rather than the other. To make matters worse, he realizes he left the crutch up at the house. It had got in the way during dinner and he'd leaned back and propped it against the wall.

He gropes forward, trying to disentangle himself from the chair, and sits up. Twisting around, he runs his hand eagerly along the up-turned side of the chair, slips it into the opening of the side pocket to grab the hard, cool flask. Thank Christ for that: emergency rations. He takes a long swig, and another. Fumbles forward for the cigarette that flew right out of his mouth when he hit the ground.

He remembers a jar of fireflies his sister Ann brought him the time he was sick with fever, after Pieter died.

"In case you get scared of the dark," she whispered, standing by his bed, placing the jar gently next to some books on his bedside table.

He remembers lifting the jar up onto the pillow beside him. When the twilight fades, draining from the room like the ebb tide, he un-screws the lid and lets them fly out. Watching each one as it slowly crawls to the lip of the jar, then lifts off, up into the dark eaves of his room. Where they blink on and off. Glowing like tiny, floating Chinese lanterns. Yellow-green. Like lighthouses. On, off.

Beetles really, not flies. From the family Lampyridae. It's not the whole beetle that lights up, only the final section of the abdomen, or if it's female, the last two sections. Each species flashing its own specific pattern, which is how they recognize each other. He tried to time the on-off cycle. If the periods of dark are longer than the light, it's called *oscillating*, as opposed to *flashing*; those are the words you use for a lighthouse. Marked *Osc.*, as opposed to *Fl.*, on a chart. Except that the purpose of the fireflies' light is different—to lure rather than warn, to attract a mate.

Jim cried and when he cried his face and eyes felt even hotter and more swollen. His body shivered with fever. Here I am, the fireflies flash. See me. Love me. I am here.

It's Stillman who finds him. He hasn't much to contribute after dinner's over, so he excuses himself, thinking he'll have a drink with Jim. He'd heard the old man had moved down to the boathouse. It hadn't surprised him.

"Forgot my crutch up at the house," Jim says simply when Stillman almost stumbles over him in the dark. "Can't right the goddamn chair." He's more shaken than he lets on. So's Stillman, to find him tumbled onto the ground.

"Guess we'll have to fix you up with a horn," Stillman remarks, pulling up the chair. Leaning forward, he takes Jim's hands between his. "Steady, steady," he mutters as if talking to a runaway horse or rabid dog. Jim's arms are surprisingly strong though Stillman can feel his hands shaking. He lowers Jim into the chair and wheels him down into the boathouse, paying no mind to whether Jim likes it or not.

"Hold on please," Jim pipes up before Stillman can flip the light. Not ready for the glare of electricity, he strikes a match, holds it to the wick of the kerosene lantern. For a moment the flickering yellow flame lights the deep creases of his forehead, the old scar running down the left side of his face, his reddened eyes, the terrible shaking in his hands set off again by the fall. Ravaged, Stillman thinks and wonders if he should ask Jim just how much he's been drinking. Or is it best just to offer up a steady, silent comradeship? It's what Stillman himself would want.

"Came to join you for a nightcap," Stillman says.

Jim produces a flask from nowhere. He must keep one in his pocket. Then swivels the chair to grab two glasses from the counter and Stillman sits, surprised to find himself looking right out the doors at the dark of the sea and sky. He wonders if it's safe to leave them open and

the question makes him feel old and disloyal. He so clearly remembers the boy Jim hanging from his knees.

He listens to the night sounds. The water lapping against his lobster boat moored in the cove. A gull's wing beat as it flies past in the dark. He looks at the stars.

"Orion's belt," he says. The Dipper turned on its side now in late summer. Jim nods.

After throwing back the Scotch—he has some catching up to do— Stillman slides his glass along the table for a refill. He leans out of the light, which casts a yellow glow like a campfire, and drinks more slowly. He hears the short bark of a night heron. Breathes in the good smell of Jim's tobacco and the sea. Each of them aware of the other sliding away into his own thoughts. Both familiar enough to guess what these thoughts might be—or how utterly unknowable—Helen. Stillman's wife Esther, his son Elias. The war.

Stillman raises his glass and it all comes back to him so strongly, he can't recall afterward if they said anything out loud or if they just drank together in silence.

Layla Island, Wanawana Lagoon, Solomon Islands, July 1943

It wasn't difficult. A brief scuffle, what you might call a scrap. Looking back, it was shamefully easy. Not even a fair fight.

Jim hears the soft rumble of the boat asserting itself in his sleep. Then Tosca is shaking him awake, already kicking over the lean-to, scattering dirt and leaves over their campsite while Jim struggles into his boots, which are tight because he'd been going barefoot. They hurry down the narrow path to the beach, wedge themselves under a thick cover of branches and palm fronds propped against a jagged outcrop of coral—one of several camouflaged blinds.

A whaleboat. In the dark, they can see the darker circle of the rising sun painted on its bow, hear the whisper of strange guttural voices across the water. A searchlight like a cyclops eye flashes on and scans the shore. They keep quiet, flatten themselves against the rough coral, glad they took such care with the blind, positioning it to watch both a nearby sea eagle nest and the beach.

The eye blinks off. They hear the sound of men splashing down into the shallows. Three, Tosca signals, holding up three fingers. His eyesight far keener than Jim's. It's a relief. There could have been more. Now Jim can make out the dark silhouettes of packs and guns—the shadows of the men wading in across the reef. Once on the beach, the Japs bend earthward and scurry into the shelter of the bush. They are surprisingly close.

Jim curses himself for his carelessness, for having left so many signs. The bamboo racks of birds wedged into cones of leaves, the small shelters they'd built to keep them dry. They'd stopped birding the week before D-day and the American landing on Rendova Island. They've been hiding, keeping watch, sleeping in turns. But they'd left tracks. Jim wonders if the boy could get away safely in his canoe. If confronted by Japs, he could pretend to be alone and know nothing of the specimens collected on the island. Whether he could save himself by leading them to Jim.

Too late to consider that now. Jim concentrates on the Japanese, who will stop in the bush, regroup in a circular, defensive position, and wait for dawn. Are they out looking for him, or are they just Coastwatchers like himself? Here to spy on Rendova.

The rain comes down, loud and heavy, smacking the thick leaves and splashing in the sea. The sound is welcome cover, as is the trill of bugs, which have started up again, the screeching of night birds, the engine of the whaleboat backing out. Jim watches its dark shape retract, the pupil of the cyclops eye. And hears three metallic clicks, the Japs loading their guns.

In the dark, every sound is loud and distinct. His whole body so finely attuned, it seems he can feel the tiniest filaments of his auditory canal straining, searching for signal. His eyes become black holes, absorbing the faintest light, the slightest movement. Keen as an animal. A wild dog. Every muscle primed. Ready. He turns to Tosca and their eyes meet for an instant in the dark. They don't need to exchange a word or gesture. They move forward, instinctually, like pack animals accustomed to hunting together. Along the coastal trail they've made circling the island those past weeks trapping parrots and rails.

They don't have far to go but it seems to last forever. Jim's muscles cramp from holding still after each step. He moves in slow motion like a master of Chinese martial arts. As if in a deadly game of Grandma's footsteps. He feels the long proboscises of mosquitoes penetrating his drawn flesh, the sticky gauze of web clinging to his wet face, the light scurrying of a spider on his neck. The sweat drips down his back.

Remembering his own first night on the island, he imagines the Japanese waiting, listening. Half-deafened by the sound of their own hearts, their blood beating loud as the surf. Trigger-happy maybe, though Japs usually aren't. He sees them so clearly, it's as if he's crouching right beside them. Both hunter and hunted, predator and prey. This sense becomes so real, he feels a sharp premonition of his own death, as if he's stalking himself, the man he'd been his first night alone on the island. A sorrow that he'll not discover the schools of bright fish, or baptize himself in the turquoise-blue sea, or meet the boy Tosca.

They move closer, until he isn't sure if he hears the men breathing or himself. He hears a man clear his throat very gently, very close. It's a highly disciplined patrol. They make no other sound or movement. Jim's glad the rain had washed the smell of sweat off him.

Now Tosca touches his arm lightly, almost a brush, and he freezes and hangs back. Instinctively they fall into an encircling maneuver. The boy must have seen them and Jim sees something too, the faint glint of a gun, or is it a sword—so close he could touch it. He focuses on the dark in front of him until his eyes depict the outline of a man squatting, the faint glow of skin around his neck and wrists. He waits, holds back. Then, using the cover of a bird rustling, or is it Tosca moving in, he lunges forward with his knife.

He can hear Tosca nearby. He can feel resistance against his knife as it cuts through skin and trachea. The Jap tries to cry out but the only sound is a wet burbling through the slit in his throat. A mangled gurgle as he dies. Pushing his knee hard into the Jap's back, Jim feels the struggling body go rigid, then limp.

He lets go, grabs his pistol, turns to shoot the others, but Tosca's rifle blasts out, deafening them both, and there he is grinning in the dark.

"Japan soldia, me killim two," Tosca crows, with boyish exultation. He'd knocked one dead with the butt of his rifle, then shot the second.

After Stillman goes, Jim lies on the cot fully dressed, unable to sleep. Rolling over on one shoulder, he reaches for the refilled flask on the floor and cradles it at his side. He takes a swig to dampen the pain in the stump, to try to stop himself from thinking.

Layla Island, Wanawana Lagoon, Solomon Islands, July 1943

The next morning at dawn, they return to the scene. Riffle through the men's packs and pockets with the unabashed pleasure of children looking for flotsam and jetsam washed up on the tide, the greed of Stevenson's pirates.

They take anything they can use. Ammo, knives, grenades. What they're really after is food. Jim feels humbled by how little the Japs carry, barely enough to keep them alive. He'd noticed it before on Guadalcanal, how thin and malnourished they are, how little they need to survive. Their faces are almost skeletal. He can feel the bones of the Jap he killed through the man's shirt.

Jim's Jap has a small piece of soap, a ceramic flask of sake, half full, in his pack. Also, wrapped in a bit of cloth, a delicate bamboo brush and a small, flat porcelain pot with a block of dry ink. In his breast pocket, a small book wrapped neatly in leaves to keep it dry.

Jim unwraps the book and fingers the thin, translucent paper, admiring the scratchy inked characters, black marks that run top to bottom, right to left. Indecipherable to him as hieroglyphs or prehistoric scratching but nonetheless beautiful. Like the markings of a shell. The unintelligible words of an oracle. A lucky charm. He folds the book up in its leaves, carefully wipes off the blood, and sticks it in his own pocket.

One of the other Japs has an ornamental sword, which the boy draws out, admiring its sharpness.

Jesus Christ, he can't remember what they did next. At least, he's been pretty goddamn careful *not* to remember.

They drank the Japs' sake. Jim poured large cupfuls for himself and Tosca. Maybe that emboldened him. Unless it was just another ploy, a ruse to keep the war at bay. Some desperate reasoning: if the Japs are creatures to be stalked and collected, if they're not men, then he might still be his former self. A hunter and collector, not a killer. He can still be the boy he'd always been.

Or was it deliberate payback—for the USS *Helena* going up in flames, the oil drums exploding on Rendova, all the men he'd seen die?

He pulls himself upright, giving up on any pretense of sleep. Lights a cigarette and blows out the smoke slowly. The pain in his leg makes it hard for him to think straight. The Scotch in his veins too. He looks out at the stars.

One of the Japs is still alive. How could Jim have let this happen? Even as they scavenge, emptying the packs, he moves, emitting a harsh cry. In his death throes, drained of blood and unable to lift himself off the ground, he reaches for a grenade in the small stash Jim has left too close, along with the Jap guns. And Jim, who's been admiring the sword in its decorated sheath, spins round and hits him hard between the shoulder blades. The man slumps forward and whether he's dead or not, Jim's not taking chances this time.

He's so angry at the Jap for coming back to life, angry at himself for putting the boy's and his own life at risk, he draws the sword and hacks the Jap's head off. And maybe that's what spurred him. Gathering the packs and guns to take back to their camp, he picks up the Jap head by the hair.

Japanese Bones,
American Museum of Natural History,
New York, August 1973

*T*he great Japanese bone scandal *is what Mann calls it, waving his
hand dismissively in the air. "It was not the prettiest part of the
war." Laina's presented the chairman of the department with the copy
of the letter he wrote some thirty years before. He lays it on his lap,
lowers his reading glasses to the end of his nose, and runs a large hand
through a shock of white hair.

It's not just Mann's professional reputation or the half dozen books
to his name that make him intimidating, but also his large stature and
austere Germanic manner. Laina gives him the seat of honor in her
office, a comfortable green leather armchair. While Michael, lithe and
slight, sits perched on an antique wood swivel chair, his discomfort
heightened by a growing sense of irritation.

It's not as if he'll be able to use any of this. The *Auk* is hardly the
appropriate outlet to expose a war crime. He suspects Laina's using

248

his article as cover to excuse her determination to follow each lead to its end, to shake each clue until it gives up its secrets—to feed her infatuation.

She leans forward to serve tea from a tray Michael notices is balanced on a pile of books she hasn't quite managed to put away. Laina prettily exempts herself from any reasonable order, he thinks, looking around at her Pacific artifacts. She gets away with it too, with her red hair, her charmingly old-fashioned tea set. The fact is she's so far from home.

The teacup and saucer look particularly small and dainty in Mann's large hands. He leans back and studies them both with pale, milky eyes. He's sizing us up, Michael thinks, deciding what to say and what to hold back. He squirms in the chair, certain he'll be found wanting. Not Laina, who's happy to play the part of a bright-eyed schoolgirl, or dizzy tea server, Mann's favored student—whatever it takes to get her facts.

"Jim wasn't the only one," Mann says hesitantly. "Many were guilty. Collecting bones, ears, dried hands. Stringing teeth around their necks. Extracting the gold from teeth. If you could get a skull—even better.

"You could think of it as hunting trophies," he continues, warming to his topic, beginning to find his voice as lecturer-philosopher. "The thing is, if you were sent to the Pacific, your friends, your girlfriend, your kids *expected* you to send or bring something home. They wanted proof of your strength, your cold-bloodedness. Proof you were there.

"And if you worked behind the lines, if you were a Seabee or on a supply tanker, you could buy something. The Americans, as ever, were natural salesmen." And artisans too, he thinks, remembering photos he's seen of Japanese skulls mounted on jeeps. A Japanese arm bone and fingers used to point the way to U.S. headquarters. He sips his tea, blinks, looks at Laina with half-lidded eyes.

Mann was twenty-five when he first went to New Guinea to collect for Rothschild, then on to the Solomons to join the museum's South Sea Expedition. He only spent two years in the Pacific, not long compared with some of the other collectors. But for a man of his analytical skills, those early travels fostered a life's worth of deductions. His evolutionary theories had started with studies of white-eyes from the Solomons. It doesn't surprise Laina that, thirty years on, Mann can recall this letter and its related circumstances so clearly. He's precise, intellectually exacting. She remains quiet and attentive, not wanting to interrupt.

"The problem came to a head, so to speak," he begins again, smiling, "when *Life* magazine ran a full-page photograph of a girl, from Arizona I believe, writing a letter to her sailor beau with a Japanese skull sitting on the desk before her.

"The photo caused an uproar, because it displayed so publicly the extent of the practice. It was seized on by the Japanese military as proof of American barbarity and racism. As mentioned here," he points to the letter, "it led to a swift attempt to crack down on these practices. Photos like those could be turned against us, making the average Japanese soldier even less likely to surrender, encouraging him to mistreat our own dead. It was not good PR.

"Collecting body parts, mutilation of the dead, is outlawed by the Geneva Conventions." He blinks. Putting the teacup down, he interlocks his fingers. Laina offers some pastries but he shakes his head.

"The fact is, defilement of war dead started the moment the marines set foot in the Pacific. And it's hard to explain the savageness of it. Partly, you could argue, it was a response to the particular brutality of the Japanese, which had been well documented. We'd all read about the slaughter and rape of women and children in Nanjing, later the point-blank executions of Americans at Wake. Another explanation might be that there were no prisoner-of-war camps on those islands. Taking prisoners was inconvenient.

"Then, of course, there was the psychological motivation," Mann continues. "The need to assert your power, to dehumanize the enemy. A part of any war, I suppose. Though Jim's case was a little different."

He trails off into his own thoughts. And Laina jumps in, not wanting to miss her chance to find out what she really wants to know.

"What did Jim send?" she asks. Michael admires her well-crafted tone of regret, as if she's really sorry to have to ask.

"Three heads," Mann says quietly. "But they never reached us."

"Heads not skulls?" she persists with her usual specificity.

"Heads," he confirms. "Skinned. The irony of it was that the skins were so professionally executed, so impressive, that the navy postal workers mounted them, up in their tent or Quonset hut or whatever sort of office they had." Above the mailbags, Jim had told him. "Expressly ordered to confiscate body parts, they evidently didn't want these treasures to go to waste. So there they were, on display, exactly what the navy inspectors were looking for when they came to town looking for fall guys."

"Fall guys?" Michael pipes up. "Surely you're not suggesting Jim was innocent?"

"No," Mann says a little wearily. How can he explain it? Wounded servicemen brought back skulls in their duffel bags, some still green with flesh. And who was going to stop them, when they were also coming home without their own legs or arms? On Halloween, he'd once seen some American children trick-or-treating with a lantern fashioned from a Japanese skull. It was not just soldiers who collected, but congressmen, businessmen, churchmen out on fact-finding missions. Even President Roosevelt was implicated when it came out that a senator had presented him with an arm bone carved into a letter opener.

"Look at it this way. The situation was like this." Mann leans forward, directing his slightly intimidating gaze solely at Michael, spelling it out for the one who doesn't quite get it.

"You remember the Battle of Saipan?" he asks, suddenly reanimated. Once again, Mann—the brilliant professor, the world figure in ornithology, about to reach the climax of his lecture. Saving one stunning piece of evidence for last. "The entire Japanese garrison of thirty thousand men, either killed or committed suicide?"

Michael nods.

"Many years after the war, when the Japanese navy returned to recover their dead, bringing Buddhist monks to exhume the bodies and release the souls, they found nearly two-thirds of the corpsman headless. If you'd wanted to court-martial someone, you'd have to court-martial the whole Pacific force."

He sits back, suddenly looking his age, which is about seventy-two or -three. Michael understands the point but still, he can't help feeling indignant. Jim was even more deranged than he'd thought.

"Jim had been collecting birds for us?" Laina asks, more measured. Or is she just showing she's done her homework, that she's worth talking to?

Mann nods. "Along with others."

"Gilliard. Austin," she says. Not as wide-eyed as she lets on. Isn't she appalled? Surely this will change her view of Jim. Or did her New Guinea childhood immunize her from shock.

"Yes. He'd taken his skinning set with him," Mann says. "His shotgun. I'm afraid I might have encouraged it."

Mann picks up the letter and hands it back to her. "I'd forgotten my threat about the Smithsonian," he says, chuckling softly. "That was a good one—for a German." Laina hadn't considered this before, the trickiness of Mann's position during the war.

"I am not saying it wasn't a racist phenomenon," Mann says. "It most certainly was. I don't recall that Americans treated German war dead with the same savagery."

He picks up a pastry, bites it in half. "But let us talk of more cheerful things. I hear you are going back to New Caledonia," he says. "Tell me about that."

Michael squirms. He'll have to sit even longer, while Laina goes through her New Caledonian itinerary, consults Mann for advice.

He'll wait till Mann's finished, then he'll ask her out, one last time.

Layla Island, Wanawana Lagoon, Solomon Islands, August 1943

What Jim tries hard not to remember is the Jap's skin, how it was turning slightly blue. He'll have to get it off fast, brush it with arsenic, before the head starts to smell and attract bugs. He sits cross-legged on the ground a little distance from the camp, the skinning set unrolled beside him. He cuts carefully up the back of the head, parting the hair, separating skin from bone. It's trickier than any work he's done before. Scalping like a goddamn Indian.

When it's done, Tosca, who's been watching from a distance, crouches down beside him, wraps the awful flesh-covered skull in leaves, and takes it to a coral outcrop on the far side of the island. Places it there to dry in the sun. They bury the bodies because of the smell. They stuff the heads with feathers.

Fox Island, Penobscot Bay, Maine, August 1973

When Jim finally sleeps, he dreams of swimming. He's wearing a mask and peering down into a forest of kelp.

It's hard to breathe through the snorkel. The mask keeps filling with water. But he takes a deep breath and dives down. Reveling in it because he realizes he has his leg back. He can feel his two feet chafe against the tight fit of the rubber flippers. Both calf muscles straining against the drag of water. His body, whole, alive, and young. He kicks down until his lungs strain for air. The sun angles down sparkling off flecks of mica in the sand below.

He's about to turn back, swim up, when he sees a bird. Its wings beat through the kelp. And all about him, birds swim. Brightly colored green and red sunbirds. Species they haven't seen before.

He spins round to signal to Delacour, who must be somewhere close behind. Look here, look what I've found. But when he turns, a Japanese is swimming right behind him. He opens his mouth to shout and it fills with water. He can't breathe, he's swallowing water. He struggles toward the surface, fighting his way through the kelp, which now threatens to entangle him and hold him down.

He wakes, sitting bolt upright in the dark, gasping and choking for air, and drenched in sweat. So feverish and disoriented, he's not sure if he's back in the Pacific suffering from malaria. The stump's hard throbbing brings him harshly back to the present. The dream still holding him in its terror and rhapsody.

He finishes the whisky in his flask.

The following morning, Fergus brings Jim's papers and mail, and two large cups of black coffee. Stillman had told him about Jim's fall and he's relieved to find his pa already at work, though looking a little roughed up and shaky.

He puts the mail and one mug next to the typewriter. His father's books and papers make it hard to sit at the table, so he perches on the cot under the tied-up mosquito net. Glances around at the empty glasses, the Scotch, the stubs of cigarettes Jim shouldn't be smoking.

"I'm planning to drive Cadillac down to Yale at the end of the week," he says. "She needs to be there for orientation day."

Cadillac was to leave just after Labor Day. Yes, Jim does remember that. He hadn't realized it has come about so soon. The girl leaving. The goddamn end of summer. He picks up the coffee.

"I'm wondering if you'd like to come with us," Fergus asks. "Your old alma mater. We could make a jaunt of it." He does his best to sound upbeat and enthusiastic, though he can tell the word *jaunt* grates against Jim's more caustic mood.

Jim grunts and shifts in his chair. His leg seems to be causing him some discomfort, which encourages Fergus to get right to the point.

"I know you won't like this, Pappy, but it'd also be a good idea for the doctor to check up on your leg. I can make an appointment."

Strange Fergus should mention it now—this morning. It's too bad he hadn't asked before—yesterday for instance. Even then, Jim could have shown his son the stump. He could have unwrapped the bandages, unveiled the clean, pink skin to put the boy's mind at ease. The wound had healed nicely. Jim had taken care of it. He'd followed the doctor's instructions as to creams and bandaging, even if he hasn't always managed the exercises. Hell, the last thing he wanted was to fetch up in Rockland with some skin fungus. The whole thing had been healthy-looking if revolting.

Up until this morning that is, when he'd woken early and changed out of his clothes from the day before. Overnight, the stump had turned a startling blue. The skin is swollen and tender to the touch.

He'll not show it to the boy now.

"You'll need to see the doctor," Fergus persists. Goddamn self-appointed nurse.

"Make an appointment for me in Rockland then," Jim says, "I'll ask Stillman to take me in." Which means no to New Haven and to coming down with him to Greenwich, but yes to seeing the doctor. Fergus is relieved; he hadn't expected Jim to agree to that so readily.

He looks out the open doors, the sea right there, almost as if you are in a boat. It makes him think of an illustration of a coot's nest afloat which he saw in one of Jim's bird books. The seaborne roost of the Never Bird.

Jim peruses the mail. A response from Avery Wright at Harvard to Jim's query about a species of ant he remembers from Old Providence. The latest issue of *Tin Can Sailor*, a navy rag. A postcard from Delacour—*Lunch at the Dominican Place. Ordered our old favorite huevos. Michael asking after you.*

"Goddamn fool Michael," he says. "Been pestering Delacour too."

Fergus smiles. This man's another person his father dislikes. Jim's so easily irritated.

"Listen, I'll come back up and take you to Rockland myself," Fergus says. He'll want to hear what the doctors have to say and knows he'll never get a clear report from Jim. The old man doesn't look so well.

Jim nods, not paying too much mind. When they leave, he'll have the whole place to himself. Well, he's glad, if he can just hold out until then.

War Worker, Public Library, New York, August 1973

There's the photo—just as Mann described it. A clean-cut, all-American-looking girl, wholesome, prim, pen poised over paper as she gazes down at her Japanese skull. *Arizona war worker writes her navy boyfriend a thank-you note for the Jap skull he sent her*, the caption reads. Mann even had Arizona right.

Laina has searched through thick collections of *Life* magazine in the public library to find it. Michael had asked her out for a drink as soon as Mann left but she'd put him off. Pretending she had a date, she'd come here instead.

The photo is very posed, professionally arranged. You can see that at once. The girl's blond hair pulled neatly into a bun pinned with a flower. Her starched collar carefully folded over the lapel of her fitted jacket. Chin in hand, she looks at the skull vacantly, fondly almost, the way you might look at a small dog. At the moment the shutter clicked, she would have been more concerned with her looks than what anyone would think of the trifle before her. Or even the letter to her beau. She would have been flattered by the attentions of the press photographer. Unaware of the furor her image would cause.

The skull—once a man—stares with black empty eye sockets. It's artfully turned toward the camera, so you can see the shadowed temple, the high nose, the jawbone with only half its teeth. Had the sailor and his friends extracted the others for their gold fillings?

Laina wonders if the boyfriend had been reprimanded afterward, or threatened with a court-martial like Jim. Whether he would have held this against his girl when he came home.

Then again, he might not have come home. May 1944—the bitter war in the Pacific still had a year and three months to go. The Allies poised to take Biak Island in New Guinea, then the Marianas, Guam, and Tinian. The battles for Okinawa, Leyte, and Iwo Jima all still ahead.

But if he had come home? Then Laina wonders if they had lived happily ever after—neatly groomed, hardworking, emotionally callous, all attributes the photo suggests. Or whether her sailor beau might have brought back other demons to haunt them, less tangible than a skull?

Or perhaps, despite it all, they'd found a wholly different kind of love, one that would excuse the barbarities of their youth. The sort of love she'd always hoped for.

And what about the Japanese? Who was he?

Munda, New Georgia, Solomon Islands, September 1943

Jim was summoned by Halsey, who demanded to know just what the hell he'd been doing skinning birds when he was supposed to be looking out for Japanese ships. He mumbled some explanation about the South Seas collectors but Halsey cut him off. It was easier for Halsey to understand why Jim scalped the dead Japs.

By then, a cable had come from navy headquarters threatening Jim with a court-martial. Colonel Harding had submitted his medical report. Jim waited to hear whether he'd be summoned home to Washington. He'd seen men commit worse crimes. He thought he could manage the disgrace, so would Helen. But he'd worried what it would mean to his young son Fergus, who'd want him to be a hero.

"They've let you off," Halsey said gently. He placed a firm hand on Jim's arm. "But do me a favor, would you? No more head-hunting."

And that was it. All it amounted to at the front in Munda. Just this gentle rebuke from Halsey. Even then, Jim could tell The Bull's heart wasn't in it. It was Halsey who'd spurred them on with his edict—*Kill Japs, Kill Japs, Kill more Japs*—posted on a huge billboard at the entrance to Tulagi Harbor for everyone to see. The admiral needed his men to be bloodthirsty, and if beheading Japs, or taking their teeth or ears, boosted morale, then it helped the war.

He read out two conditions. One, Jim was forbidden to engage in any further *scientific activity* for the duration of the war. Second, he was being reassigned to an aircraft carrier, which would steam up toward the Philippines. Back to his pilot training, work for which he'll later be awarded a Bronze Star and citation.

It's only once they were winning, once Operation Toenails had secured its foothold, that the military could afford to play by the rules. Dropping the atomic bombs on Hiroshima and Nagasaki, for example. Up thousands of feet in the air, the pilots who released those weapons would not have heard a single cry, would not have even seen the cities flattened in an instant. Those were bloodless killings, a mass incineration. No chance of defiling the dead there. There wasn't enough left.

Layla Island, Wanawana Lagoon, Solomon Islands, July 1943

It was Jim's idea to skin the heads. His own reenactment of the depraved white man going native in the jungle. A derangement of his scientific ambition and skill. He was the older man, the scientist. He owned the skinning set, for Christ's sake. He takes full responsibility.

But damn it, Tosca had his own *kastom*, and head-hunting lay at the heart of it. Taking heads marked a rite of passage to manhood. It was a way of gaining earthly and spiritual power, the islanders called *mana*. And raids had continued right up to the end of the nineteenth century, and in a more haphazard way beyond that.

Tosca would have grown up with tales of the great Chief Inqava and his warriors, *tie varane*, who journeyed hundreds of miles across the sea to Choiseul and Isabel to collect heads. Of their vast war canoes, *tomoko*, each paddled by thirty or more warriors. Intricately carved and inlaid with mother-of-pearl. Their carved ebony *nguzunguzu* figureheads lashed low on the prows, dipped into the waves, protecting the warriors from reefs and evil water spirits.

To announce their return, Chief Inqava would blow a conch shell and the warriors would bring the severed heads before a priest. Each man striking the ground with his club when his name was called, to tell how many heads he'd taken. And there would be feasts with sacred puddings, which could only be passed to the men by women's feet. And dancing, with men in one line, women and girls in another. The men decorated their bodies with white lines of lime and red dye extracted from leaves. They wore rings cut from giant clamshells and carried their weapons carved with frigate birds and sharks and lines of human heads.

Maybe Tosca was happy to get a chance at it.

Years after the war, Jim had read articles by the anthropologists Hocart and Rivers. Rivers pioneered the humane treatment of shell-shock victims during the First World War. But before that war, the two men had traveled to New Georgia and spent three months on Eddystone Island.

Rivers described head-hunting as the hub at the center of the wheel, the central tenet that held all parts of society together. When it was outlawed by the British, the birthrate in New Georgia had plummeted. Listless, lacking purpose or interest in life, the islanders had simply started to die off, he warned. He argued that a substitute be found—perhaps in the hunting of animals.

The white man must have appeared so hypocritical. First came the missionaries, then the colonial agents. Both preached the evils of warfare and outlawed ancient rites. *Thou shalt not kill. Thou shalt not steal.* More severe sects, like the Seventh-Day Adventists, took the prohibitions further. *Thou shalt not sing. Thou shalt not dance.* Terrified as they were by the islanders' open display of power and sexuality.

Then, only half a century later, within the lifetime of many, war was back. This time the white man was killing on an almost unimaginable scale, with unimaginable weapons. There were battleships, planes, machine guns, mortars, rifles. No more simple club or ax or spear. A war the islanders called *Bikfala Faet*.

All these years, Jim worried he might have scarred Tosca, mistaught him, led him down a dark path. He wished the Coastwatcher Donald Kennedy had never sent a scout, and had just left him alone, which is what he'd wanted. He saw himself as unfit to be any sort of officer, or friend, or teacher.

But Tosca had become a man, a father, a birder too—curator of the Solomon Island Museum's natural history displays. This was the gift Cadillac had delivered to Jim in the form of a golden whistler. The news that despite it all, he might have been some goddamn use to someone.

The boy carried the skulls in leaves and placed them on a coral outcrop, looking out to sea. He laid the empty flask of sake and the ornamental sword beside them.

Layla Island, Wanawana Lagoon,
Solomon Islands, July 1943

Tired and wet, after watching U.S. ships bombard Munda in the night, Jim returns to camp to find the boy gone. He's not down on the beach either, or inside their blind on the coral headland. Jim peers in, hoping Tosca might have fallen asleep.

Alarmed, he bushwhacks through the mangroves to the place he knows Tosca hides his canoe. Gone too, which at least means the boy has left on his own accord and Jim doesn't have to worry about finding his young body mutilated and tied to a tree. He hasn't been abducted by Japs, by a second patrol coming in to search for the first. Turns out he's just goddamn unreliable. He's just gone. Absconded.

Jim treks back to the camp, surprised by his disappointment, his sense of abandonment. He wonders whether the heads spooked Tosca.

He's become too reliant on the boy, too used to Tosca's company. Maybe it's for the best he's gone, now that the war's here. It's better for

Jim to be on his own. *Fireworks over Munda last night,* he radios late. *0500, three Jap transport ships heading into Kolombangara.*

That night, a blast like a trumpet erupts at the bottom of the canarium tree, loud as a ship's horn. Jim grabs his rifle, peers down through the ferns. That was the second time he might have shot Tosca. Jesus fucking Christ.

Scrambling up the tree, the boy presents Jim with a conch shell, a hole cut through the spiral for a mouthpiece. He's brought two, he says, for signaling—one for either end of the island. His canoe's hidden back in the mangrove swamp.

Jim takes the gnarly shell with its skin-smooth pinkish lip. Jesus Christ, a noise like that should be sounded only in an emergency, he scolds, not to play a trick. They can't afford to take any more risks. They have to keep quiet. Make their radio reports. Stay alive.

He's glad it's dark so Tosca can't see how pleased he is. His delight and gratitude. Without Tosca, he may never have come home.

Fox Island, Penobscot Bay, Maine, August 1973

Jim's finished the *Treasure Island* piece. Just as well, as the swelling in the stump is becoming worse each day, rather than easing.

Avery Wright's letter identified the black ant on Old Providence as *Solenopsis geminata*, the little fire ant, which will do until someone says otherwise. Jim scribbles its name at the bottom of his addendum, *The Flora and Fauna of Old Providence*. Then gathers his papers together. Twenty pages in all, if you include the chart and addendum. The whole thing scruffy, coffee-stained, full of typos. Still he's pleased with it. All the likenesses of Treasure Island and Old Providence adequately set out.

Just this morning, he'd typed out a final argument. The way Stevenson makes use of the naval surveyor's warning about the tricky channel through to the harbor, the unreliable depth readings due to tidal drift. *"There's a strong scour with the ebb . . . and this here passage has been dug out, in a manner of speaking, with a spade,"* as Silver puts it.

Straightening the pages, he slips them into an envelope and scribbles Laina's name on it. Just in time for Fergus to take it to the museum. Now it's done, he'll fix himself a drink to celebrate. An icy martini maybe, five shots with just a splash of vermouth—a drink they call the Lone Pine. He'll wheel himself outside, where the sun is just beginning to set, casting pink reflections across the cove.

He puts his hand on his hot thigh. Finds it painful to stand.

It was just at sundown when we cast anchor in a most beautiful land-locked gulf, and were immediately surrounded by shore boats full of negroes, and Mexican Indians, and half-bloods, selling fruits and vegetables, and offering to dive for bits of money—Stevenson's description of the port the *Hispaniola* hobbles into, unprovisioned, undermanned, demasted after the mutiny on the island.

It's the place Stevenson lets his chief scoundrel free. Where Long John Silver escapes by shore boat with his single bag of treasure. Most likely on the coast of Nicaragua, Jim has argued. *I think we were all pleased to be so cheaply quit of him,* young Hawkins says.

It was far less than he'd hoped for. But still, Stevenson allows Silver to evade the gibbet or any other comeuppance that might await him in Britain. The dire fate of Ben Gunn, who winds up keeping a lodge *exactly as he had feared upon the island* and singing in church on Sunday.

Of Silver we heard no more . . . but I daresay he met his old negress, and perhaps still lives in comfort with her and Captain Flint. It is to be hoped so, I suppose, for his chances of comfort in another world are very small.

An earthly paradise then for Silver, complete with its piratical trinity: Flint, Silver, Silver's island wife.

It was just the sort of place Stevenson would soon set sail for himself. Taking his royalties from *Treasure Island,* and his tubercular cough, the great writer would leave dour Edinburgh and bleak Britain for good. Sail to the South Seas, to the Gilberts, to Tahiti, and finally to Samoa, where he is buried.

Jim finishes his drink and watches the sky light up across the cove. Stevenson dreamed it all before, Jim thinks. He sent Silver ahead to scout, to reconnoiter, to lead him in.

VIII

Hieroglyph

I have never seen the sea quiet round Treasure Island.
The sun might blaze overhead, the air be without a
breath, the surface smooth and blue, but still these great
rollers would be running along all the external coast,
thundering and thundering by day and night; and I
scarce believe there is one spot in the island where a
man would be out of earshot of their noise.

—Treasure Island

Fox Island, Penobscot Bay, Maine, August 1973

Cadillac and Fergus are out in the rowboat, hauling up the tall plywood frame they've been constructing on the lawn. They must have towed it from the dock. Jim crutches out the door across to the picnic table to watch.

"Owee." He hears Cadillac whistle her approval as the structure rises out of the sea. In shape, it's a simple tripod consisting of three tall, thin legs of plywood, two bound with struts like a ladder, the third angling back to give support. In the Thoroughfare, the racing dinghies risk their positions at the starting line to take a look, luffing and tacking at the mouth of the cove.

Jim lowers himself quickly onto the picnic bench, the sudden rush of blood to the stump sharp and overpowering. He takes off his jacket, thrusts it under his thigh to alleviate the throbbing. Tinny music from a radio on the race committee boat spills across the water. The boat idles off the green gong. On board, the teenage boys will peel off

T-shirts to suntan, it being a fairly hot, windless day. If they've any sense, they'll have set an upwind leg to start, counter to the tide, allowing the sailors to drift back.

It must be near the last race of the season. Jim feels the drawing in of winter, the ends of past summers. He imagines his mother bustling about, Frau Leiber overseeing the packing of swimsuits, tennis rackets, summer clothes. Pieter in his blue fisherman's hat coming to take him for a last adventure. The fearful apprehension of school, the cold drunken stupor of his past winter. The cruel cut of age.

Now Fergus clambers over the gunwales of the rowboat onto the bottom strut of the frame, jumping up and down to dig its legs into the seabed. Whorls of mud rise in the clear water.

"You go first," the girl directs from the boat. Jim can hear their voices clear across the water. He notices the male fish hawk circling above, casting an eye over this unusual activity in the cove.

"What if it breaks?" Fergus worries. "Then you won't get a chance." Ever considerate. The frame shudders under his weight. Cadillac laughs. If it breaks, she evidently thinks that will be worth seeing.

She leans forward to reach for the wet suit in the bow and steps into it. The dull black of the suit slipping over her blacker skin. While Fergus's chest gleams city-white above knee-length Bermuda swimming trucks.

How unlikely it is that these two should ever have met. It seems to Jim they've materialized unsummoned from two distinct parts of his past. He would not have predicted they'd get along so well, almost as if the girl is Fergus's long-lost sister after all—he remembers his son's accusation on the phone. His son. Jim can hardly take credit.

Adjusting his hot thigh, Jim realizes all of a sudden what he's seeing—Tosca's great New Georgian diving frame. The one they'd never built, resurrected here and now in the Penobscot. He remembers Tosca tracing an outline in the sand, pestering Jim to let him build one. Boasting how he could *swim long sky*, flip like a fish leaping from the sea.

Christ, the thing would have been a goddamn beacon for the Japs.

Do you regret it? Jim imagines Cadillac asking him this in her direct manner. She'd sit across the table from him, arms up on his books and papers, ask him that with an unabashed directness—if she knew. He looks out at the muddied water.

Not then. That is an answer.

Not even when the navy threatened to court-martial you? Jesus Christ, he'd killed other Japs on Guadalcanal. Why should this man be any different? He was following orders: *Kill Japs*. The way you killed them, what you did with them after, was it relevant?

But later? Ever? He looks at the girl out in the rowboat.

Maybe. Yes, when he visited Helen in the hospital and felt there was his punishment, his retribution. And again, years later, when the dead man's words were read aloud to him from the thin rice paper with the hieroglyphic characters. He'd kept the book all these years. He could show it to Cadillac now.

He pulls a cigarette from the crumpled case, watches a blue damsel-fly alight on the bare skin of his arm, and thinks of another girl who came in and out of his life just as fleetingly as Cadillac. Just as unasked for, unwanted.

Her name was Misako. She was a young Japanese doctoral student who came to the museum to research the tongue structures of the nectar-feeding birds of Hawaii. It was work he'd begun before the war when he and Bryan had been the first to suggest that the honey-creepers, Drepanidinae, be classified by tongues rather than plumage and bill shapes. Their work cut short by the attack on Pearl Harbor. Because, after that, all Jim and Bryan and anyone else cared for was signing up.

At first he'd felt angry. He resented the fact that a Jap was continuing his own work. He was taciturn and unhelpful. It made no difference to him that Misako was a second- or third-generation Japanese Hawaiian and spoke with a gentle West Coast lilt. Any mention of Japan could make him spit. But she'd remained so impeccably polite and quietly determined, bringing in skins for him to look at and pickled tongues, some fleshy, others tubular, some with highly evolved brushlike tips. In the end, he'd done about all he could. He'd helped her craft her dissertation though he never earned a goddamn degree himself.

She was fastidiously neat, handsome, so elegantly dressed you'd never have guessed she was a birder or any kind of naturalist for that matter. Hardworking when most other kids her age were squandering their youth, taking drugs and playing guitar and hanging out on the streets. Fergus too for a while. It could make you want to weep.

He remembers one day bringing in the rice paper book to show her. He didn't offer how it was he came by it. Even showing that book to a Japanese was a confession. She took it from him in her small, white hands. Her fingernails painted, he remembers, a bright, unusual color, blue as this damselfly.

"Go on," Cadillac shouts. "Fly off the top."

At home, her father used straight saplings and tied the wood together with rattan. He could make a diving frame in an hour. When they were small, they'd beg and beg and he'd put them off, claiming he was busy with his birds and other things. He liked to aggravate them with his delays, laughing at their childish impatience, their eagerness, fanning their desire. You can get what you want but not that easily, he seemed to be teaching them.

Then on their way back from school, they'd see the tall structure jutting up far across the water, beckoning them. They'd run up the thatched pier, shedding clothes and school satchels, which had little in them: a single Solomon Islands School jotter, a pencil; both were scarce. Race down to the beach.

From a distance, the diving frame looked like the big A the teacher drew on the board with chalk. Her brothers flinging themselves from the top looked like dark punctuation marks that had broken loose. A comma, a question mark.

"Jump like a frog," Cadillac would instruct, happily dangling from the bottom rung, her arms looped over the smooth wooden strut, her legs splashing in the warm blue of the bay. She'd laugh as they bent their arms and legs, stuck their heads forward in midair. "Drop like a coconut." Her brothers drop, curled up like balls. "Be an exclamation mark!" She liked to test them on things they learned at school.

"Be a knight jousting. Be Queen Elizabeth. Be a Wildcat bomber." This one they knew. Sailing out over the water with open arms, sputtering and whining like engines, they plunged into the sea.

Misako opened the book carefully, conscientiously, with the quiet respect she gave to everything. She took her time, glancing over the pages.
It was another thing he noticed, she was not unnerved by silence. She
let it gather in, giving Jim the chance to think himself back—to Tosca
and the islands.

Would you like me to read it to you?

Please.

It was then—Jim answers Cadillac's unasked question—only then
that I truly considered the reality of the dead man's existence, the nature of his character and thoughts.

It seemed to Jim, he was being offered a glimpse of the tangled,
wounded landscape of his own mind.

She started somewhere in the middle, translating a description of
men retreating through the jungle after a failed attack on Henderson
Field. The men carrying litters, the wounded carrying the dying. All of
them hungry. And he could see it again before him—the narrow red-
earth trails, the thick brush and tangled vines. A lifeless arm dangled
from the side of a litter. He smelled the sweat, the viscosity of blood.
Ripped flesh, wounds that would soon begin to rot in the heat. The
loneliness of dying so far from home. The horror of death in youth.

The Japanese soldier was a lieutenant like himself. Guadalcanal was
also his first posting. His battalion had been devastated by General
Hyakutaki's ill-planned attack on Henderson Field, which took place
soon after Jim's arrival. Later, he was routed from the hills around
Mount Austin. He survived. Sick, delirious with hunger, the island
lost, he'd been evacuated along with hundreds of others from Cape
Esperance, only to have the barge sunk by an American PT boat. He

wrote of boats circling in the dark, American GIs picking off drowning men in the sea. Whooping like cowboys at a roundup.

He survived that. Pulled out of the water the following night by a Jap destroyer, he'd been taken to Rabaul, where he recovered and awaited his next assignment. His entries became increasingly cynical, pessimistic, and melancholy. Heavy with foreboding and resignation. With the knowledge that things were not going well.

Today No. 3 Company left for Lae in New Guinea. Though weary and with bloodshot eyes, they managed to sing as they marched, saluting the past glories of our splendid Emperors. One of the old gunka songs we learned at the military academy.

I went down to the jetty to smoke. The Captain came. He turned toward me and I lit his cigarette. We knew we would not see these men again.

Jim feels dizzy and light-headed, as if he were looking down, or back over his shoulder at something that had just moved, eluding him. The dead man's words flit all about him like sunbirds.

He'd kept the book. Even though orders were to hand over any document to Intelligence, for whatever information it might yield on Japanese intentions or morale. It was another transgression. He'd felt protective of it, covetous. As if his Jap might have written something there for him. That only he would understand. The Jap's words, smooth and pure as sun-bleached bones.

"Go on," Cadillac urges. A sailor bellows encouragement from a Herreshoff. The frame juts some fifteen feet above the water, it must be that deep underneath.

Jim has never considered Fergus brave, with his wet suit and kayaks, his mild, unfailingly considerate manner. At times, he's found his son a disappointment. But now, watching the boy scramble up the rickety frame, the struts bending, the whole structure wobbling wildly, he wonders if he's been impatient and wrongheaded. Whether bravery, freedom, delight might come later, in other forms. Whether there are qualities he's not only overlooked but has never seen. Quiet ones, like the boy's kindness and beauty.

Fergus tucks his hair behind his ears. He's at the top of the frame now and Jim doesn't think he's ever seen his boy look so free. He envies him up there, though it makes him giddy. Even from that height, the boy should have a clear view across the island, be able to see Ames' Knob, its one hill, the water tower, the small collection of houses that make up the town.

Further off, on a clear day like this, he'll be able to see Stonington, Isle au Haut, and Brimstone. He'll have a bird's-eye view of the racing dinghies blowing up the Thoroughfare, their gaff-rigged sails like butterfly wings. He'll be able to peer right down to the bottom of the cove if the mud's settled. Or right down into the fish hawk nest.

Jim's about to shout out, to ask the boy to count the chicks for him—two by Jim's reckoning—when the whole frame shudders violently and Fergus launches himself into the air. A neat swan dive, arms outstretched—as if he were embracing the sea, the whole world.

He feels the free fall in his own chest. His heart beating so hard, so loud. A sudden pounding in his ears and even more intense pounding in the stump. He blacks out for a moment, losing vision and consciousness. He finds himself clutching the table.

I'm dying, Jim thinks. If not this moment, soon. Either his heart's going to give or the stump poison him with its infection that'll spread to the blood. He hadn't realized how *well* the thing was before. He lowers his head between his hands to steady himself and clear the dizziness.

"Bravo, bravo," the sailor hollers through cupped hands. Cadillac shouts her approval too.

And if he doesn't die—Fergus will take him to the hospital at Rockland where they'll hack the rest of his leg off. Leaving him worse off than he is now. With an even more grotesque stub. Jesus Christ, he can't imagine becoming completely dependent on Fergus, or his brother Cecil. Being fully immobile or sick. They wouldn't relish the prospect either. He'd make their lives a hell.

He can't imagine anyone loving him that much.

He pulls himself upright just in time to see Cadillac fly off the top. Her body curls to execute two perfect somersaults—just as Tosca boasted.

Hemingway's wife had it wrong, Jim thinks. That first time, when she stumbled across Papa in the front hall of their house in Ketchum, Idaho. With the breech of the gun open, a note to her propped on the gun rack.

What she might have done was leave him to it. She might have walked past, run if she had to, out into the front garden with its view of the Sawtooth Mountains. It might have been a better thing to do, though maybe impossible.

Jim's been rereading his old copy of *Across the River and into the Trees*, and discovered an article tucked in the back flap. Front-page news of the great man's death by shotgun accident, datelined Ketchum, 1961. He unfolds it on the table before him.

A gun accident by the great hunter himself? Who would believe it? He skims the article, noting how all the facts point to a different conclusion. Hemingway, given his first shotgun at age ten. His experience in three wars: Italy, Spain, then France. The fact that his father had shot himself too, with a Civil War pistol.

Papa had been discharged from the Mayo Clinic just days before his death, after being treated for "hypertension" and kept there for two months. After three months the year before.

Tapping the edge of his cigarette pack, sliding one out, Jim remembers the sad and sordid details that came out after. The times Papa had tried before and been stopped. Interrupted by his wife. Tackled by the local doctor. Held back from pushing himself out of a plane, the private one chartered to take him back to the clinic. Stopped from walking into its propellers when it landed.

And all for what? So they could subject him to their rounds of electric shocks, to the treatments that damaged both his manhood and his memory. The things he relied on to write, and to live. His friends later told of the great author standing all day in front of his typewriter, typing out gibberish, or nothing.

Committing Hemingway to a hospital must have been like caging a wildebeest, a great wounded animal. Jim had seen the sheer inhumanity of it. Jesus Christ, how do you cure hypertension, depression, paranoia, delusion, all things Papa suffered from? Harding's true psychoneuroses? And was it an inherent weakness, a disease to be driven out by any means, or was it a reasonable enough response to the things men saw?

He folds up the article, slips it back into the book cover. Wheels himself across the room for his gin.

Her last few days, Cadillac comes down to the boathouse bringing wildflowers that grow along the bank of the millpond. Queen Anne's lace and curling sprigs of wild pea. She arranges them in an empty glass. She cuts colorful feathery cosmos from Sarah's garden and orange nasturtiums with their lily pad leaves. Not the great sunflowers now towering taller than a man's shoulder.

"Too gah'geous to cut." Sarah beams. She says they're the best she's ever grown, owing to the unusually hot summer. She'll wait until they begin to droop, then cut the heads and dry the seeds to eat.

Cadillac brings the finds from her bedroom: her collections of stones, domed sea urchins, orange crab shells, sea glass, the jar of feathers, not knowing where to put them. "Can I leave them in the cupboard here?" she asks. She brings the pandanus mat, laughs because she says she'll have to get used to sleeping on a bed now. "But you won't mind if I sleep on the floor when I come back."

When I come back. She feels badly about going. He can tell because she keeps saying that. She's looked at the Yale calendar. Thanksgiving's her first holiday.

"May I come back for Thanksgiving?" she asks, trying out the word. It sounds nice to her. She thinks she has plenty to be thankful for. And once she's a doctor, or a surgeon if she works hard enough, she'll have something to give back. To Tosca, Jim, her brothers, her country too, which will be independent one day with its own government, like Fiji and New Guinea.

Jim nods without conviction. November, it'll be cold. The leaves will have turned and possibly there will be snow. He wonders what she'll make of snow. He doesn't celebrate Thanksgiving particularly, or

Easter, or even Christmas for that matter. Not since the war. Though Fergus always makes some attempt with him. He wheels himself around to get a drink. He hasn't got out of the chair these last days, due to the pain in the stump.

"Mr. Jim, are you going to move back up to the big house?" She makes room for her shells in the closet. "I can help move your things back up before I go." *Going.*

"No," he says, inhaling the sharp tang of gin before turning round to face her. "Not now." She looks at him, drink in hand, the crumpled pack of cigarettes in his chest pocket, the habit he has of tilting his head to one side and pulling an earlobe, and considers whether he might be happy to have the place to himself again. The way he was when she came—like a Japanese MIA.

Mr. Jim's numbawan man, Tosca told her. The problem is he can't see that for himself. She doesn't think Jim's looking well and she examines his face more closely, with professional scrutiny. Flushed, she notes, the skin around his eyes, blue and puffy. He may be feverish beneath the flush. His skin looks unhealthy and drained of color. The way he moves too, is slow and cautious, as if he might be in some pain.

"I can stay longer if you are not well," she says with some concern.

"Damn that!" Jim snarls over his gin, anger surging through him as he makes eye contact. "Jesus Christ, you came here to be a doctor. Don't tell me you changed your mind? Don't tell me you want to be a goddamned nurse!"

He's shouting and Cadillac smiles, happy to have roused this ferocity. The mean dog. Jim's been too quiet and withdrawn the last few days.

"Of course, I want to go," she says. A determined excitement in her voice, for the now fast-approaching day when the rest of her life begins. She remembers writing her application with Ms. Sethie. How long ago that was, when Yale seemed a fantastical dream.

"Then goddamn do it!" Jim snarls. "Besides I want my house back!" He picks up the books she's returned and puts them back in her open hands. "Keep these." Pulling her by the arm, he wheels to the cupboard, lifts out the canvas skinning set, and puts it on top of the books. "Take that too." Maybe she'll find some use for it.

He'd like to give her more. He'd like to give her the kettle and the tin cups, the fishing tackle and rods, the butterfly nets. He looks at her shells, the sea glass, the golden whistler Tosca skinned. He'd like to give her the storm lanterns, the mosquito coils, the box of charts. He'd like to give her the whole goddamn house, the cove, the point. Everything but the guns maybe. He'd like to keep those.

It's the last entry Jim remembers most clearly. So it seems he might have written it himself, dipping the bamboo brush in water, brushing it against the dry inkstone, tracing small black characters down the thin rice paper. The lieutenant's final entry—written the night he and two colleagues are given their assignment to scout on Layla, or maybe in the wakeful hours of the morning.

This evening we received our own assignment. To patrol an island near Rendova. An island they tell us is uninhabited. Ide, Kiyoshi, and myself were all permitted a cup of sake. Later the CO secretly slipped me the rest of the flask to take with us. That night, after I put out the candle I use to write with, I could not sleep. Remembering that my wife, on the night we parted, had washed my back. It weighed on my mind that I had not washed hers.

At least we are not being sent to Lae.

When Misako read Jim that, he thought of Helen's back. Her broad shoulders browned by the sun. He thought of running his soapy hands through her hair, the way her neck curved back against his hands.

They are camping, high up in the hills above Dalat, in Indochina with Lowe and Delacour. It's the time Delacour moved out of the little hut into the tent with Lowe to give Helen a proper bed. For a shower, they've rigged a barrel on stilts to catch rainwater, fixed a spigot to it. He heats a kettle of water over the campfire to pour over her long mane of hair. The others are away picking up supplies in Saigon. He runs the water along her shoulders, down her spine. Her hair is wet and heavy. The water smells of rain and the burnt embers of the fire. He can feel her shoulder bones beneath her skin. Her bright laugh rings out. Steam rises in the cold air. Soapy water catches in small eddies, swirling round, as it runs down the steep hillside.

When they go, Jim almost faints from the effort of getting up to the house. He's in constant pain now. The skin of the stump so hot and hard beneath his khaki trouser, it makes him queasy to touch it. A fever too that makes him feel cold and disoriented. He pulls a cigarette from the crumpled pack, determined to conceal his difficulties, his increasing confusion.

Cadillac's scuffed brown leather suitcase by the door, is Helen's small blue suitcase, the one he brought back from the hospital and couldn't bear to unpack.

He can't stop thinking of Helen now, and the war. As if his past, so long pushed back, now threatens to rise up and crash down on him like a giant wave and sweep him under. It's taken thirty years for him to even begin to look at it. It's taken this girl, all the way from the goddamn Solomons, to remind him what love felt like.

"See you in a few days Pappy." Fergus lays his hand on Jim's shoulder and takes it away. His boy wary of any further display of affection, in case it elicit scorn. Too late for it to be otherwise. Too late to apologize for being such a goddamn lousy, son-of-a-bitch father. Fergus's eyes are Helen's eyes. Fergus's hair, her hair.

He's debating whether to stand, or whether he would collapse, when the girl leans forward and takes both his hands between hers. And he lets her and doesn't pull back. And now she clasps her hands up along his forearms, as if to fortify him and give him strength. And she's saying something about Tosca, Tosca telling her Jim's a good man. And Tosca's right here, alongside him, crouching down to skin a small bird. And Jim hears the far-off rumble of the reef and he smells the sun beating down, the rough weave of pandanus, their rain-soaked clothes.

Good-bye Tosca. Good-bye Helen. Fergus lifts the brown blue suit-case into the back of the car. Jim glimpses the skinning set, resting atop the other bags, Tosca's, Cadillac's, before the trunk shuts and the car doors slam—one, two. He lifts his hand with the cigarette. Watches them drive off, their hands wave out of the windows.

He closes his eyes, puts the cigarette between his teeth, and sucks in the good tobacco as if it were oxygen. He listens as a flock of flickers swoop down and settle on the lawn, their communal chattering a busy *wick-a, wick-a, wick-a.* Gathering for autumn migration.

They should have left Papa to it the first time. Instead Mary distracted him, sat talking until the time she knew the local doctor would arrive to take Papa's blood pressure. The great man had been obsessed with that for years. He'd kept charts on his wall, detailing precise measure-ments, fluctuations in his weight, along with the number of pages he'd written each day. It was the same doctor who helped tackle Papa to the ground, the second time they took him to the Mayo Clinic.

This isn't what Jim wants to think of. It's what he wants to forget most of all. He presses his eyes more tightly, tries to listen to the flick-ers, to the chicks in the fish hawk nest. How did he ever let it happen to the only person he loved?

Like Hemingway's doctors, Helen's doctors were optimistic. They claimed they were curing her. They subdued her all right. Her bright eyes, dead, drowned Jim with a dull accusation. Her shoulders slumped. She was overweight, limp, listless. It seemed as if they'd drawn the very marrow from her bones. She dragged rather than walked—like the soldiers in Rendova.

Her doctors insisted she was improving. Christ, they certainly had an easier time of it after. Helen no longer raving, shouting out, no lon-ger seeing things, or hearing voices that weren't there. She'd let Jim touch her now, hold her hand, only he wasn't sure it was her anymore he was holding.

Subdued—but not broken. Because a week later Helen hung herself in the institutional green-tiled, multicubicle shower room, using strips of towels, which she'd braided to strengthen them. Jim insisted they take him to see the exact place.

He brings his arms up around his face, burying his eyes in the crook of his elbows. Weeping.

If only he had looked after her, if he hadn't gone to war. He thinks that, wonders about it every day now. Why it wasn't him who died instead of her? Goddamn, it would have been better for the boy.

Why had he survived? How had he come through it all—the killing, bombing, shelling, strafing, knifing, torpedoes, the boats exploding in the night, the planes falling from the sky—to return to Helen sick in the hospital and, soon after, her suicide?

He wishes he'd just brought her home and not let them do anything more to her. And just let her be, however that turned out.

"Knock, knock," Sarah says, nose pressed up against the screen door. She has a jar of unruly nasturtiums from the garden. A pie for his dinner. "Thought you might need some good food now that the chef's bailed out." She calls Fergus, *the chef*.

Jim thanks her from behind the book he's reading, asks her to put the pie on the small stovetop. It's Sarah's practical eye he has to guard most vigilantly against. The others will have instructed her to watch out for him, no doubt, until Fergus gets back.

"Anything else you need?"

He glances over at the counter. "Another bottle of gin."

She laughs. It could be back to the old ways then, if Sarah's agreeable. His diet of gin, eggs, and hash.

"Well you take care then." She'll be back in the morning with the newspapers and gin, if he's lucky.

Fox Island, Penobscot Bay, Maine, September 1973

Jim waits. He waits for a bright day. A warm day when there are no shadows, no presentiment of winter to put him off. A day Sarah's away.

He's thought it through, made plans. Jesus Christ, he's dying. Waves of dizziness overtake him. At night, dreams hold him with their hard grip. The infection in the stump wreaking its havoc.

Fergus will have dropped Cadillac in New Haven by now. He'll be delivering Jim's article to the museum before heading back to take Jim to the hospital in Rockland. To hell with that. Jim's not going anywhere. He's not going to leave this place. There's just about anywhere he'd rather end up than a hospital.

Feverish and jittery, he eases a clean cloth down the barrel of the gun and polishes the wood one last time. Allowing himself to be comforted by the task performed since boyhood. Then wheels the chair over the wide floorboards toward the open doors where there will be less of a mess.

The gun is heavy and solid. There's purpose in the loading, in the firm catch of the well-oiled breech.

Just past noon. He inhales the tranquillity of the place now that the others have left. The seductive quiet at the end of the season, with no pleasure yachts or sailing dinghies rushing up and down the Thoroughfare, only the slower chug of lobster boats working the bay. The ferry half empty as it glides past. It's a quietness most summer folks don't know. One he'd savor if he wasn't so sick.

The sun's high and it glints all sparkling off the water. He feels its warmth full against his skin, although it doesn't stop him shivering. He listens to the high chirrups of the fish hawk chicks, soon to be testing their wings. Gulls chivying. The clang of the green gong.

Out in the cove, the diving frame juts from the placid water, looking foreign and out of place. Like one of the Japanese characters loosened from the rice paper book. He thinks he can read it now. The character says, *jump*. It says, *freedom*. It says, *I love you*.

Hemingway, the great hunter, loaded two cartridges. Did that show just how far gone he felt? Jim wouldn't ever want to be that unsure of himself. His own gun's single-barreled in any case. But Jesus, how do you miss with the gun in your mouth?

He takes a long swig from the whisky flask to sharpen his mind. Finishes it off. Turns the gun to wedge the butt against the side of the cot. His hands suddenly steady, resolute.

Now's the time—before any shadow of afternoon creeps in to undermine his confidence.

He's young again, back on the Mekong with Delacour. Or up in their mountain hut at Phu Kobo. Confounded by the mist that keeps them from hunting, he aches for Helen, wondering why he ever left her. But then, all at once, the mist begins to lift, they head up to the mountains to shoot, and he's rapturous, happier than he's ever been.

He sees his son Fergus, Helen's boy, teetering at the top of that hieroglyph, fifteen feet in the air, then diving down, arms wide, as if he'll embrace the whole world after all. And Cadillac there to love him. He sees Helen smiling with Lowe's lemur curled asleep in her lap.

They came into a cloud forest in the hills above Hue, Le Col des Nuages. Green with tree ferns, epiphytes, and moss. Everything wet, hushed, dreamlike, with glimpses of the emerald sea and coastline snaking far below.

They trekked up the high peak of Phu Kobo, its slopes covered with orchids, ferns, and ginger. At the top, they came to a tree, devoid of leaves but covered with great red flowers, with hundreds of jeweled sunbirds coming in to feed like bees.

He hears the whir of fast-beating wings all around him. The gentle brush of ink on rice paper. He feels Helen's lips barely touch his. The cold of the gun's metal in his mouth. A quickening of his soul, urging him to leap.

He brings his foot up along the gun, curls his toe around the trigger. Not yet. Ever the hunter, he holds back, waits just one second longer. Now—just when the iridescent yellow, green, red of the sunbird alights on the red flower of the bombax tree.

Afterward, Fergus thinks his father had done about everything he could to throw him off. He curses himself for falling for it, for not taking Jim to the doctor immediately when both he and Cadillac had noticed a decline.

This is what Jim was good at, what he'd trained for. Hiding out. Going to ground.

Their last evening together, Jim had wheeled himself up to the house and made a noticeable effort to be civil. He'd pressed a thick envelope on Fergus—the article he'd been working on all summer—and asked him to deliver it to the museum. Inside was a chart of Treasure Island so shaky and trembly it makes Fergus ache to think of it. But Jim had seemed pleased and excited to show Fergus his work.

"Portable No. 3 Corona. Best goddamn present I ever had," he'd enthused. "Just like Hemingway's!" It seemed the closest he'd ever come to saying thank you, or I love you for that matter. Should Fergus have caught the allusion to Hemingway?

The postmortem showed that Jim's body was rife with blood poisoning and equally lethal levels of alcohol so that the doctors said he might have died from either, if he hadn't shot himself.

He'd planned it. You couldn't dismiss it as a sudden act of rage. He'd waited for the day Sarah went to Rockland, called the island cop to ask him to come round later that afternoon, and scribbled a short note to him apologizing for the *goddamn mess*.

When Fergus arrived the day after, rushing from New York, he'd searched for something more. Another letter addressed to him. An explanation. All he found were Jim's notes for the museum piece. A field book his father was keeping of birds on the Point—great horned owls, a snow goose, eider ducks, loons, red-winged blackbirds, the fish hawks' nest.

September 6, the day Jim died—an entry about sunbirds was the only evidence that Jim was suffering from some sort of delirium, because there are no sunbirds in Maine.

Three weeks later, the morning of Jim's funeral, Fergus stands in front of the boathouse, which has been closed up and shuttered. He pushes open the door and steps inside. Alone in its slatted shadows, he presses his palm against the weathered pine of the wall and allows himself to imagine Jim's face determined and hard-set, the intensity of his blood-shot eyes, the fishhook scar down the side of his cheek that made the boy Fergus think of pirates.

When he called Laina at the museum to tell her of Jim's death, he could hear her weeping on the end of the line. Fergus had been unable to weep until now. He walks across the room and throws open the big doors over the cove. It's no use to keep the place closed up, no use to keep anything closed up—better to open it wide.

Through the doors, he sees Cadillac sitting down at the end of the dock, her knees drawn up to her chest and her arms around them. He walks out of the opened house and down the steep gangway to join her.

Fergus looks severe and uncomfortable in his black suit and tie. His face is drawn, his eyes red.

"I am thinking it would have been nice to keep Mr. Jim's skull in a small shrine down here by the sea," Cadillac says, as he sits cross-legged down on the dock beside her. "It's the way we used to keep our ancestors close."

He tugs at the tie around his neck to loosen it and when he tucks his hair behind his ear, she notices him pull at his earlobe, the way Jim did.

"Of course that doesn't happen anymore," she assures him. It's the first time she's seen him smile since he came to New Haven to pick her up. Apologizing for interrupting her work and promising to get her back in time for Monday classes.

"I'm not sure what was left of it," he says bitterly.

A bullet at that range wouldn't have left much intact. Still, they might have mended it, she thinks. They might have sat here and bound the broken pieces with ivory nut leaves and creepers. Refashioned the eye sockets with rings of clamshell. There must have been something left.

Cadillac's been trying to cast some light on the news of Jim's death, to see it as a release, a new beginning, a reunion with others who died before. In this way, the old island beliefs weren't so different from Christianity. The main difference, it seems to her, is that the Solomon Islanders managed to keep their dead close at hand. So they might go and talk to them sometimes.

"At home, the old people believe that the dead pass over to an island called Santo," she says. "Some of them say they have seen the dead or heard them passing by in their canoes. They say a man's spirit can come back in the shape of a shark or snake, a bonito fish, or a frigate bird."

Sunbirds, Fergus thinks. The dead returning for Jim. And what bird or fish would Jim come back as?

It's time to leave. But he sits a while longer, letting Cadillac's thoughts of shrines and frigate birds wrap around him. Hell, they're not going to start the service without him. Looking out across the cove and all its bright reflections, he sees clearly what she's offering him. Another way of seeing, acceptance, a hope that stands apart and directly opposed to the gloom of his doubly crossed inheritance.

When he stands, she raises a hand for him to help her up, then keeps his hand firmly in hers. They walk up the dock together toward Stillman, who's waiting to drive them in his pickup truck.

Island Funeral, Fox Island, Penobscot Bay, Maine, September 1973

Jim's funeral is timed to begin shortly after the arrival of the noon ferry. Michael disembarks with a small clutch of fellow birdmen and they walk up a slight hill to the small white clapboard church just back from the waterfront. Its bells call out in the brisk, clear sea air. They pass the small post office, shut for the day. The town library. A provisions store, where they linger a minute, drinking some bitter overbrewed coffee.

Fergus had invited him, along with the rest of the bird department, and an impressive number have shown up, given that Fox Island is a full day's journey from New York. That many had only just returned from summer holidays. And that Michael isn't the only one Jim's offended and alienated. They are here for his better days.

Oliver Austin—or Iggy as he's called, the expert on Japanese birds—is here. Farrell, back from studying parrots in Central America.

Inside the church, Michael looks about him and studies Jim's family from behind. A large jowly figure he recognizes as Jim's brother, dressed rakishly in a cream-colored suit and panama hat. A tall, younger man who must be Jim's son, though his full, shoulder-length hair is unusual for Wall Street. Next to him, a tall, striking black woman. Her bright flowered dress and hair mark her as foreign. Delacour sits with them.

Toward the back, Laina slides in late just as the organ sounds. She wears a stylish hat but looks terribly pale beneath it.

It's an eclectic gathering. The delegation of crusty ornithologists dispersed amid a smattering of islanders in their Sunday best, looking as though they feel slightly displaced in their own church. There's an old, hunched man wheeled into the aisle, a medal from the war pinned on the lapel of his suit. A large sturdy man with thick calloused hands who later stands to read Psalm 23 with a slow Maine accent and sonorous gravity that makes the whole journey worth taking. Stillman, he's called.

And that's before a voluptuous soprano teeters up to the altar in high heels and sings Bach's *Bist Du bei mir*. This followed by an aria from *Tosca*. Actually Michael distinctly hears her say "for Tosca," but perhaps she misspoke. She's German. He remembers that Jim's brother helps run the Met.

The soprano sings again as they file out, this time gesturing to the foreign woman, who joins her in an apparently impromptu descant to Shubert's *Ave Maria*. Their voices spill out the open door, across the Penobscot.

Someone's been busy gathering flowers. Cutting them ruthlessly from every garden on the island it seems; there are so many. Dahlias, cosmos, daisies, and black-eyed Susans in every alcove. Up on the altar, giant sunflowers beam like big, colorful defiant suns.

At the door, the island cop in full uniform stands so stiffly, it appears to Michael that he's waiting to arrest Jim's ghost.

It's a beautiful afternoon, a *spah'kler,* he hears someone call it. The guests gather on the wide porch of Jim's house and spill out over the lawn, where they drink champagne and are served New York delicacies, such as Jim would never offer.

The foreign woman and Jim's son go hand in hand. Michael overhears Laina talking to them about a museum in the Solomon Islands, so he's confused as to whether she had some relation to Jim or is Fergus's exotic girlfriend from the city.

"Michael!" Laina greets him, as he joins her at a small picnic table under an apple tree. She's taken off her hat and has been sitting with her face to the sun.

"I hear you're taking a break from the museum and heading back to Argentina?" she asks with interest. He nods.

"Will you be finishing your reference work on local bird names? Such a terrific idea."

He's flattered by her enthusiasm, her exact recollection of his work. "Actually not," he confides quietly. "I'm going back to find my wife, Nita."

He looks out to sea, unsure what she'll make of this, wedded as she is to incessant research. Curious whether she'd ever had any inkling of his feelings for her. And is taken aback when she almost jumps with pleasure and clutches his hand.

"But Michael, that's wonderful," she says. And Michael is relieved to find he's immune to this physical contact. His infatuation has vanished. Not that he doesn't appreciate her hair, her pretty hat.

"To your luck," she says, raising her glass. "To birds of paradise and their showy courtship displays." Michael's not sure what to make of this either, it seems so out of character.

"I'm wondering if you might do me a favor," he says, seizing the moment. Laina looks at him, wide-eyed. "I'm wondering if you might finish off the piece for me, the profile of Jim."

"I'd love that," she says. She squeezes his hand.

"You'd do him better justice."

And here is Mann lumbering down the lawn toward them with a bottle of champagne. It seems a long time ago, much longer than this one summer, that he assigned the profile of Jim. Strange that it had turned into an obituary after all. Although Michael had never got past the note-taking stage, it seems the work has changed him. That Jim's secrecy, his isolation, his temper had stood as a warning. He'd been an ass to let Nita go.

Standing to greet Mann, he looks out across the cove, its green-brown water, its clutch of lobster pots, a single lobster boat on its mooring, the weed-strewn rocks, the reflection of trees and sky. Both wild and workaday, which suits Jim somehow.

No one at the funeral had mentioned how Jim died. Most likely, it's another fact that's not going to appear in the retrospective. He wonders what Laina will do with the Japanese material. The heads Mann had told them about.

Suddenly, Michael feels eager to get away. To be back in the colorful, dusty streets, the forests and hills of Argentina. It will take explaining and apology. It will take changes. But he wants nothing more now than to join Nita. To be a proper husband to her, which will mean staying there in the wilds of Argentina. On a farm on the pampas maybe.

Now that he's decided, he feels he hardly has time to get there fast enough. He hopes it's not too late.

EPILOGUE

*S*et out, you people of Enogai, you people of the Kula Gulf, you people
of Roviana, you people of the Wanawana. Go up to Noro, launch four
canoes; go to Mbanga, launch four canoes; go to Kokenggolo, launch four
canoes. Paddle four embracing nights, cast out four anchors. Shout people
of Enogai, shout people of the Wanawana. Let him come down sounding
your conch, let him come down casting.

"Stop that witch talk," Cadillac's mother scolds, overhearing the old
aunties. But she's too busy grilling fish and preparing pudding for a
proper church burial to interfere. And other women draw in to listen,
nodding and recalling their own memories of how it was a dead man
used to be sent on, remembering stories they'd been told.

They sit under a mango tree a way off from the thatched Methodist
church, enjoying the shade and the rapt attention of this young girl,
who is smart and quick. Already they see something special in her.
They are chewing betel with lime. One or two are weaving a decorative
altar of rattan and dyed pandanus leaves for the church.

In the old days, the souls of the dead were picked up by the ancestors and paddled across the sea. As far as Cadillac can make out, this doesn't happen right away, the moment a person dies, but sometime after. After all the proper rites and ceremonies have been performed. First, you have to leave the skull to bleach in the sun, one auntie says. Then, you bind the jaw with lave creepers and decorate the ear and eye sockets with rings of clamshell.

She's seen the skulls tucked between slabs of coral, haphazardly arranged, on what is still considered *tambu* or sacred ground, in the rubble of old canoe houses. The Australian scuba divers pay money to the chief to see them, though most of the skulls have lost their decorations and jawbones. The creeper has rotted and not been replaced.

In the old days, an auntie says, a dead man's body was tied with vines, slung on a pole, and carried down to a sacred rock by the shore. A remote rock where it was tied in a sitting position looking west out to sea and left to rot, and to be picked clean by the corpse-eating spirit. As well as by the birds and bugs and great hordes of flies, and crabs, another auntie adds. And you wouldn't want to go near that place because of the smell.

"Stop now, why are you are filling the girl's head with all that nonsense?" Cadillac's mother tuts from a distance. But they only laugh and spit betel juice and slap Cadillac on the shoulder or pat the back of her hand affectionately, conspiratorially, as if the girl can understand things her mother doesn't. Even the most devout, who are weaving the altar, join in.

In the old days, when a man died, fresh young coconuts and areca nuts were broken and left as offerings for the ghosts and the ancestors to eat. Also puddings of cassava and betel nut with lime. The dead man's most precious belongings—his shield and spear, his shell arm rings—were broken and cast about. And in his garden, all his betel nut trees were cut down and his cassava plants uprooted, which was a way of displaying grief and fear and anger, as well as protecting against thievery and jealousy, Cadillac supposes. And his relatives would wear pepeu leaves around their necks to protect them from the corpse-eating spirit.

This was the old way to mourn. The aunties nod their approval, quietly question whether Christianity had left a few things out.

There were other traditions and rituals they are more abashed to speak of. Customs they're well rid of, and others some of them won't admit ever happened. Like the kidnapping of children from other villages to be tended until the day a skull might be needed for an important ceremony like the funeral of a chief, for instance, or the launching of a canoe. The way a chief's widow was expected to commit suicide, and how the others might be called on to help her. The way the bodies of suicides and lepers and stillborns were not tended to, but taken and unceremoniously dumped at sea.

The way menstruating girls had to seclude themselves in a *bisi* hut at the edge of the jungle and pregnant woman had to give birth there. Though that, in fact, had the advantage of allowing the women some rest, Cadillac thinks.

If you ask them about any of that, they tut like Cadillac's mother and shake their heads—as if it was another world where those things happened.

Her old aunties' murmurings have sunk so deep, Cadillac supposes she'll carry them around with her forever. Even here in the United States, even when she returns to the Solomons as a proper doctor.

Jim would have liked the stories too and the old way of burial. He would have liked being left down here a while looking out. Even if, as a suicide, he was rudely dumped at sea, his body floating down into the deep forest of kelp to rest on the mica-flecked sand, he would have liked to be picked clean by fish and crabs and lobsters.

It's the end of the day. The sun drops low across the cove, turning a brilliant orange. She's sitting on the thick plank that runs across the threshold of the boathouse, the exact place Jim died. Tomorrow, she will be heading back to Yale, but now she lets her legs dangle toward the cold water.

Go off to Baanga, slap the water four time to attract bonito fish. Go to Kohinggo, slap the water four times. Go off to Wanawana, she murmurs. A prayer used to summon the ancestors and usher a spirit on its way. When she whispers it aloud, then closes her eyes, she can hear their paddles slapping the water, the guttural utterings, the whistling of ancestors. Here they are. They have come for him, to this place Jim died.

Jim's spirit is as truculent as ever. She has to scold him and wave him on his way, just as Tosca shooed the hornbill. She can tell he's pleased, though he'd never say. And who has come? His doctor father, his father's friend, who first taught him about birds, a boatman who taught him to sail. Dead men from the war. The lovely woman in the photograph he hides.

When a man becomes a spirit, he is a child all over again and has no knowledge of the ways of the ancestors, or even their language, her aunties told her. For Jim, it's a relief. He doesn't like talking. And now there's no demand for explanation, in fact there's no possibility of saying anything. The ancestors don't rush him, they don't hurry. They paddle slowly all the way around the cove, four times.

Nor will they steer a direct route back to Santo but will take their time, paddling along the reefs and islands, putting into familiar coves and sacred places. Along the way, they will fish. They will cast. They will shout and blow conch shells. It's as if the new spirit has given them a chance to come home, to visit their old haunts and pasts.

And Jim is glad to be on a boat again, out on the sea. Fishing. Moving along the coast in the last reflections of the sun. *Go now, and wait that they might take you to Santo.*

She keeps her eyes shut and listens to the sound of spirit paddles.

NOTES

ON NAMES

Bird names change over time as scientists reclassify species based on new information about molecular data (DNA), behavior, and geographic distribution. To the best of my ability, I have adopted the scientific names my characters would have used. For simplicity's sake, more modern spellings are used for place names.

ON SOURCES

The description of the Laysan Rail and quotes come from J. Greenway Jr.'s article "Remarks on the Preservation of Birds" delivered to the International Technical Conference on the Protection of Nature in Lake Success, 1949. The theory and arguments for the whereabouts of the true Treasure Island are adapted from Greenway's unpublished article "Isla de Providencia: Or Old Providence, Providence of Pirates."

The songs Cadillac sings are "Auki Love Song" and "Walkabout 'Long Chinatown," written and recorded by Solomon Dakei and by Edwin Nanau Sitori, respectively. As well as leading the capital's top bamboo band, Dakei was chief radiologist at Honiara's Central Hospital. He served as a scout in the war. I have not been able to track the origin of the popular war tune.

The incredible story of Jean Delacour can be read in his memoir *The Living Air*, published by Country Life Ltd. in 1966.

Highly informative local accounts of Solomon Island traditions and lives include *Maekera: The Life Story of Hereditary Chief Nathan Kera*, as told to Russell Parker (1994); *Tie Varane: People of Courage*, a series of biographies compiled by the Methodist minister Rev. George C. Carter (1981); and *The Big Death: Solomon Islanders Remember World War II*, 1988.

One of the first books I read on the Solomons, *Aloha Solomons*, by Gwen Cross, who worked as a missionary teacher between 1929 and the late 1960s, made a vivid impression. I would recommend Arthur Grimble's *A Pattern of Islands* to anyone interested in the South Seas.

John Miller Jr.'s *Cartwheel: The Reduction of Rabaul*, published by the Office of the Chief of Military History in 1959, served as a constant reference and provided key details of the New Georgia Campaign. As did Eric A. Feldt's *The Coastwatchers* (1946).

The book Jim sends Tosca is modeled on Ernst Mayr's *Birds of the Southwest Pacific* (1945), the first field guide to birds of the area. Modern birders are in luck with Guy Dutson's 2011 *Birds of Melanesia*. Jared Diamond's article on Northern Melanesian Birds (published in *Pacific Science*, 2002), Charles Sibley's "Notes on the Birds of New Georgia" (1951), and Walter R. Donaghho's "Observations of Some Birds of Guadalcanal and Tulagi" (1950), both published in *The Condor*, were particularly useful for me as local studies. Sibley and Donaghho collected and observed during the war.

All Native American bird names mentioned come from Joseph Kastner's history of birding, *A World of Watchers*, Alfred A. Knopf, New York, 1986.

The *Life* magazine photo was published as "Picture of the Week" on May 22, 1944. James J. Weingartner's "Trophies of War: U.S. Troops and the Mutilation of Japanese War Dead, 1941–45," published in *The Pacific Historical Review*, gives an account of the furor it caused.

A. M. Hocart's fascinating and hugely informative article "The Cult of the Dead in Eddystone of the Solomons" was published in two parts in *The Journal of the Royal Anthropological Institute of Great Britain and Ireland*, vol. 52 (1922). W. H. R. Rivers's lecture, "The Dying-Out of Native Races," was delivered to the Royal Institute of Public Health in 1918 and later published in *The Lancet* (1920). The anthropologists travelled to New Georgia to conduct field research between 1908 and 1909. During World War I, Hocart's served in France with Army Intelligence, while Rivers, more famously, treated shell shock victims in Edinburgh.

The Japanese diary is inspired by Lietenant Kiyoshi Yamamoto's beautiful journal entry, published in Richard J. Aldrich's *The Faraway War* (Doubleday, 2005). Four lines are directly quoted with kind permission.

ACKNOWLEDGMENTS

This book is inspired by the character of my grandfather, James C. Greenway Jr., a noted ornithologist who served with distinction in Naval Intelligence during the Pacific War. Without him, I could not have written this story. It should be stressed there is no Layla Island in the Solomons and the events portrayed there and elsewhere are my own invention.

As an amateur wanderer into the worlds of ornithology, war and medicine, I have no doubt made mistakes. Still I owe great thanks to the people who tried to set me straight. I am immensely indebted to Dr. Mike McDonnell, former District Medical Officer in the Solomons, who gave me a crash course in Solomon Island culture and medicine, adding to that friendship, hospitality, and such delightful storytelling that I can only hope he writes his own book soon. Also to Francois Vuilleumier, a kind friend and editor, who spent several days introducing me to the American Museum of Natural History, and who has, over some years, patiently and painstakingly answered the endless questions of a novice. Ms. Alison Pirie, a peerless guide to the hugely atmospheric ornithology department at the Museum of Comparative

Zoology in Cambridge. John Lawrence, who served with Naval Air Intelligence and on Admiral "Bull" Halsey's staff, dragged his zimmer frame defiantly behind him as he took me to see the Japanese sword he brought back from Guadalcanal. Taska Sasamara, who introduced me to the war wrecks in New Georgia and to people who remember those times. Gordon Beti for his war collection in Munda. Keithie Saunders, the American consular agent, for taking time to talk to an unknown tourist about Solomon Island politics. Wilson Maelauna, my guide on Guadalcanal. Dr. Jimmy Macgregor, former Director of Medical Services in the Solomons. Ian and Louise Gardiner for lending me a room and Bici Pettit-Barron—a boathouse.

I would like to thank my father and mother, my Uncle Jim, my Auntie Hooblie, and my cousin Dinny for helping me with research, and for their encouragement. Bob and Diana Harding for sharing their personal observations on Maine birds.

I would also like to thank my agent, Felicity Rubinstein, a true champion. My editor, Joan Bingham, for her unflinching support of both books. My editor, Elisabeth Schmitz, for her careful editing and her astonishing ear for language. Karen Duffy, my savvy and elegant publisher at Atlantic Books in London. And all those at Grove Atlantic who helped make this book happen: Charles Rue Woods, Zach Pace, Deb Seager. My Los Angeles writing teacher Les Plesko for his astute reading. Darren Woodhead and Julia Greenway for their beautiful illustrations. Chin-yee Lai for her gorgeous cover. And Jun Shibata for helping to put my disordered world back in some order.

Finally, I would like to thank my daughters, Annie and Eliza, for being so absolutely wonderful. And my husband and childhood friend, Timo, who supported this far-too-lengthy project, travelled with me to the Solomons, and skillfully and generously read these pages many times over. I love you all three.

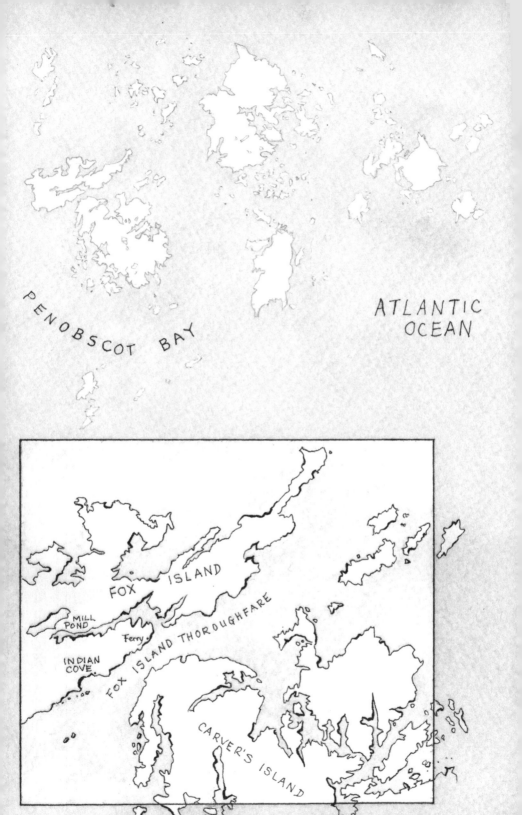

ATLANTIC
OCEAN

PENOBSCOT BAY

FOX ISLAND

MILL
POND

Ferry

INDIAN
COVE

FOX ISLAND THOROUGHFARE

CARVER'S ISLAND